On the Hook

Also available by Betty Hechtman

Crochet Mysteries

Yarn Retreat Mysteries

On the Hook

A CROCHET MYSTERY

Betty Hechtman

CROOKED LANE

NEW YORK

Copyright © 2018 by Betty Hechtman

All rights reserved.

Published in the United States by Crooked Lane Books, an imprint of The Quick Brown Fox & Company LLC.

Crooked Lane Books and its logo are trademarks of The Quick Brown Fox & Company LLC.

Library of Congress Catalog-in-Publication data available upon request.

ISBN (hardcover): 978-1-68331-565-0
ISBN (ePub): 978-1-68331-566-7
ISBN (ePDF): 978-1-68331-567-4

Cover illustration by Jesse Reisch
Book design by Jennifer Canzone

Printed in the United States.

www.crookedlanebooks.com

Crooked Lane Books
34 West 27th St., 10th Floor
New York, NY 10001

First edition: May 2018

10 9 8 7 6 5 4 3 2 1

Acknowledgments

I want to thank my editor, Faith Black Ross, for her invaluable help with this book. Her suggestions were perfect. I am eternally grateful for Jessica Faust's help in keeping this series going. Jenny Chen has been a pleasure to work with. The Crooked Lane art department came up with a fabulous cover.

Thank you to Linda Osborn for suggesting I include who went on the Hawaiian trip with Barry. Explaining it made for a nice moment between Barry and Molly.

I am forever grateful to everyone in my knit and crochet group for their friendship and yarn help—Rene Biederman, Terry Cohen, Lynn Dubrow, Sonia Flamm, Lily Gillis, Winnie Hineson, Reva Mallon, Elayne Moschin, Vicki Stotsman, Paula Tesler, and Anna Thomeson. We all miss Linda Hopkins, and I know that she is with us in spirit.

Roberta Martia remains my staunchest cheerleader.

Thank you to Jakey for being my baby-blanket tester and for giving me someone new to love. Burl, Max, and Samantha—as always, you guys are the best.

Chapter One

"I'm telling you, we Hookers have gotten away from our core business. We used to be more concerned with giving service instead of just pleasing ourselves." After years of being an actor, CeeCee Collins naturally projected her voice. The trouble was, she didn't realize how it carried—or notice how the diners at the next table were reacting to what she said.

The three thirty-something women wearing bowling shirts that said "Wilbur Avenue Elementary" on the back were nudging each other and snickering as they stared at the five of us around the small table. They all looked similar with their assorted shades of blonde hair, trendy clothes, and attitudes that said they knew it all. Though obviously they didn't, since it was clear that they were taking what CeeCee was saying way too literally.

"Isn't it sad to see what she's turned to now that her career is in a downward spiral?" one of the bowling team said.

Totally oblivious to them, CeeCee continued, only making things worse. "I wish our whole posse was here," she said. "I'd like to get everyone to agree to go back to our old ways. Just think of all those people we made happy."

The women started checking out the rest of us at the table. "I wonder who their customers are," one of the women said.

All I had to hear was something about a retirement home and old geezers and I was out of my chair. I should have just let it go, but I have never been good at minding my own business or staying out of trouble. So, before I thought it through, I barged into the three women's conversation. "You can't honestly believe CeeCee is some kind of streetwalker. I mean, really, she's an Academy Award–nominated actress, and she'd be playing Ophelia again if there was going to be another one of those 'vampire who crochets' movies. But everyone knows that vampires are pretty much yesterday's news now." I pulled out a red metal crochet hook from my purse and waved it in front of them.

"When CeeCee said Hookers, she meant as in the Tarzana Hookers. I'm sure you understand the Tarzana part," I continued, using my other hand to indicate the area of the San Fernando Valley we were in. Surely they knew that Edgar Rice Burroughs had owned the land in the area at one time and had named it after his star character.

"And the hooking we do is all about crochet. We used to use our get-togethers to work on projects to give to charities, but lately everybody seems to have gotten more into working on their own projects. And this woman you were whispering about wants us to get back to making things to help others."

"I'm sorry," one of the women stuttered, trying to distance herself from us. "I'm glad to hear that what we thought isn't true."

"And there is no need for sympathy about my acting career. I'm doing just fine, thank you very much," CeeCee added. "Actually, we're here for the unveiling of a dish named after me." She pointed to an open spot on the wall of photographs. "Next time you come in, there will be a picture of me and the CeeCee Collins Mélange."

Restaurants that served only breakfast and lunch had been popping up along Ventura Boulevard, but the Petite Café had been around way before the trend. As its name implied, it was small, and the tables were close together. It had an interesting clientele. The photographs covering the walls were a testament to its many entertainment business customers, but you were just as likely to see average Joes who lived or worked in the area.

As if on cue, the owner of the Petite Café brought over a plate of food and set it in front of CeeCee. He had no idea what was going on between the two tables and, after he set the bowl down, stood behind her to pose for a picture. CeeCee did a little hand fluffing of her brown hair. She had smartly stayed with the same simple style throughout the years, which gave her the appearance of never aging. Her makeup seemed a little overdone in person but would be perfect in the photographs. She struck a pose with her merry smile and held her fork above the large bowl.

The "mélange," as CeeCee called it, was basically a salad made with organic baby lettuces, fresh sprigs of dill, sugar plum tomatoes, and shredded carrots, topped with a couple of poached eggs and a drizzle of balsamic dressing. There were several more photos with CeeCee holding her fork over the bowl before the owner and the server taking the photos went back to their duties.

Meanwhile, I continued the conversation with the women. "We meet at Shedd & Royal Books and More." I mentioned that there was a yarn department. "It's part of the 'more,'" I explained. Then I held out my hand to introduce myself. "I'm Molly Pink, and I'm the assistant manager of the bookstore and in charge of the yarn department."

"You mean that bookstore has a knitting department?" one of the women said.

I heard a shriek from behind me and, before I could stop her, Adele Abrams Humphries had popped out of her chair and was standing next to the woman who had made the comment.

"Why would you call it a knitting department?" Adele demanded. She was tall and amply built and had a loud voice as well. The woman who spoke shrank back as Adele stood over her.

"I just thought knitting and crochet were the same thing," the woman said feebly.

"Knitting and crochet, aren't they the same thing?" another of them said.

The poor women had no idea that the mere word *knitting* to Adele was like a red cape to a bull.

4

"Knitting and crochet are not at all the same. One of them is so much better, and that is crochet, which is what we do." As if to add a visual to the explanation, Adele modeled the tunic she was wearing. It was made of multicolored granny squares. It was attractive and over the top at the same time, but then, when it came to crochet and, well, just about everything, Adele was always over the top.

I noticed that the women were all looking a little uncomfortable by now. They paid their check quickly and were already pulling on their coats when the server came back with the change.

Just before they went outside, they all turned back and gave us a last once-over. "They're certainly a rowdy bunch. I thought that people who sat around and"—the speaker's eye stopped on Adele—"and did *whatever* with yarn were all sweet old ladies." The woman made eye contact with me. "I suppose you overheard that too."

And then they were gone.

"Sweet old ladies," Adele repeated, starting to get up from the chair. I had to grab her tunic to keep her from going after them.

"We're certainly not sweet and for sure not old. They were right about rowdy, though," Dinah Lyons said with a chuckle, looking out the picture window at the three women as they pulled their coats shut and made a run through the rain for their cars. It had been raining steadily for hours, but then it was February and the height of the rainy season in Southern California.

None of us ever talked about age. Dinah thought it was

better to leave people guessing about her age so they wouldn't judge her once they knew. But since I was her best friend, she had told me she was fifty-eight. I couldn't imagine, though, how anyone could consider her old. She was full of energy, and there was a dash of pepper in her personality. Her dark hair was sprinkled with gray, but the short spiky style she wore it in had an edge.

Adele was one of those people who looked older than her years. It was partly her ample build and height but mostly her manner. If I'd had to say, I'd have put her at around forty.

CeeCee Collins seemed ageless, but according to her online listing, she was "in her sixties."

The other Hooker at the table, Elise Belmont, had a fragile, ethereal look about her, as if a good gust of wind could knock her over, but the truth was she had an iron core that would keep her upright in a hurricane. She was forty-something.

As for me, I'd turned the big five-O. But I didn't care since fifty was the new thirty.

Adele was eyeing the wall of photographs.

"Are you looking at the spot for my new photo?" CeeCee asked, following her gaze.

"No, I was thinking more about where a picture of me would go," Adele answered.

"You do realize they're all photographs of performers who eat here," CeeCee said.

"You never know what the future holds," Adele said

with a secret smile. The other three of us looked at each other and shook our heads. What was Adele up to now?

I had thought of the pictures as all being of celebrities, but what CeeCee had said was more accurate. They were all performers, but not all exactly A-list stars. There were a lot of people I didn't recognize.

"That was embarrassing," Elise Belmont said, looking at the table the women had exited. "It doesn't matter for the rest of you, but I have to be concerned about my reputation."

Huh? This was from a woman who had been so vampire crazy she had worn mostly black clothes with splashes of red for the past few years. Everything she had crocheted was done in what she called the vampire stitch, which was actually half double crochet, and I had to admit it did look a little like a fang. She had made a cottage industry of creating crochet kits for vampire-themed items we'd sold at the bookstore. All because she'd gone gaga over Anthony, the vampire who crocheted.

Anthony was the main character in a series of books that had been red hot. So red hot that the first book had been made into a movie—the movie that got CeeCee her Academy Award nomination. But then readers had cooled on the books and moved on to the next hot topic. We didn't even have the Anthony books in stock anymore.

It all seemed like past history now. The kits had stopped selling, and I'd noticed Elise had begun to add some color to her wardrobe and broaden the types of stitches she used.

Before Elise could give any more details about what

reputation she was worried about, Adele took over the conversation and started talking about her newly wedded state. She alternated between the wonders of being with Cutchykins, as she called Eric Humphries, her motor cop husband, and the miseries of having his mother living with them in a condo townhouse. "Wherever I go, there she is. I mean, it's hard for me and Cutchykins to have any privacy."

"You need a bigger place, a real house," CeeCee said. She had smartly bought a mini estate a long time previously when she'd had *The CeeCee Collins Show*, and she had no idea what it was like to buy a house now.

"I mentioned that to Eric, but, well, it's turning out that he likes to save everything. He figures his mother will move to a retirement community someday and then the condo will be fine for us. He won't even consider looking at anything bigger." It was the first time Adele had admitted that everything wasn't exactly going smoothly in her new life.

I had seen their condo, and while the grounds around it were very pretty with lots of trees and even a pond, the best I could say about their place was that it was cozy.

"Men are so difficult," Elise said. She had a wispy voice, but she packed enough punch in the word that we all turned toward her in surprise.

"Does that mean you're having a problem with Logan?" CeeCee asked.

Elise leaned closer and dropped her voice, not wanting to share what she was about to say to the rest of the diners, though it had reached that slow time between breakfast and lunch and all the tables around us were now empty. "You would think he would be glad that I wanted to take up a new profession and work side by side with him." She let out a discontented sigh. We all knew that Logan Belmont was in real estate and well known for it around the Tarzana area. "When I told him I wanted to get my license and then we could work as a team, he went nuts and said it was a bad idea. Can you believe he said I wouldn't be good at selling real estate?"

Given Elise's persistence, she would have been good at selling anything. I mean, she had actually made a business out of vampire kits. I had a feeling it was probably more that Logan didn't like the idea of working with her.

"Well, he can't stop me," she said with a touch of defiance. "He doesn't know it, but I got my license on my own. I figure I'll sell a few houses and then he won't be able to say no." Elise stabbed the last piece of lettuce in her mélange and put it in her mouth, chewing with a vengeance.

CeeCee turned to Dinah. "Dear, I noticed that you didn't join in with the husband complaints. I hope that means the transition is going well." Like Adele, Dinah was newly married. Actually, they'd had a double ceremony at the bookstore. Really, it had been a triple ceremony when, at the last minute, Mrs. Shedd and Mr. Royal had decided to join them in tying the knot. I had been the maid of honor for all of them. Well, matron of honor, according to Adele.

Dinah gave the actress a Mona Lisa smile as an

answer—her way of saying she didn't want to talk about it. Dinah began to gather her things and said she had a class. She taught freshman English at Beasley Community College.

Only I knew the truth. Dinah had been on her own for a long time after divorcing Jeremy, her skunky first husband. Dating Commander Blaine had been an awakening for her. It was hard for her to get used to the fact that he didn't have a jerky bone in his body. But that didn't mean that being married to him was easy. She was used to being the captain of her own time, whereas he thought she should stick to his schedule.

CeeCee wrapped a scarf around her neck and pulled on her trench coat, saying she had to leave as well. "I have a meeting with my agent." She looked to the owner, who was standing behind the counter, and bowed, holding her hands together. "Thank you for naming the dish after me." She turned back to us. "When the Hookers meet this evening, we can talk about doing a charity project."

At that, she and Dinah went to the door, preparing to deal with the rain. Yes, we were wimps when it came to rain, but really, when it rained here, it poured. The street just past the tiny parking lot was flooded, and every time a car drove past, it sent up a huge spray of water. It was one of those times when rain boots would have been nice. The problem was, they seemed irrelevant when it was sunny, which was most of the time, and would be sold out by now.

With CeeCee and Dinah gone, our gathering started winding down. As I was draining my coffee cup, Elise turned to Adele. "Maybe we can work something out that benefits both of us. I could help you find a house first; then you could talk Eric into it. And Logan doesn't have to know anything until we're ready to write up the contract. What a great idea, if I say so myself," Elise said, perking up. She stopped for a moment and thought. "And I know just the house to show you. Logan just listed it. It has two stories with a bonus room you could turn into a separate area for your mother-in-law." She muttered something about knowing the code to open the door. "The only thing is that unless you decide to buy the house, Logan can't know that I showed it to you. It has to be just between the three of us."

"Fine with me. But we also have to agree not to say anything to Eric or anyone else that I'm looking at a place. If Mother Humphries found out, she'd use it against me," Adele said. I agreed too quickly, and she seemed to think that meant I wasn't sincere. "Pink, this is serious. If you talk, relationships could crumble and my future could be ruined."

You could always trust Adele to be overly dramatic, but to keep the peace, I didn't chuckle at her drama and assured her I would keep everything under wraps. Adele was already getting out of her chair. "Let's go."

"Good luck," I said, draining my coffee cup and grabbing my coat.

Adele appeared stricken. "You have to come with." She and I had a strange relationship. We both worked at Shedd & Royal Books and More. By now she had gotten over the fact that I had been given the position of event coordinator that she had wanted. She was even dealing with the fact that I was in charge of the yarn department and that I had recently been appointed assistant manager as well. She still called me by my last name, though I don't think she even remembered she'd started doing it to bug me when I got the position she was hoping for. But she seemed to have made peace with the fact that she was head of the children's department. When she'd been given the job as a consolation after not becoming event coordinator, she'd been less than thrilled. Adele didn't particularly like children, but it turned out they really liked her. Or at least all the costumes and drama she brought to story time.

Somewhere along the way, Adele had decided that I was her best friend, but it was more about me being a friend to her than her being one to me. Whenever there was trouble, she dumped it in my lap. That's why I was surprised it was the first I'd heard of the not-exactly-happily-ever-afterness of her marriage.

I really wanted to beg off the house-hunting excursion. With all the "Don't tell anyone" stuff, it sounded like a mess waiting to happen. But before I could say no, Adele looped her arm in mine and pulled me along as she walked to the door.

Just before we went outside, I made sure my scarf was tucked under the collar of my coat to keep it from getting wet. I had a particular affection for the one I was wearing. It was the first scarf I'd made from a pattern I'd designed myself. It turned out to be unnecessary, though. As we went outside, I saw that the rain had finally gone down to a drizzle for the moment. Not that it wasn't still dreary and wet.

"We'll take my car," Elise said, trying to appear professional. "That's the way it's done. The agent chauffeurs the client." The three of us went toward her white Lexus, which was parked right in front of the restaurant.

Adele commandeered the shotgun seat, saying that she was the client, leaving me to squeeze into the back of the two-door car.

"If you're going to make a business of this, you might want a different car," I said as Adele flipped the front seat back and my leg room disappeared.

Between the foggy windows and being in the back seat, it was hard to see where we were going. I recognized Wells Drive, the back road that wound around the base of the Santa Monica Mountains. At Serrania Park, Elise made a sharp turn and then another, and I figured we were on Dumetz. I'd driven the area often and never paid much attention to anything beyond the houses that faced the street. Elise bent low over the steering wheel as if looking for something and then abruptly made a turn. The road began to climb and twist. Of course, we were in Woodland Hills now, and "Hills" was in the community's name. I just hadn't realized what was beyond the houses I'd driven by.

It was suddenly like a different world, as if we were in one of the canyons where the houses were built into the hillsides. The road was narrow and most of the houses hugged the street. The ones that were set back had driveways that seemed almost vertical. Elise pulled the car off the street onto a bricked area in front of a house that sat just feet from the curb.

As I squeezed out of the car, I checked out the design of the house. It was very plain looking, almost like a long box with a roof. There was a double door and a couple of small windows.

"Now, remember, no word to anyone we were here," she said as she went up to the door. There was something hanging off the handle, and she punched in some numbers and extracted a key. Elise made a point of leading the way as she pushed open the door. She poked her head in first, called out "Hello!" a couple of times, and waited for a response. When there was only silence, she walked us inside. She stopped short on the mat just inside the door, and the two of us bumped into her.

"We can't drip all over and make a mess. You have to take off your shoes and coats." She pointed to a coat tree next to the door.

Adele kicked off her shoes and dropped her coat on a hook, and I did the same.

"The bedrooms and the bonus room are downstairs," Elise said, pointing out the stairway that was cut out of the floor. "I'll just go down there and check that everything is shipshape." She dropped her voice and seemed to be speaking to herself. "The agent should always check that everything is presentable before showing it to the client." I thought I heard her squeal as she went down the stairs and figured it was part of her pep talk.

The outside of the house hadn't even hinted at what the inside was like. The upper floor was really one continuous space that included a living room, dining area, and kitchen. The ceilings were vaulted, making the space seem airy. The furniture was sparse, which only added to the open feeling. I was drawn to the far wall, which was all windows and sliding-glass doors. A patio ran the whole length of the place, but it was the view that entranced me. We were perched on the edge of a hill. There was no yard, but rather a sheer drop to the street below. I looked down on the flat area beyond and saw rooftops and backyard pools. In the distance, another hillside was dotted with houses. Turning another way, I could see all of the western part of the Valley to the Santa Susana mountains. I shivered as I felt a blast of cold air coming up from below and wished I'd been able to keep my coat on.

"You can see the cars going around the bend at the top of Topanga Canyon," I said to Adele, but she was too busy opening cabinets and doors.

I was about to open the sliding door for a clear view— since the windows were splotched with water—when I heard a flurry of footsteps.

"We have to go. We have to go now," Elise said as she reached the top floor. "C'mon." She waved her hands impatiently when neither of us moved right away. "I just got a text from Logan that he's showing some properties to clients. He's very anxious to sell this place, so I'm sure it will be his first stop." I'd never seen her so unglued. All I could think of was that old saying about a chicken with its head cut off. She was already at the door with her shoes and coat on and fussing at us to hurry. She grabbed our coats off the rack and pushed them on us as we slid into our shoes and then herded us out.

"Remember, none of us were here," Elise said as she pulled the door shut behind us.

Chapter Two

"Do I ever need this," Dinah Lyons said. It was just about five o'clock and time for our happy-hour gathering, and we were the first two at the table in the yarn department of the bookstore. Dinah was still going by Lyons despite having married Commander Blaine. Everybody knew her as Lyons and she wanted to leave it that way—even though Lyons wasn't the last name she'd been born with but rather had come from her jerky ex, Jeremy.

Originally, the Tarzana Hookers had met a couple of times a week during the day, but recently we'd changed our meetings to five PM and called it happy hour. Some people had a glass of wine to relax from their day; we did our relaxing with crochet.

Shedd & Royal Books and More had a lot of space, so creating a yarn department had been no problem. From this back corner of the store, I could see the whole place. Aside from the main part of the store, which was all bookcases and display tables, there was an alcove for music and movies and another alcove that was the children's department.

We had set aside an area for events near a big window that faced Ventura Boulevard.

"This is the perfect antidote to the stresses of the day," Dinah said, watching me take out a pair of knitting needles and several balls of yarn. "You better not let Adele see those. What are you making?"

I glanced around quickly and was relieved that Adele was nowhere in sight. "I'm making swatches of some new yarn we got in. Let me know when you see her coming and I'll put them away." We liked to have made-up samples of all of our yarns. There was no problem with the crocheted versions, but since we welcomed all yarn crafters, I thought we should have knitted ones as well. I had to do the knitted ones in secret or deal with a hissy fit from Adele. We all agreed that crochet was the better yarn craft, but she was over the top about it.

But then, she had her reasons. It had to do with a story straight out of Cinderella. Adele had an unpleasant step-mother and stepsisters who were knitters and had mocked her crochet.

As I began to cast on the stitches, Dinah pulled out her work and, as she did, the metal crochet hook came loose from the tangle of delft blue yarn and hit the table with a ping. She retrieved it and started crocheting. "Just when I think my students can't surprise me, they do."

Dinah taught freshman English to reluctant students. She got them when they were still acting like goofy high school kids and did her best to whip them into real college students. It had always been a challenge but was even more so now thanks to all the new ways of communicating.

"I tried to have them handwrite a letter." Her eyes went skyward at the memory. "They couldn't understand why 'Hi' wasn't a proper salutation. They didn't know how to write in cursive and could barely print. And they couldn't spell without presumptive type. When I suggested a dictionary and held up my *Merriam-Webster*, they all gave me blank looks."

She finished a row and moved on to the next. "I think this group of students might be the one that breaks me. They might be totally hopeless." She held up what she was making and showed me the rectangular shape. "Am I really making place mats?" She let out a resigned sigh. "I knew it would be different once we got married. It's always hard, but at our age, it's even harder. He wants us to sit down to dinner every night at a whole setup. Candles, cloth napkins, the works. The place mats were his idea when I said I wanted to make something for him. I was thinking more along the lines of a scarf." She moved down the row of crochet. "I liked the way we used to set up dinner on the coffee table. All casual and spontaneous. Now you see why I had cold feet about getting married." She got to the end of the row and turned her work. "But enough about me. What happened after I left you this morning?"

I knew I wasn't supposed to tell anyone, but Dinah was my best friend, so it seemed as if it would be okay. Besides, she wasn't likely to be talking to Adele's Cutchykins or Elise's

Logan anytime soon. I told her about the whole episode. "We never even saw the whole place. Elise got a text that Logan was showing property and she was sure he was on his way there and she rushed us out." I gave Dinah a brief description of what I'd seen of the house, spending most of the time on the view.

"Here comes Adele," Dinah said, nudging me. I stowed the knitting needles in my tote back and pulled out a crochet hook just as Adele came in to join us. She was followed by Lara-Ann Wilson, our new hire.

"I'll keep an eye on everything while you two are back here," she said, picking up a skein of yarn that had fallen out of the row of cubbies along the back wall and replacing it. "I hope it wasn't a problem that I had yesterday off."

I smiled and told her we'd managed okay.

Now that I was assistant manager and the two owners of the bookstore, Mrs. Shedd and Mr. Royal, had finally gone public with their relationship and gotten married, we had hired some more help. Lara-Ann was perfect for the job. She loved books, particularly mysteries. She was divorced with a grown daughter, so working all kinds of hours wasn't a problem. I was actually glad she wasn't a crocheter so there was no chance she'd want to join the group instead of looking after the store.

"She sure has great hair," Dinah said as Lara-Ann went back into the main part of the bookstore.

"It makes you want to have gray hair, if it can look like hers," I said. Her hair was long and wavy and hung to her shoulders. I was sure the color was premature. Lara-Ann couldn't have been older than her early forties.

Eduardo Linnares passed Lara-Ann as he headed toward us. I watched as the few patrons in the bookstore stopped and looked at him as he walked by. As a former cover model for romance novels and later a commercial spokesperson, he had charismatic good looks. He was tall, and even his slacks and sport jacket couldn't hide his nice build. His face had all the stereotypical features of a romantic hero, including the strong jaw and angular cheekbones. His lustrous black hair was pulled into a ponytail.

When he'd started being cast as the cowboy's father on book covers, he'd decided it was time to move on. These days, his time was spent running The Apothecary, a high-end drugstore and sundries shop in Encino.

The Hookers mostly carried cloth totes or reusable bags from Trader Joe's. He carried a tawny-colored leather tote.

"Ladies," he said with a warm smile and a bow of his head as he dropped the tote on a chair. He eased his large frame into his chair and then leaned back with a sigh. "I'm glad for this hour. Then I have to get back to my store. We're having a special event. Tyler Penner is signing the silver hairbrushes she designed." We all nodded, recognizing the name. She was the current hot model/reality star/social media influencer, and her name on any product made it a huge seller.

He took out a ball of ecru thread and a thin silver hook and began working. His Irish grandmother had taught him

Irish crochet when he was a child. He could turn out the lacy patterns with ease. He was currently making runners for the shelves in his store, thinking they would show off the high-end shaving and grooming items he sold. He understood better than most that presentation is everything.

CeeCee and Sheila came in arm in arm. Our actress leader seemed to have forgotten all about the skirmish in the restaurant and appeared in high spirits. Sheila Altman was the youngest in our group. I think our happy-hour get-togethers were most important to her. She had anxiety issues that she kept at bay with crochet. She worked at Luxe, the lifestyle shop down the street. *Lifestyle* seemed to mean an eclectic and expensive selection of merchandise. I loved to look in there. It smelled wonderful from all the handmade soaps they sold, and there was always so much to look at— handmade shoes, dresses made of sari silk, the occasional piece of furniture fashioned from reclaimed wood. Sheila had developed her own style of crocheting and knitting as well, though she kept the knitting on the down-low from Adele. Her pieces were done in blues, greens, and purples and had the dreamy look of an Impressionist painting. She mostly stuck to wraps, blankets, and scarves and was able to sell them at Luxe, as they fit in perfectly with the other merchandise.

"Tell this to those women who thought my career was in the toilet," CeeCee said before she even sat down. It was a given that she sat on one end of the rectangular wood table and Adele sat on the other, giving the appearance that they were co-leaders of our group. We all still thought of

CeeCee as our leader, but this kept the peace. "I had a meeting this afternoon with my agent and the representative of a dog food company. They want me to be the spokesperson. You all know how much I love animals," she said in her musical voice. She had a sparkling smile as she spoke that seemed to pour out warmth.

"Are you sure you want to do that?" Adele said from the other end of the table. "One minute you're known as an Academy Award–nominated actress, and the next minute everybody sees you and thinks of the smell of dog food. Are they giving you some kind of catchy line to say, like, 'Where's the beef?'"

"My, but you know how to poke a hole in my balloon of happiness," CeeCee said. Her expression had dimmed, and I knew she was not only thinking over what Adele had said but also considering if it might be true.

"If it was me, I'd want something with a yarn company. Maybe a whole line with my name on it." Adele had gotten a dreamy look.

"You should really think it over carefully. You don't want to be so defined by dog food that you get passed over for a real role," Lara-Ann said. I was surprised to see she had come back into the yarn department. "That's what happened to my daughter, Paisley." Then she looked embarrassed. "Sorry, I couldn't help but overhear."

CeeCee went back to addressing Adele's comment. "I had my own sitcom, and there were all the guest shots in other shows, and then the part of Ophelia in the Anthony movie. I even hosted a reality show. The public isn't going to connect me with the dog food. It's because of who I am that the dog food company wants me. The point is they'll connect the dog food with me, which incidentally is really a super product. I'm feeding it to Talulah and Marlena now," she said, referring to her two tiny Yorkies.

"You forgot the skin cream infomercial," Adele said, and CeeCee gave her a sharp look. She had deliberately not mentioned it, as it had turned out badly and was ancient history now.

Finally, Lara-Ann was able to get a word in to tell me she was having trouble finding a book someone had ordered. It was easier for me to go with her and find it than it would have been to explain where it might be.

When I returned to the group, Rhoda Klein was sitting at the table with an unfamiliar man next to her. Even though she'd lived in Southern California for twenty years or more, Rhoda had a thick New York accent. The best way to describe her personality was blunt. She always got right to the point of a situation. That was how she looked as well, with a solid build, no-nonsense short brown hair, and comfortable clothes.

"That's Molly," she said, turning to the man as I returned to my seat. "She's the one I told you about." The man leaned forward to get a better look at me. I took the opportunity to check him out as well. He was ordinary looking, with plain brown hair that seemed a little uneven.

"This is Leo Klein, my brother-in-law," Rhoda said. She turned to him. "Well, you've met everyone now. You can go look around and I'll find you when I'm ready to go. Molly can tell you about the other activities they have going on here then."

Leo pushed away from the table reluctantly and then wandered off toward the main part of the store. She waited until he was out of earshot. "Whew." She leaned back in relief and let her arms drop to her sides. "You have no idea." She took another breath. "His wife died six months ago. He was living in Newark, but he decided that he ought to get a change, and so he came to stay with us while he figures out what to do." She took out a lapghan she was working on and began to crochet. "His wife did everything for him. Cooked his dinner, picked out his clothes, and handled all the money. Now he's like a lost puppy. He's lonely and he wants to find someone else." She rocked her head with dismay. "I tried fixing him up with a woman in the book circle I belong to." Her eyes went skyward. "It was a disaster. He showed up at her house expecting her to cook dinner, and she was expecting to go out. He finally took her to McDonald's and was reluctant to get her one of their ice cream cones, saying something about how she ought to skip dessert. He came home thinking she'd had a good time, but she called me and told me to make sure he never contacted her again. He is clueless that he's clueless."

We all looked toward the main part of the store, where he was wandering among the bookcases. Rhoda had mentioned that he was just about my age, but he looked older somehow. Since Rhoda had said Leo's wife had picked out his clothes, I wondered who had chosen his current outfit. The navy-blue sweater seemed baggy over the navy-blue pleated cotton pants. And he wore white sneakers that were definitely not the current style.

"Pink can help him," Adele said. "Her husband died and she had to deal with the whole older people dating thing."

I looked across the table to Dinah. "Maybe it would be better if Commander gave him some advice. He was widowed, and he had to start a new chapter with someone new," I said.

"He won't listen to a man. Hal tried to talk to him, and Leo just didn't get it. He needs a woman's touch." Rhoda gave me a hopeful smile. "Would you? I know you'd be great."

"Flattery will get you everywhere," I said with a smile. "I hope I can live up to your expectations. Call him over and we can do it now."

Rhoda seemed unsure. "He'll be uncomfortable with everyone listening. Maybe he could go over to your house when you have a day off."

"Are you trying to set me up with him?" I asked with a laugh.

Rhoda brightened. "I hadn't thought of that, but if you're interested . . ." Rhoda let the thought trail off.

"I'll be happy to try to give him some advice, but that's it."

Leaving nothing to chance, Rhoda locked in a time for him to come to my place.

"Enough about dating," CeeCee said, projecting her voice over the conversations that had broken out at the table. "I think we really should get back to our core hooking and start making things for charities again." She looked out into the bookstore to see if anyone was listening and had misconstrued what she had said this time. There was no one.

"I mentioned it earlier when some of us met for the unveiling of the CeeCee Collins Mélange at the Petite Café." She glanced around at the group. "I hope you'll all go in and try it. But I'm getting off the subject. So what do you all think about getting back to our original mission?"

"Absolutely right," Rhoda said, and the rest of us all nodded in agreement.

"Good," CeeCee said with a big smile. "I'll check around and find something special for us to do." She looked around the table. "Elise hasn't shown up, has she? She was in the group this morning, so I'm sure I have her okay." She turned to Adele. "Did she say anything to you after I left about not coming?"

Adele shrugged and seemed tense. "I don't know anything about her plans or what she was going to do today." Her voice sounded forced. She nudged me. "Right, Molly?"

I was about to say, "Huh?" until I got what she was doing. Adele was trying to say nothing by saying too much. I gave CeeCee a vague nod. "As far as I know, she was planning to be here," I said. But I couldn't help but wonder if her not showing up had something to do with her showing us the house.

Chapter Three

I intended to call Elise when the happy-hour group broke up, but a bunch of teenage girls came in looking for what appeared to be the next big thing. Apparently Irene, the hottest YouTube goddess, had been telling her minions that books were "the thing." She had sold them on the idea that there was no greater way to get away from the craziness of teenage life than to read a real book. In physical form. The latest book Irene had been pushing was *My Gal Ella*, which was a modern-day retelling of Cinderella.

"She said if we went to a bookstore, we could get a copy right away," one of the girls said. She glanced around Shedd & Royal with awe. "This place is really nice. I didn't know it was here."

I had to search around our stock to find enough copies to appease them and then put in a rush order for more books.

By the time I got home, I had forgotten all about Elise. My menagerie was waiting by the kitchen door when I came across the yard. The door was all glass, so I couldn't miss seeing them. The rain had stopped for the moment, but everything was still very wet. There were puddles on the patio, and the bark of the orange trees was so shiny it reflected the floodlights I had on the back of my house.

Felix and Cosmo slipped out as I went in. Felix was a small gray terrier mix and loved going outside no matter the weather. Cosmo was an unknown mix of breeds, had long black fur, and resembled a black mop. I expected them to return with muddy paws and pulled out the old towel I used on them to have it ready.

I made sure not to let the two cats out, though they hung by the door. They were allowed outside only during the day and when they could be escorted. Otherwise they got into too much trouble.

"Everybody has been fed," my son Samuel said. He was just slipping on a vintage sport coat over his jeans. His sandy-colored hair was in a ponytail, and I was glad my twenty-three-year-old son had resisted the trend of wearing a man bun. "I let them out before and tried to get Blondie to join them. But you know her. All she wants is to sit in that old chair in your room. I did take her for a walk, though. That dog has some nerve claiming to be a terrier mix." He glanced out the large kitchen window as Felix rushed out in the yard, got beyond the floodlights' reach, and disappeared. "Now that's a terrier," he said. The small dog with wiry gray hair was definitely truer to the breed. He was feisty and smart. He barked when the doorbell rang and had to be locked away on Halloween because he wasn't happy with all those strangers in weird outfits coming to his front door. "See, he's even giving lessons to Cosmo," Samuel joked.

Samuel followed me as I walked out of the kitchen and went to hang up my coat and stow my umbrella. He saw me looking into the living room. The coffee table had been pushed off to the side again, leaving the center of the room clear. "My mother and the girls were here again?"

"Grandma—I mean Liza—said to offer her apologies. They thought they could use the community room in their building, but it turns out they've been banned from using it as a rehearsal hall."

My mother was the lead singer of the She La Las, a girl group from the sixties that had had one big hit, "My Guy Bill." She and the girls, Lana and Bunny, were back doing gigs. Personally, I didn't know why they needed to rehearse so much. I was sure they could do the songs and choreography in their sleep.

Samuel must have read my mind. "They wanted to warm up before tonight, and they're working on something new—well, at least new to them—for that charity event. So they'll be back. That's why we left everything as is." He straightened his tweed jacket. "Gotta go. They have a gig at a small club in Burbank. I'm playing keyboards." Samuel was a barista by day and musician by night. When he wasn't acting as musical director for my mother, he played his own gigs at local bars. He could play just about every instrument, though he usually stuck to guitar or piano.

Samuel had been living with me off and on, and it seemed that every time he moved back, he brought some animals with him. I had planned on just one dog, Blondie. When Charlie died, I'd adopted her from a local shelter. She had an aloof personality, and I was sure that she'd been adopted once and returned to the shelter. We'd both been feeling pretty abandoned when I brought her home.

By now I was used to her personality. I called her the Greta Garbo of dogs because of her preference for being alone. I accepted that she wanted limited attention and didn't even care much about food. The only thing she got excited about was her nightly walk.

The two cats had come with Samuel. They had started out with different names but were now known as Mr. Kitty and Cat. Samuel had gotten them from a shelter. They were adult cats—Mr. Kitty was seven and Cat was ten—which had given them little chance to be adopted until Samuel came along.

Cosmo was a whole other story entirely. I'd gotten custody of him in a breakup.

Felix was the latest addition to the group. Samuel and his then girlfriend had found him somewhere. And Samuel had gotten the dog when they broke up.

I followed my son as he walked through the kitchen to the door. As an afterthought, he looked back. "You could come with. It would be good for you to get out there instead of sitting here alone."

Says who? The idea of an evening alone sounded great to me. I planned to make myself a nice dinner and cuddle up in front of a romantic comedy and watch Hugh Grant stumble around until he managed to win over Sandra Bullock,

Julia Roberts, or that woman in *Love Actually*. It didn't matter that I knew them all by heart; I enjoyed all the silliness and the always-rosy endings. Though I had pretty much given up on it happening in my life. I had been relegated to giving romance advice now. What was I going to tell Leo, anyway?

After Charlie died, I had tried starting a new chapter. It had started with me getting the job at Shedd & Royal and had included some attempts at relationships. I had married young and had never thought about dealing with dating ever again. I wished it was as simple as my catalog of romantic comedies made it seem.

With Samuel gone, I went and rousted Blondie from the chair and got her to go outside while the cats watched. All the dogs came in, and I did a number on muddy paws, gave them all a treat, and let them spread out through the house.

I was happy to find a bunch of white containers in the refrigerator, which meant no cooking. One of the positives of my mother and group using my house was that they always ordered in food. My father did the ordering, and his motto was, better to have too much than not enough. I poked through the containers and saw they had gotten Thai food. I made myself a plate of pad thai with its orange-colored sauce, some thick noodles with a brown sauce, vegetables simmered in a yellow curry, and a big mound of jasmine rice. I left it sitting on the counter while I set up the TV in the room where I kept all my yarn. The plan was to eat first, then crochet while I watched the movie. I popped *Two Weeks Notice* into the DVD player. The food had inspired my choice. Sandra Bullock had a thing in the movie about ordering lots of white containers of food, though in her case it was Chinese.

I polished off the plate and began crocheting. I had a bunch of works in progress that served different purposes. For tonight, I wanted something simple that I didn't have to think about and pulled out the thing I most liked both to make and to wear. The one skein of yarn went from burnt orange to turquoise, and, when the cowl was finished, it would be a colorful accent to my usually bland work outfits. Not that I really had to pay attention to the movie. I'd seen it so many times I practically knew the dialogue.

I had settled into crocheting, and the movie was just at that part in every romantic comedy where they realize they're made for each other and somebody has to run somewhere, when the phone rang.

It was late enough to stir some worry as I reached for the cordless. The phone I had now no longer announced the caller in a mechanical voice, and I always forgot to look at the small screen to see who it was. "Hello," I said with a breathy touch of concern.

"Detective Greenberg here," a familiar voice said in a flat, professional tone. Before I could ask why he sounded so formal, he added, "It's official police business."

Barry Greenberg had been part of my attempts at dating. What had we been to each other? Boyfriend and girlfriend? It sounded so juvenile. I supposed the best way to describe it was that we'd been a couple. It hadn't worked out for a number of reasons. Mostly, it had seemed that he'd wanted to make all the decisions and his job would always come first. That and he wanted to get married and I didn't.

I hated to admit it, but even though we'd been broken up for a long time, I still couldn't help but feel a flutter when I heard his voice. I was guessing that would never go away, but this time there was another feeling too—concern.

"What kind of official police business?" The flutter had been knocked out by worry.

"It's better if we talk in person," he said. He was all authoritative cop voice, and it was impossible to tell if he felt any sort of residual feeling talking to me.

He was a master at controlling his feelings, whether tiredness or hunger or anything connected to romance, probably. He kept them hidden behind the benign cop face and flat voice.

When I agreed, he told me he was parked in front of my house. By the time I got to the front door, he was coming up the stone path. It had started raining again, but it was a soft sort of rain. All the moisture in the air made the atmosphere feel close, like being in a chilly steam bath. As he reached the front porch, the overhead porch light reflected off the droplets in his short-cropped dark hair. In his tough-guy fashion, he'd left off his raincoat, and more droplets glistened on his dark suit. I did feel a tug when I looked at his face. There were shadows under his eyes and a faint dark stubble on his stubborn jaw.

It was only when he came inside that I noted he had a folder under his arm.

"I thought I'd avoid a rush of dogs if I didn't use the doorbell," he said, and I nodded.

He stopped to wipe his feet on the mat. He cocked his head and seemed to be listening just as Hugh Grant called out, "Darling, where are you?"

"Do you have company?" There was a flicker of consternation in his mouth.

"It's a movie," I said. "I was enjoying an evening alone with a romantic comedy."

"Right," he said, going back to his stone face. I didn't make a move to bring him farther into the house, and finally he suggested it might be better if we were sitting down. I led him into the living room, and he looked at the readjusted furniture.

"My mother's using it as a rehearsal space again," I said by way of explanation. I was trying to stay cool, but my nerves were on edge. Part of Barry's job was delivering bad news. I wanted to demand that he tell me whatever it was right away, as the tension was getting to me. But I was also determined to be as controlled as he was.

"Where would you like to sit?" I said. I had two leather couches that were adjacent to each other. There was usually a table with a lamp between them, but it had been moved and now they formed an L and were touching.

"It's your call," he said. I offered him one of the couches and pulled a chair up from across the room for myself. "Maybe I'll just stand," he said, realizing the couch made it seem too much like a social call.

"Maybe I will, too," I said. I wasn't about to have him towering over me. Much as I had tried to hide it, the worried looked showed in my face.

"Everyone you know is okay," he said, apparently picking up on my expression. I took a deep breath and let it out, which didn't go unnoticed. "I'm sorry. I should have said that right away."

He took the file from under his arm. "I'm here about this." With no coffee table to use, he put it on the arm of the couch and then opened it to reveal an eight-by-ten photograph of an orange-colored scarf on a wood floor. "Do you recognize this?" he said.

Of course I did. It was my go-to scarf that I was particularly proud of, since I had created the design myself. As an accent, I had added yellow flowers using yarn that glowed in the dark, though that had turned out to be a disappointment. The yarn glowed for only a few moments and no one had even noticed this unusual trait. That might have been why the yarn had been discontinued. Barry had seen me wear the scarf numerous times, and it was obvious he knew it was mine, or else why would he be here? But where had he gotten this picture and why was he asking?

I took a moment to think. I remembered that I had thrown it on that morning as I was leaving. I retraced my steps in my mind. I'd gone directly to meet everyone at the Petite Café. I was sure I hadn't left it there, as I remembered going back to the table to grab my umbrella, and there had been nothing else left. I'd gone to the bookstore afterward. Could I have left it there? And then I remembered the stop before the bookstore. Elise had rushed us out of that house. She had grabbed my coat off the clothes tree as I was stepping into my shoes. It must have fallen on the ground.

Barry was too much in serious cop mode for this to be merely a lost-and-found sort of thing. If he had just been returning my scarf, he would have brought it with him. Why all this nonsense about sitting down? Unless there was more to it.

"Why do you want to know?" I said. I saw his shoulders drop, and there was the slightest noise as he blew out his breath in consternation.

"Just answer my question with an answer, not another question," he said.

"I'm not saying anything until you tell me why you're asking," I said, thinking of my promise to Elise to never disclose that we were at that house. "I doubt you have time in your busy cop schedule to act as the lost-and-found of women's accessories, so I'm assuming it's somehow connected with your core business of crime investigation," I said, trying to be light about it.

Barry stepped closer to me. "Molly, stop it. You're not going to trick me into giving you any information. You do realize that we can test the scarf and get DNA from it?"

"Maybe you can and maybe you can't, but it takes a long time and you have to have something to match it with," I said, and he closed his eyes for a moment.

"I should have known you'd be difficult," he said, shaking his head with frustration.

"Only because you won't tell me what's going on."

"It doesn't work that way. I'm in charge," he said.

"And that was the problem, wasn't it? You wanted to make all the decisions." Oops, I'd strayed into personal matters. I tried to cover it, but his eyes had flashed and he'd dropped the cool-cop thing for an instant.

"Forget I said that," I said.

"Then you'll answer my question. Do you recognize this scarf?"

"Not answering until I know why you're asking," I answered.

"You're impossible," he said, and the benign face cracked.

I knew that he probably hadn't eaten, and maybe I felt a little bad about giving him such a hard time even though there was no way I was going to say anything until I knew what was going on with the scarf. "My mother left a lot of Thai food. How about I make you a plate?"

He started to shake his head, but I think the mere mention of the food got through his ability to keep his hunger at bay. "Maybe I will take you up on that. It's been a long day, and I'm not sure there's anything at my place. But don't think you're buying me off with a plate of pad thai. You're going to tell me about the scarf."

"Don't bet on it," I said with a smile.

I don't know why I always seemed to end up offering him food whenever I saw him, which actually hadn't been much recently. I mean, we were finished as a couple and he wasn't interested in being friends. Our only connection was Cosmo. When he and his son had adopted the small black dog, I'd agreed to let him stay at my house, since I had a yard and a doggy door. When we'd broken up, Cosmo had just stayed with me, though Barry's son, Jeffrey, had visitation rights. Being a typical teenager, the visits were spotty at best and recently had gone down to nothing, since Jeffrey was staying with his mother for the moment.

I went into the kitchen, made a generous plate of the leftovers, and put it in the microwave to heat. Berry had followed me into the kitchen, and I told him to help himself to something to drink in the refrigerator.

"So what are you working on these days?" I said casually as I pulled the plate out and carried it into the dining room. The table was littered with stuff my mother had moved off the coffee table before it had been pushed against the wall. The junior detective set my son Peter had given me as a birthday present was among the junk. Barry's eye went to it as he set a can of soda on the table.

"I should have known," Barry said, looking up at me, "that there would be strings attached to the food. I know what you're doing. How about we talk about something else? How are things with you and Mason?"

Mason Fields was a hugely successful attorney with a lot of celebrity clients. We'd had a casual, no-strings sort of relationship at first, but I couldn't leave well enough alone and had been upset that he'd never introduced me to his two daughters. In fact, I'd made it kind of a deal breaker. It turned out to be like opening Pandora's box. I met the daughters and then his ex-wife, and then one of his daughters moved in with him while she went to law school, and then his ex was living there too, supposedly while she got her house remodeled. It went from not knowing his family to knowing way too much. Did I mention that the daughter who moved in didn't like me and his ex-wife was campaigning for them to get back together?

"If you have to know, I sort of broke up with him." I didn't go into any details or mention that the reason I'd broken up with Mason was because I was sure his wife had won the campaign and they were back together. I noticed Barry's expression perk up. "And I'm so busy with work and all now, I don't really have a lot of time."

"Married to your job?" he said with almost a smile. There wasn't any one reason we'd broken up, but the fact that he was married to his job and kept insane hours was part of it.

"Okay, you got me on that."

Barry seemed to be inhaling the food, and I wondered when he'd last eaten. I offered him seconds and he gratefully accepted.

"When Jeffrey was living with me, I had to remember to keep food in the house, but now that he's at his mother's, it's been breakfast sandwiches at the all-night doughnut shop."

I was thinking about asking him how he was doing on his own and then thought he might consider it too personal. But before I could finish debating with myself, he'd already begun talking about it. "It was hard adjusting when he came to live with me, and then there was all that stuff about wanting to be an actor that I didn't understand. But now . . ." He let out a deep sigh. "What's that saying about not realizing what you have until it's gone?" He was staring down at the plate, poking a piece of broccoli with his chopstick.

"But he's coming back?" I said, concerned that he sounded so forlorn.

"I hope so. His mother is doing a whole number supporting his acting ambitions and not even minding that he's going by a single name—Columbia. And her new husband is being quite the involved stepdad."

It seemed that Barry suddenly caught himself and realized he was being too open about his feelings. He reached over and took the detective set and flipped off the lid. Then he turned to me with a grin. "And what is that you've been working on lately?"

"Why are you asking?" Then I smiled. "I get it. You think it's somehow connected with that scarf that may or may not be mine."

He answered with his blank cop face. I put on my thinking pose, and maybe it was a little over the top when I pulled the Deerslayer hat out of the box and put it on. "You don't have to be Sherlock Holmes to deduce that you're asking me about the scarf because it's somehow connected to a crime." I looked at him expectantly. "That's it, isn't it?"

I had to be very careful here not to divulge anything, but my mind was racing. What if there was something valuable missing from the house and the owner was trying to track down who had been there?

Barry wouldn't talk, even when I offered him ice cream.

"Thank you for the food," he said as we finally walked to the front door. He looked back and our eyes met for a moment. He said, "You do realize this isn't over?"

* * *

I didn't really care if Hugh Grant and Sandra Bullock got together anymore and just took out the DVD and turned off the player. The exchange with Barry had been upsetting. It wasn't really the scarf or our mutual determination not to give away any information. It was simply realizing that seeing him had set up a tempest of feelings.

Then I got annoyed all over again that he wouldn't tell me why he had my scarf.

The TV had gone to a replay of the news. A story had just ended and it went to a commercial. It was another of the cute ones that seemed so popular. This one featured Cauli Flower, the vegetable fairy. Just as she was wandering through a forest of broccoli—which she called little trees— Cosmo and Felix ran past, playing a late-night game of chase. Felix got his foot caught in the yarn I had been using, and when he ran out of the room, the yarn and my work went with him. I managed to grab him before he did too much damage.

When I came back into the room, the news was back on and in the middle of a story. I looked at the screen and then did a double take when I saw a reporter standing in front of the house we'd looked at earlier that day. There was no mistaking the boxy shape of the house, the bricked area in front of it, the dark-red double doors with the lockbox, and, of course, the FOR SALE sign with Logan Belmont's name on it.

The reporter was saying, "Timothy Clark was well known for his role as Binkie MacPherson on *Bradley V, P.I.*"

The live feed cut away to a tape of an even-featured man with a haughty expression wearing golf knickers and holding a cocktail glass as he spoke to his cousin Kiplington Bradley the Fifth about a case the ultra-wealthy amateur sleuth was working on. He delivered what was his punch line for the show: "Oh, no, not another kerfuffle. Shall I call the butler?" Since the show had been filmed in front of an audience, their laugher was heard in the background.

The reporter came back on and said that Clark had been nominated for an Emmy but, when the show ended, had turned to helping others make their dreams come true through his acting coaching and workshops.

"I got it; so it's Timothy Clark's house. So what's the problem?" I said to the TV. Then something struck me that the reporter had said. It was just one word. He had said Timothy *was* known for the role of Binkie MacPherson. *Was* as in past tense. I felt a catch in my stomach. Did that mean Timothy was dead?

And if he was, why was Barry investigating? I flipped to another station, hoping to find another replay of the news with more of the details. Channel 12 was in the middle of the story. The reporter said Timothy had been found by a real estate agent who had brought clients to see the house. The picture went to tape, and I immediately recognized Logan Belmont. He was pretty bland looking except for his odd hairline that made him look like he was wearing a hair hat.

I was impressed by how in control of himself he seemed

for someone who had just come across a dead person as he spoke to the TV reporter. "I had brought my clients downstairs, and when we got to the den, I saw Timothy from the back. It looked like he was just sitting there, and I was going to introduce my clients to him. I'd told them the house belonged to a celebrity, but having them actually see him in person would be even better. Or would have been. I brought them into the room with me and was about to introduce them when I noticed his head was slumped forward. I thought he was asleep or maybe drunk—there was a cocktail glass on the table next to him. When I got a good look at him—" Logan suddenly looked a little pale as he remembered the moment. "I hustled my clients out of the room and called the authorities."

The reporter returned to the screen. "The manner of death of the forty-four-year-old hasn't yet been determined."

I sat back on the couch, stunned, as it all began to sink in. I knew enough about investigations of dead bodies to realize that the manner of death could be natural, accidental, suicide, homicide, or undetermined. I was hoping it was the first one. Then the presence of my scarf wouldn't mean much—not that I planned to acknowledge it was mine—and Barry would let it go. I shuddered to think what would happen if it was determined to be a homicide.

Then I began to put two and two together. Logan had gone there right after we left. Did that mean Timothy Clark had been sitting there, dead, while I was admiring the view? I knew that Elise was probably nervous doing her first house showing, but how could she have missed that?

If I could find out what Logan had seen, I might have a better idea if I was in trouble or not.

I ignored the late hour and called Logan and Elise's house. I was disappointed when not only did I get their voice mail, but the message said their mailbox was full so I couldn't even leave word to call me.

And then there was Adele. She had made a big fuss about not telling Eric about looking at a house, but Adele wasn't very dependable about sticking with what she said. I thought she'd be more likely to keep it to herself if she knew the owner had been found dead. I tried her number, but I didn't even get voice mail, just a message that Adele and Eric weren't accepting calls at this time.

I really wanted to talk to somebody about the situation. My natural instinct was to call my best friend, Dinah. Before, it had never been too late for either of us to call each other with news or problems, but lately I'd gotten to feeling funny about it. It was all because of the time that Commander had answered the phone. He'd given the phone to Dinah but had apparently commented afterward that the late call had worried him and sent his blood pressure up.

I had no choice but to put everything off until the morning. Needless to say, I spent a fitful night trying to sleep.

Chapter Four

As soon as I arrived at Shedd & Royal the next morning, I went looking for Adele. When I didn't find her in the children's department, I got worried. Lara-Ann was setting up some books on a display table. "Have you seen Adele?" I asked, trying not to sound frantic.

"She's in the café. You seem upset. Is there anything I can help you with?" She added a pat to my arm for reassurance.

"Thanks, but I need to speak to Adele." I didn't wait for a response but rushed back to the front of the bookstore and the café entrance. I spotted Adele immediately. Adele did not merely read to the kids at story time; she dressed in a costume that went along with the chosen book or theme. Based on her outfit today, I wasn't sure what she had going on. She wore a long, spring-green crocheted tunic over green tights. A pair of wings made out of green chiffon with glitter accents were strapped to her back, and a tiny sparkly crown finished the look.

She was standing at the counter having a conversation with Bob, our barista, and took a moment before she

46

responded when I called her name. "Pink, I'm glad you're here. Since you're now the assistant manager, you need to tell Bob that my hibiscus punch is top priority. We're having a fairy tea party at story time."

Now I understood the costume. Bob looked at me, and I gave him the nod to handle her request despite the line waiting for coffee drinks. I looped my arm in Adele's and pulled her off to the side while he went to fill a pitcher and get cups. "Did you happen to watch the news last night?" I asked, and she rolled her eyes as if I had asked an absurd question.

"It was Tuesday night," she said, as if I was supposed to know what that meant. When I didn't immediately respond, she threw me an exasperated look. "Everybody knows Tuesday night is our special evening. Mother Humphries goes to movie night at the senior center and Eric and I have what we call our cocoon time. No distraction, like phones or TV. It's just us together." She looked at me directly. "You should keep that in mind for the future. Maybe if you had done something like that, you wouldn't be alone now."

I was used to Adele's comments by now. They could seem barbed, but I think she believed she was handing out useful advice. I merely ignored what she said and got to the point.

"I think you should know that the house you looked at yesterday belongs to Timothy Clark, and he was found dead—"

"Wha-what," she stuttered. "That was his house. That's where he lives. Dead?" She seemed to choke on the words.

I had never seen Adele behave quite this way before. "He can't be." Her face had gone white, and she seemed to be coming unglued. "He can't be dead now. Just when—" Her eyes went skyward. "I can't deal with story time. You'll have to handle it." She tore off the wings, pushed them on me, and fled the café.

A moment later Bob came from behind the counter and glanced around. He saw the wings hanging off my arms. "I guess this goes to you now." He handed me a tray with a pitcher of ruby-red liquid and a stack of tiny paper cups.

There was no time to think about Adele's reaction, as I could already see a bunch of small kids rushing toward the children's department. So I strapped on the wings and went to join them.

I knew that Adele had some kind of procedure for checking kids in and making sure the adults who had brought them didn't come into the area with the carpet featuring cows jumping over the moon. I didn't have time to find her checklist and allowed whatever kids were there to find seats. I didn't have to worry about telling any adults not to come in, though, as they all rushed off, seeming happy to leave the kids in my care.

"You aren't Queen Adele," a little girl in a pink dress said. *Queen Adele?*

I made up some story that Queen Adele had been called away to take care of some important royal business and had left me in charge. "I'm Fairy Princess Molly," I said, showing them my wings. And then I picked up the book Adele had left. I knew she was a far more dramatic reader than I was, but I got through the book and was handing out cups of fairy tea when I sensed an adult cross the threshold into the children's department.

"Sorry, no big people allowed until after the tea party," I said, turning in the direction of the entrance. "Barry? What are you doing here?" The words were out of my mouth before I could stop them.

He had stopped just inside the line where the kids' department started. I saw his gaze go to my wings, and for a moment, his mouth quivered as he restrained a smile. He was wearing a fresh suit and was clean-shaven, so after my house he must have actually gone home and called it a night.

"I was looking for Adele," he said. I finished serving the fairy tea and stepped closer to him.

"She's a little under the weather at the moment," I said warily. "Maybe I can help. What did you want? Are you looking for a kids' book?"

He pulled the folder from under his arm and took the photo of the orange-colored scarf out. "I thought that since you couldn't help me identify the owner of the scarf, maybe she might be able to help me. Maybe she would recognize the yarn and know who bought it."

"Sorry to burst your balloon, but she wouldn't be able to help you identify the owner by the yarn." I pointed toward the fringe that hung off the end. "It's worsted weight and it looks to me to be an acrylic blend. It's probably Lion Brand or Red Heart. They are both common brands and sold lots of places besides here." I purposely left out the yarn used for the flowers.

Barry didn't seem happy with the answer. I decided to take a shot and see if I could get him to talk about Timothy Clark's manner of death. "Why is it you're so interested in who the scarf belongs to?" I asked, doing my own version of a cop face.

"How is it that you know Timothy Clark?" Barry asked.

I froze at the mention of the name and restrained myself from insisting too quickly that I didn't know him, since I knew it would be a giveaway that I knew he was connected to the scarf.

"You mean that actor who was in *Bradley V, P.I.*?" I asked, attempting to sound nonchalant. "Didn't I hear that he died?" I picked up a spare cup of the fairy tea and held it out to him. "Have some fairy tea."

Barry's mouth tightened. "Molly, why don't you make it easy on both of us and just admit that it's your scarf? Then you can tell me what happened and we can work everything out."

Did he really think I was going to fall for that? I knew that was his standard way to try to get suspects to talk—the idea that if they spilled their guts, it was somehow going to help them. Sure, help them get charged with something. Then I backtracked in my mind. *It's the way he talks to suspects.* He couldn't think I was a suspect, could he?

Frustrated that I continued to stonewall about the scarf, Barry left.

I hung around the children's area until all the kids had been picked up, but I had other things to do and couldn't cover for Adele any longer. I had no idea where she'd gone or if she was even still in the bookstore. I looked around the main part of Shedd & Royal, hoping that I would see her coming across the bookstore with all the drama behind her. I hadn't had much of chance to think about it, but it really was an overreaction, even for Adele.

I saw Lara-Ann hand a customer a book in the travel section and then part company. Thank heavens we'd gotten more help. I waved her over.

"I need you to take over the kids' department for a while," I said when she got within earshot. I stepped aside to allow her entry. I was surprised when her face clouded over.

"I was just going to take an early lunch." She glanced toward the big window that looked out on Ventura Boulevard. I wondered why she seemed so interested in the new topiary giraffe that the Tarzana Chamber of Commerce had recently placed outside the bookstore. Someone had decided that the various San Fernando Valley communities needed to have individual identities. Thanks to our Tarzan connection, we got topiaries of wild animals and street signs with monkeys hanging off of them.

Then I realized she was really looking at the young woman who appeared to be in her early twenties standing next to the fancy-shaped bush. She looked remotely familiar, but then everybody in town did. That was the result of working in the bookstore. After another moment, I realized the young woman must be Lara-Ann's daughter. Before I could ask, she confirmed I was right. "She has an appointment and I was going to go with her."

This was the part of being a semi-boss that I didn't like.

I had to tell her she couldn't go and remind her that she couldn't just arbitrarily change the schedule.

"Of course," she said. I was relieved that she seemed to take it well. She just asked for a moment to go outside and talk to her daughter. That I could let her do. Since I had two sons, I was always curious what it would be like to have a daughter. It was nosy of me, but I watched anyway. It's amazing how much of communication is body language. I couldn't hear them, but from the way Lara-Ann was standing and gesturing with her arms, she seemed to be giving the girl a pep talk and trying to smooth things over.

If I'd done that with my older son, Peter, he would have crossed his arms and given me a withering stare. Samuel would have rolled his eyes as if he'd heard it all before but sort of liked it anyway. I couldn't see much of Lara-Ann's daughter's expression, but she seemed to have a defiant pose. Lara-Ann reached out to touch her, but the girl pulled away.

Seeing that her daughter really seemed to need her, as a person I felt bad about not letting her go, but as a boss I had to be tough. However, I did say I was sorry when Lara-Ann came back inside.

"It's okay," Lara-Ann said, relieving my guilt. "She's going to be okay now." Nosy me wanted to ask for details, but boss me told me to leave it be.

And now to track down Adele. She didn't answer her cell, but when I went to the parking lot, her car was still there. I checked around the whole bookstore and finally found her sitting in the small storage room where we kept the holiday decorations. With her green tunic, tights, and sparkling crown, she blended right in. Only, the giant cardboard Easter Bunny and the Santa Claus all looked happy, but Adele was crying.

"Go away, Pink; you can't see me this way." She had put one arm over her face to block my view of her tears, and she was waving me away with the other. Oh, dear, this was serious. I'd seen Adele do a lot of things but never have a meltdown like this.

I shut the door behind me and found a box to sit on. "Okay, tell me what's wrong," I said in a kind voice, but at the same time I was thinking, *And do it quickly*. I glanced back at the door, thinking that I'd left the bookstore largely unmanned except for our cashier Rayaad and Lara-Ann in the kids' department.

Ever since Mrs. Shedd and Mr. Royal had gotten married, they had been taking more and more time away from the bookstore. Previously, he'd been the one to take off on an adventure and leave her to run things. But now she'd begun to join him—though they were tamer adventures than he'd taken on his own. Whereas he'd gone off to Kenya for a safari, together they were more likely to take the boat to Catalina for the day.

While Adele stalled about answering me, I thought about how confusing the whole name thing became when you married later. Since the owners of the bookstore hadn't wanted to change the store's name, Mrs. Shedd had stayed Mrs. Shedd. Dinah had kept her name, since it was how she was known professionally, and Adele had just added another last name to hers. I wasn't thinking about getting married again myself, but for a moment I considered what I would do. What if I had married Barry as he wanted? Would I be Molly Pink Greenberg?

I'm afraid I chuckled at the thought, and Adele scowled at me. "Pink, it's not funny." She dabbed at her eyes and let out a sigh. It was useless to explain that I had been thinking about something else, so I just wiped the smile off my face and tried to appear sympathetic.

Adele always went for the dramatic and was big on letting the tension ramp up, so I imagined that was what she was doing now. I stole a glance at my watch and wished I could get her going.

Finally, I couldn't take it any longer. "Adele, let me know if you don't want to talk. Lara-Ann is watching the kids' department, but I need to get back."

Adele sat forward with concern. "I can't believe you're rushing me and my life is in ruins." She let out a sniffle I assumed was for effect. "It was going to be so wonderful. Timothy and I had it all figured out."

She got my interest at the mention of his name. "Then you knew him personally?" I said, surprised, wondering if she was an obsessive fan with some fantasy thing going on. Did she have secret photos of him stashed in her wallet? I hadn't meant to, but somehow I must have spoken as if I thought she knew him in a romantic way, because she grabbed my arm.

"No, no, it was nothing like that. I'm a one-man woman. Timothy and I were more like partners in an artistic endeavor." She stopped for emphasis and gestured toward herself with both hands. "You could say Timothy discovered me."

She had become the usual Adele, and her tears had dried up. "What do you mean, discovered you?" I asked.

She looked me in the eye. "As an actress—well, no, he really thought I was more of a personality. You do know that he taught workshops?" Then she abruptly lowered her voice. "No one knows it—well, except for the others in my group—but I was his star student." For a moment her eyes glazed over and she seemed to be remembering something. "He recognized my passion for crochet and, instead of setting up an audition for the Canoga Park Community Theater revival of *A Streetcar Named Desire*—which of course would have been for Blanche—he said he had bigger plans for me. We put our heads together and came up with an idea for me to host a crochet show. You know, there are so many outlets these days. We've been working feverishly for weeks, putting together my reel." She stopped to explain that this was a show biz term left over from the days when things had been on film that was rolled up on a reel. "He directed me in a series of snippets that show off my skills and personality. We did them all there with his cell phone," she said, gesturing toward the kids' department. "He edited them together and sent the finished piece to me. He even gave me a discount, since he was so sure I was going to be a big success. And then he told me he'd arranged a meeting with someone at the Craftee Channel." She heaved a big sigh. "It was supposed to go down in the next few weeks."

She gave it a moment before she continued. "My fortune

was about to change. I figured I'd get the show and then a line of yarn like Vanna White. That's why I let Elise show me the house."

I didn't know what to say, but she continued muttering to herself. "If only I'd found out who we were supposed to be meeting and where, I could proceed on my own."

"Why don't I call Eric? Maybe you'd feel better if you talked to him." I'd already taken out my cell phone, but she batted it away.

"No. He doesn't know anything about the workshops or my plans." Then she actually put the back of her hand to her forehead in a move straight out of an old-fashioned melodrama. "I've been deceiving him. He thinks I was going to a yoga class the nights I went to the workshop. I wanted to surprise him and Mother Humphries when it was a fate complete."

"I think you mean fait accompli," I said.

"Whatever," Adele said, and then she seemed to catch herself. "Of course, I'm very sorry that he's dead. What was it, a heart attack? I tried to tell him that all those French pastries and things like foie gras weren't good for him. If you think CeeCee has a sweet tooth, it's nothing compared to his. He even drank sweet cocktails."

"The reporter didn't say anything about what the cause of—" I began before Adele interrupted me.

"The important thing is that no one knows I'm connected with him. I went by my professional name, Lydia Fairchild, in the workshop. It has a nice ring, doesn't it?"

Adele had returned to her the-universe-revolves-around-me self, though she seemed to have outdone even her usual self-centeredness today. For the first time, she noticed I was still wearing the green fairy wings. "I hope you didn't mess up story time. I've given the kids pretty high expectations."

I sat, shaking my head, trying to keep my frustration in check, but I finally couldn't take it anymore. "Adele, maybe you're acting career is dead, but everything is dead forever for Timothy Clark."

I heard Adele whimper behind me. "Oh, you're so right. What would I do without you as a friend? I'm sorry that Timothy is gone, but I know what he would say." She paused and I cringed, afraid of what was coming next, and then she said it: "But the show must go on."

"There's something I have to tell you," I said, preparing for another meltdown when I told her that Timothy might have been dead when we were there and that my scarf was in the cops' hands.

"You'll have to tell me later," Adele said, getting up in a hurry. She was all recovered and looked out the open door. "I have to get back to my department and fix any damage you people might have done." She pulled off my wings and rushed out the door.

Chapter Five

A t just a little before five, I was clearing things up in the information booth, getting ready to go to the yarn department for happy hour. I had played phone tag with Dinah all day and hoped she would show up for the get-together. Commander was having a hard time understanding why she had to come every evening and had managed to spirit her away a number of times, though she usually let me know in advance when that happened.

CeeCee came bustling into the bookstore and stopped at the information booth. "Molly, I'm so excited. I have the charity project all worked out."

I hated to interrupt her, but something had been on my mind all afternoon—how to contain Adele. "There's something you need to know."

"Is it about the charity project?" she asked.

"No, it's something else." I urged her to step closer and dropped my voice. "I'm sure you heard about Timothy Clark, that actor who died?" I waited for her acknowledgment but stopped her before she could start talking about it. "It's

Adele. I don't know why exactly—maybe she was some kind of crazed fan—but she's terribly upset about what happened." It wasn't exactly the truth, but CeeCee understood right away.

"I know what you're saying. We don't want Adele to throw one of her conniptions during happy hour."

"She'll probably be okay as long as nobody starts talking about him."

"You do know that Elise's husband is the one who found him?" CeeCee said. "I suppose it was a heart attack or something."

"Yes, I heard Logan found him, and I'm sure you're probably right about the heart attack." I saw Rhoda coming in the door just as a customer stopped at the information booth. "If you could tell the others not to bring it up . . . ?" I said to CeeCee. "We don't want Adele to have a meltdown and make a scene."

"You're absolutely right, dear. I'll spread the word," she said just before she walked away.

Thanks to the customer's rather lengthy request, I was late joining the group.

CeeCee caught my eye and gave me a knowing look to let me know she'd done as I asked. "Molly, you're just in time. I was just giving the details about our project to give back to the community," CeeCee said, holding up a large crocheted square done in a yarn that morphed into different shades of blue.

I slipped into a chair just as CeeCee continued. After all I'd gone through with Adele that morning, it was amazing to watch CeeCee, who was a real star and a lot more grounded than Adele, whose stardom seemed to be mostly in her own head.

"It's a baby blanket," CeeCee explained, "and it's made on the bias so it's nice and stretchy. I'm sure you'll find them easy and quick to make. And I found the perfect places to donate them. I'm sure you all know that a newborn can be surrendered with no questions asked at a fire station, hospital, or police station. I thought we could make blankets and leave them with our local fire station, hospital, and police station so they would have something made with love to wrap those babies in."

We all murmured our approval and CeeCee continued. "There is one small issue. They pushed for a date when we'd donate them. I thought it would be good to complete this project quickly, so I said we'd have the blankets to bring over next week."

"That's not a lot of time," Dinah said.

"You'll see, they work up quickly," CeeCee said. "I'll do a demo of how to start one, and then we can all get our hooks moving."

Adele barely seemed to notice what was going on. She was facing CeeCee, but her eyes were clearly focused on something the rest of us couldn't see. Her mouth kept tightening, no doubt reacting to her thoughts. If she was like this now, I could only imagine how she would have been if I hadn't warned CeeCee to keep the group from discussing Timothy Clark. And Adele didn't even know the whole story yet. I dreaded telling her the rest of it and decided not to hurry.

"I think that's a great plan, and I'm sure we can meet the deadline," Sheila said, wiping a tear from her eye. "I'm sorry, but I'm afraid I overreact whenever I hear of any child being abandoned." We all nodded with understanding. Sheila was the youngest in our group and only in her late twenties. She'd been brought up by her grandmother, who had died recently, leaving her feeling a little abandoned. CeeCee went over and gave her a reassuring hug.

Rhoda reached across the table and touched my arm. "Leo was so excited when I told him you were going to advise him," she said, pointing to her brother-in-law, who had just come back to the table carrying a drink for her from the café. "He can't wait to go home with you."

I had forgotten that we had agreed on that evening for him to come to my place for dating advice. I suddenly regretted agreeing to it. What could *I* really tell him, anyway?

Eduardo was examining the sample baby blanket. "It will be interesting to work with a large hook and thicker yarn," he said. Most of his work was done with tiny silver hooks and yarn so thin it was called thread. Dinah seemed glad to have pushed the placemat she was making away. But there was no sign of Elise.

"You start out with just four chains," CeeCee said, demonstrating. "Then you increase on both sides, and then you decrease on both sides, and you end up with a square." The deal was that the bookstore provided the yarn for charity projects, so I went to hunt up some of the cotton yarn to show what colors we had. I was standing by a cubby when I heard something.

"Psst, psst." The sound came from the shadowy area away from the bright lights in the yarn department. Elise stepped forward just enough so that I could see it was her.

I checked to make sure no one was watching me and slipped out of the brightness. Elise had ducked back into the dark corner near the event area. I joined her and then purposely let her speak first.

"I suppose they're all talking about what happened to Timothy Clark," she said, glancing in the direction of the table. "I just can't face one more person telling me they saw Logan on television and then asking me for the real story."

"Actually, no. I told CeeCee to make sure Timothy Clark's name didn't come up. I was afraid of how Adele would react. She went bonkers when I told her about him being dead, and I was afraid she'd do a repeat performance if they started talking about it," I said with a shrug. I looked back toward the table. "They're all talking about a community service project CeeCee has us doing. She just showed us how to get started. I'm sure she'd be glad to show you too."

I gestured toward the table, but Elise took a step back. "No matter what you said to CeeCee, if I joined them I know they'd start shooting questions at me."

In the days of her vampire wear, Elise would have practically disappeared in the dark corner, but now that she was wearing what she apparently considered the real estate agent look, she was easier to spot. Even in the shadows, I could easily make out her beige linen pants and matching open jacket over a white shell complete with a string of pearls. Elise always went into things full force.

"I know you said you didn't want anyone to ask you for the real story—" I said, letting it hang.

"Okay, I'll tell you," Elise said. "Logan was showing the house, and they all walked in that room that I thought would make a perfect little studio arrangement for Adele's mother-in-law." She made a distraught sound. "Logan wouldn't give me details. He said he'd told the police what he'd seen, and now he just wants to put it out of his head and figure out how he's going to deal with his clients. I mean, showing them a house with a corpse in it doesn't exactly give a shine to his reputation."

I was a little disappointed about the lack of detail. "Did Logan say anything about how Timothy died? Was it a heart attack?" I asked, still hoping he'd died from natural causes.

She shrugged. "He didn't give me a lot of details."

I asked her if she'd told Logan that she'd shown us the house. "Absolutely not," she said.

"Good, because I need to tell you something." First I told her about the scarf, without mentioning that, since she was the one who'd handed me my coat, she was also the one who'd dropped it. "If only we hadn't rushed so fast out of the place, I might have seen it on the floor and been able to retrieve it."

I saw her eyes going back and forth as if she was thinking

about something. "Maybe we can go back and get it now," she said.

"Too late. The cops have it," I said, and mentioned Barry's two visits. She sucked her breath in with such a gasp I thought she'd fall backward. "And there's something else. Logan came there right after we left, right?" She nodded. "And he found the body."

She gasped again as she understood what I was getting at, and this time she did rock backward and I had to catch her. "You mean he was there, dead, when we were there?"

I nodded.

"How could I have missed seeing him?" She began to think out loud. "I went down the stairs. And then I went into the master suite. I went in there to do something." She turned to me. "The master suite was at the opposite end of the hall from the room Logan called the den. I lost sense of everything when I saw Logan's text. All I could think of was getting us out of there."

Elise started to panic. "And I was worried about Logan finding out that I showed the house. This is terrible. It must be a crime to leave a dead body without reporting it," she said. "Or worse, they could think we killed him."

I tried to calm her. "I can keep tap dancing with Barry about the scarf."

"But what if he proves it is your scarf and then he interrogates you? You'd have to tell him why you were in that house, and then it would come out who you were with." She grabbed my hand. "Unless you find out what happened first and settle the whole thing before we all get arrested."

She turned back to the table of Hookers. "Can we depend on Adele not to talk? She's usually such a blabbermouth, particularly when she thinks it's going to get her a lot of attention."

"Adele has her own reasons to keep it quiet. As for your suggestion, I was thinking along the same lines myself. My only requirement is that I be able to tell Dinah about it. She's my best friend and plays Dr. Watson to my Sherlock Holmes. In other words, I need her."

"She's good at keeping secrets, right?" Elise said, and I nodded. "Then okay."

"There's something else I'll need," I said. "I'd like to talk to Logan and find out what he saw."

She suddenly seemed hesitant. "Are you sure you can talk to him without giving anything away?"

"Yes," I answered.

"Okay, but it will have to be when it seems natural." Then she slipped deeper into the dark event area and I went back to looking for the cotton yarn.

When I returned to the table, Dinah looked up with a question in her eyes. She knew I'd been gone too long and had figured something was up. I mouthed that I would talk to her later.

I rejoined the group and helped pass out the cones of yarn while CeeCee gave out the patterns. When we finally broke up, Mrs. Shedd and Mr. Royal came in from their adventure of the day and took over, and I was free to leave.

Rhoda hung around while I got my things and then handed Leo off to me. "I'll pick him up in a couple of hours," she said. "Hal said to be sure and thank you. All Leo's moping around the house has really gotten to him."

It was then that I realized that this was as much about getting him out of their house for a while as it was about me giving him dating pointers. What had I gotten myself into?

The rain seemed over, at least for a while. The street was dry with just some residual water along the curb. Though the air was bracing, the lined hoodie I had on was more than warm enough. Leo was wearing a tan parka with the hood up, which definitely seemed like overkill. He followed me to my car and did a double take when he saw the blue-green color under the parking lot floodlights. "You sure have an old car," he said rather bluntly.

The comment and the way he said it put my hackles up. "I like to think my 1993 190E Mercedes is vintage," I said, trying to keep an edge out of my voice. He got in and immediately buckled himself in.

"Rhoda wasn't exactly clear on this. Are we on a date?" he said.

"No," I answered, almost before he got to the *t* in *date*. "This is absolutely not a date." I was already regretting agreeing to help him with his social life. I'd do it just this once, and then he was on his own.

It was a short drive to my house, and he kept his eye on the speedometer the whole way. I pulled into my driveway, and he looked over the exterior of my house. "You sure have a big place for one person," he said. "It doesn't seem very economical. If you sold it, you could probably afford a newer car." I don't know why I felt I had to explain anything to him, but I told him that one of my sons lived with me and that my mother and her singing group used it as a place to rehearse and that my other son stored all of his sports equipment there. "And I'm perfectly happy with the car I have. All you have to do is put the key in and drive it. And it still locks with a real key," I said, demonstrating for him. I opened the back gate and we went into the yard. He followed me across the patio, taking in his surroundings.

"Your husband must have left you pretty well off," he said.

I couldn't contain myself anymore and turned back. "Here's my first piece of advice: you don't have to say everything that crosses your mind. In fact, you might want to think a moment first about how the person is going to react to your comment."

"Oh, you mean the comment I made about your finances?"

"That and just about everything else you've said." I heard him make a *hmm* sound in answer. When I opened the kitchen door, the whole menagerie spilled out—well, not Blondie, but Cosmo and Felix pushed past us and took off into the yard. And thanks to Leo holding the door open, even went I asked him to close it, the two cats ran out. It was dark and I already couldn't see where they'd gone.

I put Leo in the living room and went back outside. The ground was soft from all the rain, and I slid more than walked as I ventured into the yard in search of Mr. Kitty and Cat. Thankfully, they didn't like the muddiness either, and they ran back across the grass and up to the back door.

They left a trail of little mud prints across the red tiled floor of the kitchen. Cosmo and Felix had no worries about the wet earth and ran around the yard in some game of their own design before they too came running to the door. I caught them as they came in and did my best to wipe off their paws. Even so, they left a few mud balls behind as they went through the kitchen. I secured the door and slipped out of my shoes and put on a pair of shell-pink Crocs I kept by the door for moments like this. I decided to wait until Leo left to bring Blondie out for her chance in the yard. I couldn't take the risk he'd say something unkind about her.

He was sitting on the sofa looking around my living room. I could only imagine what he was thinking, and I really hoped he would keep it to himself. To try to head him off, I explained that the coffee table wasn't always pushed against the fireplace and that it was just because my mother and her group had been practicing.

"I'm glad to hear that. I was going to tell you that it wasn't a safe arrangement."

I got a better view of him now. He wasn't bad looking, just sort of blah. I think the slacks he wore were called chinos. I liked them when they were khaki colored, but his were navy blue and washed out at that. The long-sleeved plaid shirt did little to spruce up his look. At least he had taken the parka off. A lock of his brown hair had broken away from the rest, which was combed across his head. It looped across his forehead in an unflattering way.

I had no idea where to begin, so I asked him if he'd like something to drink.

"Oh, yes," he said enthusiastically. "I'd like coffee with two tablespoons of half-and-half—the real thing, none of that fake creamer stuff for me. And my wife always paired my evening coffee with a peanut butter sandwich on white bread with the crusts cut off."

Inwardly, I rolled my eyes and looked at my watch, trying to gauge how long it would be before Rhoda picked him up. It couldn't be soon enough. There was just something about his personality, or lack thereof, that felt like a dead weight attached to a thick skull. Was there anything I could say that would make a difference? I excused myself to make his snack. He'd said white bread, but he was going to have to deal with egg bread. I hoped he wouldn't have a meltdown at the substitution.

After a few minutes, I returned with a tray. Cosmo and Felix followed me in. They gave Leo's pant leg a couple of snuffles, and each let out a short bark before settling on the other couch as if they were going to keep an eye on him.

"So you let your animals on the furniture?" he said as I set down the sandwich and coffee in his lap. "We never had any pets. Rebecca was allergic."

"Yes, my house is a bit of a free-for-all, and that's the way I like it." I wasn't sure he meant his comment as a judgment, but I still felt the need to defend my way of life. I took my own cup of coffee and sat down next to the two dogs. Meanwhile, Leo's attention had gone back to my offering. Before he could comment on the bread, I spoke. "No, it's not plain white bread. All I have is egg bread. You ought to try it. You might find that you like it." He looked at the coffee, and I knew he was wondering if I'd done any substituting with it. "It's homemade half-and-half. All I had was whipping cream and milk, so I made my own mixture."

I knew he was measuring my offering against his wife's, which he no doubt considered to be the correct way. Before he could say anything, I spoke up. "You seem like a rather direct person, so I'm going to be direct with you. I understand that you were married a long time and are used to things being a certain way, but if you want to meet someone new, you're going to have to open up your mind."

I expected him to be resistant to my comment, but he actually sat forward with interest. "Okay, then, tell me what to do."

I was totally stunned by his comment. "Just like that? You're not going to try to defend your ways?"

"Nope," he answered. "My wife arranged everything during our marriage. She was a lot like Rhoda—she just put things in front of me and I went along with it. It's all habit now."

"Really?" I said, wondering if he was as open to change as he was trying to appear. "Then let's see about this." I smiled as I took back the plate with the peanut butter sandwich on it. "How about we give it a little grilling?"

For a moment, he looked panicked, but then he took a deep breath. "Okay, then, grill away. But can I watch? Rebecca would never let me watch her cook."

He stood looking over my shoulder as I dropped a slab of butter in my enameled cast iron frying pan. In no time, it began to sizzle and scent the air. I slipped the sandwich in and it began to brown. Once it was golden on both sides, I slipped it back onto the plate.

"Do you really want to live dangerously?" I asked with a chuckle.

He hesitated for a second and then nodded in agreement.

I put another slice of butter in the pan before grabbing one of the ripe bananas off the counter and, after peeling it, sliced it and let the pieces fall into the bubbling butter. He watched with fascination and maybe a little fear at the idea of cooked bananas. The phone rang just as the bananas almost reached that perfect point of being soft and gooey with a swirl of buttery sweet sauce around them. I cradled the phone against my shoulder as I tried to flip them again.

"Hello," I said.

"It's Greenberg," the voice on the other end replied. I struggled to keep the banana slices moving.

"This is exciting. I've never tried anything like this before. Now that you showed me how to do it, let me take over," Leo said, and I handed him the silicone turner.

If Barry had heard Leo, he didn't let on; he was clearly in his professional mode. "There was something I wanted to ask you," he said in his cop voice. "Could we speak now?"

"How about you just ask me on the phone?" I said. I was sure it was something about Timothy Clark, and it would be a lot easier to avoid answering when I was on the phone than it would have been if we were face to face. The trouble was, he knew that too and insisted we talk in person.

"It won't take long," he said. "Or interfere with your plans." His voice cracked a little on the last part. So he had heard Leo in the background. I tried to remember what it was that Leo had said and if it could be taken another way.

"Give me a few minutes," I said, figuring he was probably out front. I'd never delayed him before, and Barry grunted in a way that sounded as if he was upset. That's what he got for just showing up.

"Okay, then," he said in a terse voice. "Suppose you just open your front door when you, ah, have yourself together."

What did he think was going on? I wanted to laugh when I looked at Leo prodding the banana slices with the turner as I remembered what Barry must have heard. The exciting thing Leo was talking about was watching bananas transform visually as they cooked. Wait until he tasted them. It was going to rock his world.

I got him situated on the couch in the living room and handed him his plate of food. I would have enjoyed witnessing his expression when he tasted everything, but much as I would have liked to let Barry stew in the images of what he thought was going on, I also wanted to get the whole thing over with.

I opened the door a crack in what was supposed to be the signal that I was okay to talk and saw that Barry was already standing just outside the door on the front porch. My plan was to keep him in the entrance hall and get whatever this was over quickly. Now that I knew why he was so interested in the scarf, the less I said, the better. I wasn't even going to attempt to pry any information out of him. I would just stonewall all the way.

Barry had his cop face on, but I noticed that he sniffed

the air when he came inside. The scent of the peanut butter, bananas, and browned butter hung in the air in a delicious bouquet. He tried to hide it, but I was pretty sure I heard his stomach growl in response. I wanted to move him out quickly before his hunger became unleashed. He was a master at ignoring it as long as nothing triggered it.

I had stopped just inside the door. A partial wall separated the entrance hall from the living room, and from here he couldn't see into the main room. But the wall only went for a short way and then the two spaces blended together. I suppose he thought he was being tricky, but I noticed that he kept stepping toward me so I'd move back.

"Do you have company?" he asked as he reached the end of the partial wall. Without waiting for me to answer, he turned and peeked into the living room, and his gaze locked on Leo happily eating the bananas and the sandwich.

"You've opened up a whole new world of sensation for me. It was never like this with my wife. All I can say is, *wow*."

I glanced at Barry and there was a flicker in his eyes, though the rest of his face still seemed impassive. There was an awkward moment, and there seemed to be no choice but to introduce the two men to each other, though I gave only names with no explanation as to who each of them was.

Leo seemed unperturbed, but Barry kept shifting around. I'd never seen him so discombobulated. Inside, it tickled me.

"Maybe we should talk in the kitchen," Barry said finally.

"Sure," I said, leading the way. He did his best not to

look around the room, but I caught his eyes going to the frying pan, where one slice of banana sat surrounded by buttery sauce.

"You wanted to ask me something?" I said.

His brow furrowed slightly, and I sensed that he wasn't happy that I'd taken to lead. Felix and Cosmo had left the couch and followed us into the kitchen. They gathered at his feet, apparently remembering that he had given them treats in the past. Barry was doing his best to keep his cop aura going and tried to ignore them, but persistent Cosmo reached up with one of his paws to give Barry's leg a reminder. Cosmo had the unique talent of acting like he thought he belonged to Barry and his son whenever it was in his best interest. Felix just went along for the ride.

Barry finally looked down at the dogs. "There won't be any peace until I give them something," he said. "Are there any of the treats that Jeffrey brought over?"

"Long gone, but the jar has been refilled." As I went to show it to him, I brushed against the handle on a cabinet and it fell off. Barry picked it up and then went to open the cabinet.

"Don't," I said, but it was too late, and, as he opened the cabinet door, it came loose from one of its hinges and hung at an awkward angle.

"Don't worry about the handle. I'll put it back on later," I said, taking over with the cabinet door. I knew if I pushed the hinge in just right, it would stay even though the screws had fallen out and disappeared.

"Are you sure?" he said, and I nodded before handing

him the treat jar. When Barry and I had been together, everything in my house had been in perfect order. He was a wizard at fixing things, but I didn't want to let him think I couldn't manage without him.

He handed each dog a treat, though it helped only momentarily. As soon as they'd swallowed the chicken-flavored snacks, they resumed their positions, hoping for seconds.

"You had something on your mind," I reminded Barry, hoping to move things along. He seemed to be struggling to hold on to his composure, but I saw his eye go to the frying pan again. The smell and the sight of the food must have cut right through all his supreme control, and I knew he was probably overcome with raging hunger. I had to stop worrying about his eating and remember that he'd come over to grill me, not a sandwich. But I wasn't good at being tough and offered him what Leo was having without the half-and-half in his coffee—Barry drank his straight.

He agreed but insisted he would eat standing up in the kitchen. I guess, in his mind, that kept it from being social. "I wouldn't want to ruin your evening," he said. I knew he was dying to ask who Leo was.

"No problem," I said. "I'll just go and tell Leo I'll be with him shortly." I was smiling to myself as I went into the living room, only imagining the expression on Barry's face.

When I returned, Barry watched while I made him a sandwich and fried bananas. He took care of the coffee him-self. As soon as it was ready, he leaned against the counter and, as he'd done before, practically inhaled the food while seeming to savor every bite at the same time.

As he set the empty plate down, he finally got down to business. "I'm curious," he said, measuring his words. "How is it that you knew Timothy Clark?"

I silently swallowed. So he was off the scarf and trying a different direction by implying that he knew that I knew the man. "I already answered that," I said. "All I know about him was that he was on a TV show and there was something on the news that he died."

"And the body was discovered by the husband of one of your Hookers."

"Really?" I said, acting amazed. "Whose husband was it?"

Barry wiped a smudge of peanut butter off his chin and tried to look stern. "You can stonewall all you want, but I know that you knew Timothy Clark."

This time my confusion was real. "I've never met him," I said.

"Are you so sure? I've seen something that says otherwise."

"What is it?" I asked, losing my cool for the moment. For just a moment, Barry lost the cop persona and became just Barry.

"You tell me about the scarf and I'll tell you what I have."

"I don't know what you're talking about," I said, recovering quickly.

He looked frustrated that none of his interrogation moves were working. "Molly, why are you being so difficult?"

I grabbed the moment. "So did this Timothy person die of natural causes?" Barry looked me directly in the eye and shook his head.

"It was homicide," he said grimly.

Not the answer I wanted to hear.

Chapter Six

I had told Dinah that I would tell all later. I was sure she was curious what was going on, and I certainly wanted to unload to my best friend. I sat looking at the cordless, wondering when was too late to call. I checked the black screen on my smartwatch and twisted my wrist until the display lit up. It told a lot more than the time, just the way my smartphone did a lot more than make calls. I saw that the temperature was fifty-two degrees, I hadn't walked enough steps to make my goal, the battery was getting close to empty, and it was 10:45 PM. The watch had been a gift from Mason Fields just before I broke things off with him. It was a standing joke that while the rest of the world was fixated on the screens of their smartphones, I mostly ignored mine and, as a result, missed most of the calls and just about everything else that showed up on it.

The Apple watch worked with the phone, vibrating when a text or email came in and emitting a longer vibration for a call. Even with all those vibrations, I still missed a lot. I liked to think I was too immersed in the world around me to care about another email rolling in.

Ten forty-five wasn't that late, was it?

Rhoda had picked Leo up shortly after Barry left, giving him enough time to ask who Barry was. I wasn't sure how much to explain and decided to keep it on a professional level. And maybe I rearranged the truth a little. I told him Barry was a homicide detective and was working on a case and he'd come over thinking I might have some information that would help him with his investigation.

"That's right," Leo said brightening. "Rhoda told me you're sort of an amateur detective."

"I've gotten lucky a few times—well, more like a number of times—and figured out whodunit," I said with a smile. I waited for him to make some weird comment as he had before, but he seemed genuinely impressed.

"She said you've gotten yourself in some pretty dangerous situations." He smiled as if he had thought of something clever. "I guess it means you got out of them, since you're here now."

I almost joked that trouble could be my middle name, but I was concerned he wouldn't understand I was joking, so I just said, "Yes."

I walked him to the door with a sense of relief that my good deed was done, but then, just before he went out, he said, "Until next time."

Until next time? He looked so hopeful, I didn't have the heart to tell him we were done, so I smiled weakly and again said, "Yes." He had zipped up his parka and carefully walked down the stone path to Rhoda's car.

Do it or forget it, I told myself. I went back to staring at the phone, debating if I should call Dinah. So much had changed since she'd gotten married. It only made sense when you put together two people in their fifties who'd been used to their own way of doing things. Again it made me glad that I hadn't taken Barry up on his offer.

It had been so much easier when I'd married Charlie. I was young and clueless and just thought everything would work out. Well, it had, because in those days I had bought into Charlie's way as being the right way and gone along with it, whether it was about leaving a light on in the bathroom at night (he was against it, I was for it) or where we should go for a vacation (he always wanted to tie it to a business trip). Once I had gotten past the grief after he died, I'd seen the light—excuse the pun—and realized my way of doing things was as valid as Charlie's. And now I was going to have that bathroom light on if I wanted and take that trip to Tuscany one of these days.

I thought to myself that I should tell Barry he was lucky I hadn't said yes because we would have had a constant battle on our hands. Maybe I'd say something about it if I saw him again.

I rolled my eyes at myself. Who was I kidding? I'd definitely be seeing him again about that damn scarf. Barry's words came back to me—that he knew I knew Timothy Clark. He had to have been bluffing. I hadn't even been a fan of the show he was on.

It was 10:50 now. There was just too much simmering in my head and I had to talk to someone. Finally I punched in Dinah's number and the phone began to ring. I prayed that Commander wouldn't be the one to answer and say something about giving his heart a start.

I let my breath out when I heard Dinah's hello. "Sorry for calling so late," I said right way, but she stopped me.

"Commander may not be happy with late-night phone calls, but it's always okay with me. I was up anyway, grading papers."

"I don't suppose you'd like to come over?" I said.

"Are you kidding? I'd love a distraction from these papers. I had my students pretend they were on an island with no electricity or Internet. Their assignment was to handwrite an essay. And they had to use a paper dictionary." She stopped and I imagined her shaking her head. "All I can say is that they better hope there's never an extended power failure and all their batteries are drained. They are dead in the water without their electronics." I heard the jingle of her keys and the sound of her opening her front door. "I'm on my way," she said as she signed off.

A few minutes later I saw her coming across the backyard. Felix and Cosmo danced around her as she came inside and the two cats did figure eights around her ankles.

"Treats for everyone," she said, walking over to the dog treat jar and the smaller one that held the cat goodies.

"What can I give you?" I asked when she was done.

"Whatever is easy. Just being out like this is great. It

feels like old times." She left it at that, but I knew she meant *before Commander and I got married*.

We rummaged around my refrigerator and came up with a pint of vanilla ice cream, a jar of caramel sauce, and a can of whipped cream. When we'd created our sundaes, we took them into the living room. Dinah laughed when she saw the furniture. I didn't have to explain; she knew right away that my mother and the girls had turned it back into their rehearsal hall.

"There's always so much going on here," she said, a little wistfully. "My house is a tomb at night." She stuck her spoon through all the layers and came up with the perfect mixture of caramel-coated ice cream with a dollop of whipped cream. After she savored the spoonful, she turned to me. "So, I'm sensing there's some kind of crisis. Tell me all about it."

She caught me just as I had put a spoonful of sundae in my mouth, so she continued. "Does the crisis have anything to do with Leo? He looked like he might be trouble. Did he turn out to have octopus hands?"

I almost choked on my ice cream, laughing at the thought. "He's not the problem," I said, and told her the peanut-butter-and-banana story without mentioning Barry's visit.

"If anybody can open up that guy's world, it's you," she said. "So then, what is it?"

"I told you about the fiasco yesterday. Elise showing a house she wasn't supposed to be showing to Adele, who wasn't supposed to be looking at one?"

Dinah laughed at my phrasing.

"It turns out there's a lot more to the story. The house belonged to Timothy Clark."

Dinah was silent for a moment. "Didn't I read something online that he died?" she said.

"Yes," I said, and then I went into the whole story, including the dropping of the scarf and Barry's repeated efforts to get me to admit the scarf was mine. "Of course, I keep stonewalling. I was hoping it would turn out he died of natural causes, but then Barry broke the news it was murder. Adele doesn't even know how much trouble we're in. I really don't look forward to letting her know, either."

"It sounds like Barry has been making a lot of visits," Dinah said with a knowing smile.

"All in his professional capacity," I said, but then told her how his last one had overlapped with Leo's stop at my place.

"I know I shouldn't be laughing. A man's been killed, but I wish I could have seen Barry's face when Leo said you were better than his wife." She let it sit for a minute. "You do realize that you and Barry aren't really finished?"

"Oh, but we are. He's trying to connect me with a murder. You know Barry; his job always comes first. Though it was priceless when he saw Leo sitting on my couch." I smiled at the memory and then got serious again. "The plan is to find out who killed Timothy Clark quickly, before Barry manages to find a way to prove the scarf is mine." I mentioned the last few moments with Barry when he had said that he knew that I knew Timothy Clark. "I think he's bluffing. I don't ever remember meeting him. I didn't even really know who he was until I saw the report on the news last night."

Dinah's expression had grown serious and she took a deep breath. "I hate to say this, but maybe you ought to get in touch with Mason. He is a criminal attorney, even if most of his clients are celebrities with no judgment. He could certainly advise you."

"We haven't talked in months," I said. "Since my phone call."

"But it was civil. It wasn't as if you had a big fight."

"No, there was no fight. I looked at the phone call as preemptive. I was sure I knew what was coming, and I took control and broke the thing off before he could."

"I knew there was going to be trouble when Mason let his daughter move into his place while she went to law school."

"She never liked me," I said, remembering how Brooklyn had done her best to ignore my presence whenever I went to Mason's house. "But when Jaimee moved in, too, while her house was being remodeled . . ." I threw up my hands.

"Too bad you didn't say something then," Dinah said. We'd been over all of this before, but she knew it was bothering me and listened as if she was hearing it for the first time.

"Mason's house is huge and Jaimee moved *into* the house, not *with* him. Besides, what was I going to say? It was his house and his family. I actually admired that he felt a responsibility to them." I dug into the bottom of the dish and scraped the last of the caramel sauce mixed with melted ice cream. "When I overheard Jaimee suggesting she and Mason get back together, I was sure he'd never go for it. Even when Jaimee and Brooklyn tagged along on his business trip to New York, I was delusional enough to believe nothing was up." I stopped and let out a sigh as I remembered what had been the coup de grace when I had gone over to Mason's and let myself in with the key he'd given me. "Jaimee was in the living room talking to an interior decorator about redoing the place. Brooklyn saw me and the key in my hand and asked for it back. That's when I finally got it. They had gotten back together."

Dinah got up, came back with the ice cream container, and dropped another scoop in my empty dish and one in her own. "This is definitely an extra-scoop story."

"I knew the inevitable was coming, so I just cut things off first—with a machete," I said with a sad smile, remembering how I had simply told him that he needed to work things out with his family and that we were done, and then I'd hung up without letting him speak. And maybe I had also not answered any of his calls after that. "But you're right. Mason would know what to do about this situation I'm in. And it would be strictly professional."

"Absolutely," Dinah said. "Now let's see if we can lighten up this conversation."

"I do have something funny," I said, glad to change the subject. I told her about the teenage girls coming into the bookstore because some influencer on YouTube had told them books were the new hot thing.

The next morning, I bit the bullet and called Mason's

office. I had considered my various options for reaching him. Calling his cell seemed too personal, and I certainly wasn't going to call his house.

When his assistant asked who was calling, I said, "This is Molly Pink," then quickly added, "And this is a professional call." I had no idea if she knew who I was, but on the off chance she did, I wanted to make it clear this wasn't personal.

"Are you a client?" she asked. I hesitated. I didn't want to say that I knew Mason; then she'd ask how and it could get awkward.

"No," I said, and she put me on hold.

After leaving me on hold for an awfully long time, a man came on the line and introduced himself as an attorney working with Mason. "Mr. Fields is tied up. Perhaps I can help you," he said.

"If I could just speak to Mason," I said. "I need his legal help."

"Then it would be a new-client interview. I can help you with that," he said. "We could start on the phone and arrange for you to meet with me first."

"If you would just tell Mason who's calling. He knows me. But be sure and tell him I need his services. That is, his legal services. And I need it to be soon," I added before he could put me on hold again. I didn't know if I was getting the runaround because someone recognized my name or because it was that hard to get through to Mason.

"You're not in jail, are you?" the man asked.

"Not yet," I said, trying to make a joke that fell flat.

After a long time, the man came back on. "Mr. Fields suggested a dinner meeting this evening, since you seem to feel you are about to be incarcerated." There wasn't the slightest hint of humor in his voice, and he offered a time and named a restaurant on Ventura Boulevard in Encino before asking for my okay.

"It's a date," I said, then regretted my choice of words. "I meant that as in the time and place are fine. Not that this was in any way going to be social."

"Whatever you say," the man said with a dismissive tone before hanging up.

"I wished I hadn't said so much," I said to myself. This was absolutely not a date. I really hoped he understood that. And then I wondered what I should wear.

Chapter Seven

"This way," the host said when I explained I was meeting Mason Fields. Donte's had a black-and-white-tiled floor and the wood-paneling look of an old-fashioned grill. The conversation level was at a low hum, and I expected to be led to one of the tables in the center of the dimly lit restaurant. Instead, the host led me to the side of the room and pulled back a curtain, revealing a private booth. He held out his arm in a gesture, inviting me to sit.

I had fretted all day, alternating between wondering if I was making a mistake and second-guessing my outfit. I had decided to go in my regular work clothes of khaki slacks and a black sweater over a white shirt, but I did redo my makeup and brush my hair. And maybe I did pop the collar on my shirt, though I hoped it would look like it had somehow happened on its own.

I slid onto the green leatherette seat and glanced at the empty space across from me. "Mr. Fields said to tell you he was on his way," the host said. "Would you care for a glass of wine or a cocktail while you wait?"

"No," I said a little too quickly. "This is a professional meeting." I wanted to laugh at myself, as if the host cared. "I'll have a coffee." I wanted to be completely alert.

The anticipation was making me nervous, and I flinched when the curtain opened and a female server dressed all in black set a cup of coffee down in front of me. I was about to take a sip when Mason sat down across from me. He was dressed in his work clothes. This time it was a light-colored suit that draped perfectly over a creamy colored shirt with such a high thread count that it had a soft sheen. His dark hair had enough strands of gray to make him appear seasoned, and the way a lock of his hair always fell across his forehead somehow made him seem earnest and hardworking. Despite my best efforts, I felt a wave of emotion.

"It's been a while," he said in a noncommittal tone as he looked across the table at me. I had expected the usual good-natured warm smile he'd always worn when we were together, but there was no curve in his lips or dancing in his eyes. If anything, they seemed to hold a question. He laid a leather folder on the table and flipped it open, revealing a yellow pad. So, he'd taken it seriously that this was a professional meeting.

I knew I had made such a point about this not being personal, but I was dying to ask him about Jaimee. Were they living happily ever after? I knew the reason they'd gotten divorced was because when their daughters were grown, they'd discovered they had nothing in common anymore and didn't really enjoy each other's company. What could have changed? Had Jaimee gotten a personality transplant?

I couldn't really ask him, since it would make it look as if the professional stuff had just been a ruse to get him there.

"Lawrence said you were concerned about being arrested," he said. "Why don't you tell me what's going on."

Okay, he was just getting down to business. I felt a pang of disappointment. Mason had always been so much fun and clear about really liking me, and now he was fine with me just being another person in trouble needing his help.

"Before I say anything, I want to make sure. This stays between us, right?"

"Yes," he said. "That's why I chose one of these booths. Other than Lawrence, no one will even know that we met." He pointed to the enclosed area. "It gives us privacy."

"Okay, then, here goes." I took a deep breath and jumped in. "It started with Adele having a problem with her mother-in-law." I checked his expression and noted that his eyes were beginning to soften. "I don't know if you remember Elise Belmont from the Hookers, but she's trying to break into real estate, and she sort of showed Adele and me a house that her husband had listed and she wasn't really authorized to show. She made Adele and me promise not to tell anyone that she'd shown us the house."

Mason was holding his pen poised. He hadn't written a thing, but he was clearly listening intently. "When I tell you whose house it is, I think you'll see the problem," I said. "You do know who Timothy Clark is, right?"

Mason's eye's opened wider. "Timothy Clark, the actor who had the running part in *Bradley V, P.I.*?" he said. "Didn't

I just hear that he'd been found dead in his . . ." Mason stopped and looked at me intently. "In his house."

"Yes, that's him, and to be clear about it, he was found by Logan Belmont, who was showing the house shortly after we'd been there." I took a breath before I got to the next part. "Did you also hear that they're saying it was murder?"

"No," he said, even more interested. "Was he dead when you were there?"

"I don't exactly know." I explained that the house had two levels, with the living room on the top floor. "Elise went downstairs to make sure everything was shipshape before she brought us down. A few moments later, she rushed up the stairs all discombobulated and said we had to leave because she'd gotten a text from her husband saying he was with some clients and was about to show a house he'd just listed. She knew he meant that house."

He put down the pen, and his expression had definitely lightened. "If you want my advice, you get together with Elise and Adele and all agree to say nothing to anybody and there won't be a problem."

The curtain opened and the server set down a glass of red wine in front of Mason along with a platter of appetizers. He picked up the glass. "Here's to an easy solution," he said before taking a sip.

"There might be something else," I said, swallowing hard. "It was a rainy day and Elise made us take off our shoes and coats so we wouldn't drip all over. If only she hadn't rushed us out so quickly, I might have noticed that I'd dropped my scarf."

Mason's expression faded as he set the glass down. "That shouldn't be a big deal. It's not like the scarf has your name on it or that anyone even noticed it."

"That's not exactly true," I said. When I described the scarf, Mason remembered it, and when he heard that Barry had it, he swallowed hard.

"It might have been okay if I'd told him right off that it was my scarf and how it had gotten there, but I didn't know why he was asking. I hadn't seen anything on the news at that point about Timothy Clark being dead. I didn't even know it was Timothy Clark's house then. You know, there's a Robbery Homicide Division, and I thought maybe something was missing from the house and that was what he was investigating. So, I wouldn't confirm or deny that the scarf was mine. I figured he would just let it go."

"But he hasn't?" Mason asked.

"No. And he says that he knows I have a connection with Timothy Clark."

"Well, do you?"

"Not that I can think of. I didn't even really know who he was until I saw that he'd died. I think Barry may be bluffing. But Adele did know Timothy pretty well." I told him about Adele's aspirations and taking workshops with the dead actor. "And it was all secret. Adele didn't want Eric to find out until she was famous, and now she doesn't want him to know she ever took the workshops. I can see her point.

Mother Humphries would be sure to have a lot to say about Adele's foolishness. There's a good chance the police won't connect her to Timothy, since she attended the workshops under the name of Lydia Fairchild."

Mason had begun to morph into the person I knew. "And I thought my celebrity clients got involved in some wacky stuff." He pushed the plate of appetizers toward me and encouraged me to put some on the small plates that had been provided. Typical Mason, he'd ordered a generous sampling of flatbread topped with cheese and tomatoes, mushrooms stuffed with crab meat, shrimp toast, and a mélange of chopped vegetables in a blue cheese dressing.

I began to load the small plate and let out a breath. It was a relief to be able to talk without being worried that I was letting out any secrets or incriminating myself. He heard the breath, and his mouth curved into a small smile.

"It's a relief to get that all out, huh? Tell me what I can do for you," he said. "If Barry comes calling with more questions, you could have him talk to me."

I waited until I swallowed the bite of flatbread before I spoke. "No, that would just make it worse."

The fact that Mason was a lawyer and Barry a police detective automatically put them at odds, but my relationships with each of them only made it more of a problem. I doubted it would make a difference that I was estranged from both of them now.

"I'll tell you what I think, and then you give me your thoughts. I don't think Barry is going to arrest me, because then he knows I'd lawyer up and not talk. More likely he thinks he'll be able to use his interrogation skills to get me to say stuff without realizing it."

Mason nodded as he poked his fork into one of the mushrooms. "That sounds about right. I'm guessing you have some kind of plan to look into who killed the guy?"

This time I nodded. "Elise asked—well, demanded— that I do something so that her husband won't find out she went behind his back showing the house and all. I'm sure Adele will be on board, too because she'll want the case closed before Eric finds out she was lying to him when she said she was going to a yoga class."

Mason couldn't help himself—his lips slipped into a grin and he rocked his head from side to side with amazement. "How do you keep getting in the middle of such crazy stuff?" It was a rhetorical question, and I shrugged in answer.

"So, just tell me what you want."

"Well, if I'm wrong about Barry's plans, will you be my one call from jail?" I said. I was half joking. I didn't think Barry would go that far, but who knew for sure.

"Absolutely," he said. "And . . ."

"I can't find out anything. I don't even know what killed Timothy. Or, for that matter, much about him. Adele is convinced that she was his star pupil and has a rosy picture of who he was. It would help if I knew some dirt that might point to who killed him."

Mason had scribbled down some notes. I knew he had lots of connections and could find out the information I needed with a few phone calls.

94

When we finally parted company, there were three things that stood out about our meeting. He had never mentioned Jaimee or his daughters or made any reference to our past relationship, nor did he suggest that we meet again.

What did that mean?

Chapter Eight

I stopped off at the bookstore after leaving Mason. I tried to tell myself that I wasn't bothered by his distance. It just reconfirmed what I thought. I was glad now that I hadn't asked about Jaimee because I might have lost my cool and said something dumb, like ask if she'd gotten a personality transplant.

I waved to Lara-Ann to let her know I was there. She was hanging by the front, talking to Rayaad at the checkout counter. The few customers seemed to be content to browse on their own. I was surprised when I glanced to the back of the store and saw a crowd gathered around the table in the yarn department. It was a permanent fixture and technically usually available for anyone to use. But this wasn't a chance person sitting down to work their needles or hooks for a while. I counted six heads, and when I saw the hot-pink beanie with a big floppy purple flower on the last one, I groaned. What was Adele up to now?

She saw me as I approached the back and pushed away from the table before rushing toward me. "What's going on?" I asked as she stood in front of me to keep me from going forward. "You know any group meetings or events are supposed to go through me."

"Shush. Could you keep it down?" Adele said, glancing back toward the table.

"Oh, so you passed yourself off as being in charge," I said in a soft but world-weary tone. Adele had a real issue with always trying to be the boss. She suddenly looked upset and grabbed my arm. Did she really think I was going to walk up to the table and say something to strip her of her imagined power?

"I'm sorry," she said quickly. "But it was an emergency. I thought that since I was Timothy's star student, I should get in touch with the people in the workshop and try to smooth things over, since tonight was our usual meeting time. Everybody seemed to want to get together anyway. You know, to figure out where we go from here. We usually met at her house." She surreptitiously pointed at a woman with short dark hair streaked with lavender. "But she didn't want the group coming over without Timothy, so I said we could meet here."

Whatever annoyance I felt quickly turned to interest. The meeting had suddenly turned into a table full of suspects. "I suppose it's okay just this once," I said.

The group was in the midst of a conversation. "Too bad I didn't get to audition for *The Girls' Club*," a woman in a straw hat said. "I would have been perfect as the lead."

The woman with the lavender streaks shook her head. "It's clear they were after someone younger. Remember, the concept is that a barely twenty-something female head of a Silicon Valley startup fights to be taken seriously while dealing with her personal life."

The woman with the straw hat seemed undaunted. "I'm an actor. I could play younger." Then her shoulders dropped. "The show's a super hit out of the box."

"I heard they already ordered two more seasons," one of the others said.

"Man, I'd like to get a shot like that," the woman in the straw hat said, sounding frustrated.

Adele, clearly worried that I was going to somehow upstage her, pushed ahead of me and got to the table first. "Everybody, I'd like you to meet Molly Pink. She works at the bookstore." I smiled at the group and, much to Adele's exasperation, added that I was the assistant manager. They went around the table giving their names. The woman with lavender in her hair was Sonia Pierson, Deana Lewis was wearing the brimmed straw hat, Brett Williamson had dark blond hair and an everyman sort of look, and Mikey Fitzpatrick was large and muscular. As they gave their names, I glanced over their faces, checking for anyone familiar. So many customers came and went in the bookstore, I felt as if I'd come across half the people in the southwestern part of the San Fernando Valley.

I could tell Adele was hoping I'd leave, but the one woman who hadn't introduced herself got up from the table and approached me. "I'm Alexandra Davinsky." She held out her hand for me to shake it and pulled me off to the side. "I love this place," she said, glancing around the bookstore.

"I'm a big fan of the café. Those new drinks you just added are delicious."

"You mean the Bobaccinos?" I said, and she nodded. Bob, our barista, had come up with the creamy party drinks and named them after himself. "Everybody says they're great, but so far I've resisted the temptation to try one."

"I know what you mean," she said in a friendly tone. "They taste so good but are deadly for my figure," she said with a smile, looking down at her hips. "I was Timothy's assistant. As you can imagine, the group is all in shock." I looked over the gathering at the table, and they were leaning on their hands as if waiting for something to happen. Alexandra stood out from the group. The best way I could describe it was that she seemed more determined than the rest of them. Her thick wavy brown hair was pulled back in a loose bun with some tendrils hanging loose. She wore a long black sweater over a white shirt. At first glance, it seemed casual, but then I noted that the collar of the white shirt she wore underneath it had definitely been popped. The silver pendant on the long chain was distinctive and one of a kind. I noticed a briefcase on the table in front of her empty seat.

"It's just sinking in that they've all been left hanging. It's different for me. Tim was a master at picking out his students' strong points. He made me realize that I was more interested in writing what the actors were going to say than in doing the saying. I wrote scenes for the group to use for practice, and then I wrote a whole screenplay." She suddenly stood a little taller. "And it's in pre-production now. He was going to tout my success along with the girl from the vegetable commercial and the woman who got a continuing part in a sitcom as part of the credits of the workshop."

She sensed that I was a little confused. "The fact that Tim was a successful actor with an Emmy nomination gave him a lot of credibility, but it helped even more to show that some of his students went on to big things."

"The vegetable fairy?" I didn't get it at first, then remembered the commercial. "You mean Cauli Flower, that girl with the raspy voice?"

"You know, that commercial won the National Children's Nutrition Council's award because Cauli Flower turned out to have the same power to influence kids' food choices as some of those elves and animals in the cereal commercials."

Adele was hanging off to the side, shifting her weight impatiently, no doubt wishing that I would go away. Alexandra seemed to have something on her mind and continued talking, "The group doesn't know this, but I was about to start giving my own workshops, though they will be for scriptwriters. I know you have events here; maybe we could work something out."

Adele'd had enough by then and butted back into the conversation before Alexandra could finish. "Since you were Timothy's assistant, you must have known about all the auditions he arranged and meetings for our group." She looked at the other woman expectantly.

"Afraid not. Timothy kept tight control on everything he set up."

Adele's shoulders slumped. "All the information is probably locked away on his phone or a computer."

Alexandra chuckled. "Tim didn't trust electronics. He did it all on a paper calendar with a lot of Post-it notes." She made a move to the table and I stuck with her, curious about the rest of the group.

Adele went right to the spot she always took at the head of the table but didn't sit. "I'm sorry about the delay." She shot me a dirty look. "I know we're all devastated by Timothy's death, but I know we were all so committed to our dream." She hesitated and took a breath. "I was just thinking that, as Timothy's star student, I could take over."

"Star student," Deana, the woman in the straw hat, said with disbelief. "If anyone was his star student, it was me. We were waiting for a callback on a drug commercial. He said I was amazing as a woman the day after chemotherapy." At that, she took off the straw hat and mussed her long, honey-colored hair before producing a scrunchie and arranging her hair so that some strands hung down. Then she leaned on the table in a tired pose and let out a long sigh. "You have to imagine me without makeup," she said, looking up from the pose for a moment.

"Have any of you actually gotten any work?" I said, interrupting.

They looked at one another and then at me. The tall, slender man who'd introduced himself as Brett spoke. "Timothy always said it was all about timing and how important it was that I worked at my craft in the workshops so that when the right audition came along, I'd be ready."

My face must have given away what I was thinking—that it sounded like a bunch of double talk—and Deana spoke up. "I'm waiting for callbacks on a play and the drug commercial. Timothy said nothing took the place of the experience of working in live theater and he was sure I would be a standout."

Sonia Pierson spoke up. "I've gone on some auditions, but so far, nothing. Still, the workshop was everything to me. For one night a week, I was an actress. Timothy kept telling me to hang in there because he knew I had star potential."

Mikey Fitzpatrick looked around at the group. "What's with you people? Timothy's dead and all you can talk about is yourselves. Just think about what he did for us all. I know he was still pursuing his own career, but he gave most of his time and talent helping us with ours. He gave me a lot of encouragement. He was there to see all of us through auditions and meetings with casting directors."

"For a price," someone muttered. When I turned to see who had spoken, I couldn't tell.

Mikey seemed undeterred and ended by saying that he wouldn't be where he was if it weren't for Timothy. Deana rolled her eyes and muttered something about him wanting to star in a comic book movie.

Adele seemed a little crushed by hearing that Timothy had apparently led all of his students to believe they were his star pupil and on the brink of stardom, but in typical Adele style, she didn't give up. "I know he had set up a meeting for me about my crochet show. It's just terrible that he's dead, but if I knew the details of the meeting, I could probably go there on my own."

There was some rumbling in the group, and I gathered that some of the others thought he'd set something up for them as well.

Brett nodded sadly. "Well, I guess there's nothing we can do." He turned to the others. "Anybody know what happened to the Big T?"

They had heard the news on TV the same way I had. Deana had checked around online to see if there were more details but hadn't come up with any more information.

I couldn't help myself and, before I could stop the words from coming, spoke. "It was murder." Their heads swiveled toward me as if they were all Linda Blair in *The Exorcist*.

"How do you know that?" Alexandra demanded.

"What?" Adele squealed. "You knew that and you didn't tell me?"

"What was it? Was he shot, stabbed, or was it poison?" Deana asked.

"I don't know—yet," I said.

Adele struggled to regain the group's attention. "Don't pay attention to her. She thinks she's really a private private detective." She turned back to me. "You should have told me you were investigating what happened." Realizing she'd only given them more reason to want to talk to me, she abruptly changed the subject. "What we really need to talk about is how we can continue to meet."

There was some muttering among the group, but then Alexandra stepped forward. "I could step in as leader."

"Not at my place," Sonia said. "Timothy and I had a special arrangement."

Leave it to Adele to offer the yarn department, and I had to explain that the table was reserved for our crochet group and the occasional yarn crafter that stopped to try out some yarn.

"I'll work on it," Adele said finally, and then the group broke up.

By then it was closing time. Adele caught up with me as I was turning off the lights. She was clearly wrapped up in thinking about something, and when I tried to ask her about Timothy's fees, she gave me a vague look and grabbed my arm. "Pink, I need you to help me get back into Timothy's."

I just looked at her and said without hesitation, "No."

Chapter Nine

Friday morning, Dinah met me for coffee and an update on what had happened with Mason. To make it a real break for me, we'd gone down the street to Le Grand Fromage, where no one would come up and ask for help finding a book. I quickly gave her the lowdown on our meeting. *Quickly* because there wasn't much to tell.

"He really didn't say anything about anything?" she asked when I finished.

"He did advise me on what I called him about," I said. "Remember, it was just professional. And he offered to see what he could find out."

Dinah saw right through my nonchalance. "It must have seemed strange."

I nodded. "I kept expecting him to be the old Mason, but he was so formal and distant." There wasn't really any point talking about it anymore, though, so I told her about Adele's gathering. "Any one of them could be a suspect. But since all I really know is that Timothy was murdered, there's no way to focus on any one of them. It would be better if they didn't know that I was investigating, but I already let on that I had inside information, and Adele mentioned that I was a private private detective."

Dinah chuckled at the title before she drained her café au lait and checked the time. "Keep me posted," she said as we both got up and went our separate ways.

I was surprised to find Lara-Ann surrounded by a cluster of teenage girls when I walked back into the bookstore. She frantically waved me over. "They're all looking for some book they heard about on YouTube," she said. "And a woman came in looking for you. She disappeared before I could get her name." I asked for a description, but she pointed at the group of girls. "I'm afraid they got all my attention."

"I'll handle this," I said, turning to the girls. "You're looking for *My Gal Ella*, right?" They nodded enthusiastically and all started talking at once about how they absolutely had to have a copy right away. I had them wait while I checked the back room with my fingers crossed that the rush order had come in. When I returned with an armload of copies of *My Gal Ella*, they emptied my arms before I could hand them out. As they walked away I heard one of them say how neat it was to get the book right away instead of waiting for it to be delivered.

I was smiling to myself as I walked toward the information desk. The smile faded as I saw Barry come in the front door. He was in cop mode and gave me a pointed stare. I let out a sigh, wondering what he was going to ask me this time.

We both arrived at the information booth at the same

time. I moved behind the small cubicle as if it would give me some protection.

"What brings you in?" I asked. "Can I help you find a book?"

"I was in the neighborhood and I thought maybe you were ready to talk about your relationship with Timothy Clark," he said.

"I've already told you I didn't know him," I said. I glanced at the phone, hoping it would ring and give me an excuse to end the conversation. The phone stayed silent, but I was surprised to see a tall plastic cup next to it on the counter. I seized on it as a way to change the subject. "Isn't that nice? Someone left me a cherry Bobaccino." Barry's lips tightened as I told him about the new drinks the café had added. "Hmm," I said as I caught a whiff of the almond scent in the drink. "I guess Bob must have added a cherry almond flavor to the list."

"You don't want to drink that," Barry said, reaching over the counter and snatching the cup.

My mouth fell open as I looked down at myself and then back up at him. "Are you saying I need to go on a diet?"

Barry's face gave away nothing; he just turned and left with the drink. I knew he was annoyed that I wouldn't talk, but really, that was a low blow.

I thought about bringing up the incident when the Hookers got together for happy hour, but then I'd have to explain why he had shown up at the bookstore in the first place. It was easiest to say nothing. I'd save it to tell Dinah later.

Rhoda had brought Leo, expecting that I would take him home with me for our next session. I tried to put it off, but Rhoda said he'd made so much progress already it seemed a shame to ruin the momentum. And then she thanked me a bunch of times and said I must have a magic touch. Okay, the flattery got to me, so I agreed. I sent him on to the living room while I checked the landline for messages. Mason had called promising inside information and told me to call his cell.

"So what's the inside information?" I asked as soon as I got him on the phone.

"For one thing, I know what killed him. A pink squirrel."

"A pink squirrel killed him?" I repeated, incredulous. "I've never heard of a pink squirrel. How could a little squirrel, no matter what color it was, kill a big man like Timothy Clark?"

I heard chuckling come through the phone. "Molly, a pink squirrel isn't an animal. It's a drink, a cocktail made with crème de noyaux, crème de cacao, and cream. It was invented in the fifties somewhere in Wisconsin. It's supposed to taste delicious, like a milkshake or some kind of dessert. My source said that Timothy had one each evening. The crème de noyaux has an almond flavor, though it's made from apricot pits, and is a perfect cover for cyanide."

"Oh," I said, feeling silly about my assumption that it was a mutated squirrel.

"There was one half-full cocktail glass on a table next to Clark. The only fingerprints on it were his."

"Hmm. Then what makes the medical examiner so sure it was murder? Maybe it was suicide," I suggested.

"From what I understand, there was no suicide note, and they found a whole bottle of sleeping pills in the medicine chest, which would have been a nicer way to go. Cyanide doesn't make for a peaceful exit. And someone cranked the air-conditioning up on the lower floor to keep the body cold, seemingly to make it harder to determine the time of death."

I thought back to when Adele, Elise, and I had been there. "And that's why we didn't notice a smell," I said. "That explains the blast of cold air I felt coming up from the lower floor." I shuddered at the memory of the cold and the thought that Timothy had been sitting there all along.

"By the way, Barry must be keeping it to himself about the scarf. As far as I could tell, the cops don't even have any persons of interest yet," Mason said.

I thought of something. "You said he had a pink squirrel every evening, and the cold air would only work so long—I bet it happened Monday evening, the day before we were there." My mind wandered back to the drink. "I wonder how the killer mixed in the cyanide."

"Before you start playing detective, I have some background information on Clark." I had pulled out a piece of paper and was about to take notes when Leo came into the kitchen.

"It was getting kind of lonely in there," he said. "I thought you were going to give me lesson number two in the art of love."

It sounded as if Mason choked before he stuttered, "I didn't realize you had company." He let out a nervous laugh. "It certainly doesn't sound like Barry. So, you've met someone new."

Leo was standing there, staring at me. There was no way I could explain the situation in front of him. "I'll be free soon. Maybe we could talk in person. What if we had one of those pink squirrels?" Leo gave me a more perplexed look at the mention of the drink.

"Hmm, this is a first," Mason said. "It seems like it was always me suggesting we get together." It was the first time he'd made any reference to our past, and I wondered if he thought I was being flirty with the suggestion.

I considered saying that it was just professional, the way our last meeting had been. But I thought making too much of a point of it would only make it seem questionable. It would be far better for me to show him that's all it was when we got together. Even the drink counted as research on what had killed Timothy Clark. We agreed to meet in the bar of an old-time steakhouse on Topanga Canyon Boulevard in an hour.

"Isn't it kind of last minute to make a date?" Leo asked. Then he laughed. "Look who's giving who dating advice."

"It's not a date. It's more of a business meeting," I said. "But let's get down to your future dates." I really wanted to change the subject because, with all my inner protesting, I was starting to wonder if I was in fact looking at it as a chance to see Mason again.

We went back into the living room and sat down. I began by reminding him of what I'd said the last time about thinking before he said things, this time explaining that he might hurt his potential date's feelings.

He seemed surprised by what I said. "I never thought of it that way," he said.

Then I moved on. I remembered the story about his disastrous date with some friend of Rhoda's and explained that he ought to take the woman somewhere and not a fast food place.

He seemed at a loss about eating out. His wife had cooked all the time, and plain food at that. It turned out there was literally a whole world of food he had never tasted or even known existed. He was curious but hesitant.

"Why don't you talk to Rhoda and Hal? I bet they'd love to take you around to try sushi or falafel."

"Hal doesn't like restaurants except for special occasions, and then it's only for prime rib."

Was I really going to say this? "How about I take you somewhere? You pick the kind of food you'd like to try and I'll find the place."

Leo brightened. "That would be wonderful. I have always wanted to try Chinese food."

"You've never had Chinese food?" I said in disbelief.

He shook his head, looking a little sheepish, probably because of my tone. As I looked at him, something else crossed my mind. He'd shown up in washed-out chinos and a plaid shirt again. They made him look old and boring. His hair was neat but dull.

"Have you ever considered updating your wardrobe?" I asked.

He looked down at his outfit and his brow furrowed. "What's wrong with what I'm wearing?"

"Your clothes are kind of faded and not really stylish."

"Really?" he said, genuinely surprised. "Stylish," he repeated with a laugh. "That's a word I never really thought about. I wouldn't know what to do."

"I suppose we could stop at a clothing store when we go out for the Chinese food," I said tentatively.

"You really think I need something new? This stuff looks okay to me," he said.

"Yes, I do," I said.

"I suppose there's nothing wrong with going to a store and looking." He seemed uncertain.

It was silly, but I felt a sense of accomplishment when he agreed. What was I doing? I thought the point was just to give him some hints on what it was like dating when you were past the point where you were going to call it dating. And now I was taking him to a restaurant and shopping.

We agreed on a time, and I handed him his parka. But he seemed overly concerned about where I was about to go. "What kind of business? I thought you worked in a bookstore. Why would you be meeting someone in a bar?"

I thought over what to say and then just went for broke and told him the truth. "Remember we talked about how I get involved in solving crimes? A friend of mine has some information for me."

"Wow." Leo sounded impressed. "I don't suppose I could go with you?"

Before I had a chance to say no, I heard Rhoda honk out front. "There's your ride," I said, ushering him out the front door.

Chapter Ten

I was about to hand the Greenmobile, as I called my vintage Mercedes, over to the valet, but Mason came up to the car and stopped me. "They don't have pink squirrels," he said. The valet gave us both an odd look, and then Mason told the guy I wouldn't be staying. "Just pull around the corner and I'll explain everything," he said.

I did as he suggested and pulled behind his black Mercedes SUV just as he came around the corner on foot. I cut the motor and got out.

"So, what's up?" I was doing my best to sound casual, but I felt a buzz seeing him again. He was casually dressed in a leather jacket on top of a sweater and jeans. I knew without seeing the label that they were some designer brand that came with the broken-in look. Instead of being upset that the bar didn't have the drink we were after, he seemed excited.

"I called around, and the bartenders all thought it was some kind of prank call when I asked if they had pink squirrels. It turns out that the crème de noyaux is a little obscure, but I found a store that sells it. I have the rest of the ingredients at my house. We could talk things over while we pick it up and then end with the actual drink at my place."

"Are you sure Jaimee won't mind?" I said. I really intended to keep my voice neutral, but a little edge crept in.

He seemed surprised at my question. "Why would Jaimee care?" he asked.

"She didn't like it when I came over before, and now that you're back together, I'm sure she'd be even more upset."

Mason had stopped what he was doing and was just staring at me. "What made you think we were back together?" he asked.

I felt like a deer in the headlights, stunned by his question. "Uh, I overheard her saying she wanted to get back together with you. And then she went along on your business trip." I swallowed before I got to the last part. "Then, when I stopped by when you all got back, she was there talking to an interior decorator about redoing your house. Brooklyn asked for my key back. What else could I think?"

Mason seemed dumbfounded. "It's actually almost exactly the opposite. Everyone has moved out. Brooklyn has her own apartment. Jaimee must have been just meeting the decorator at my place. The house she was redoing was her new one. She got a new reality show, *Hollywood Exes*. It's just me and Spike again," he said, referring to his toy fox terrier.

"Oh," I said, after taking a moment for all he'd said to register. "Then I guess she won't care if I come over."

We both chuckled at my comment, and then there was

an awkward silence before Mason said something. "I don't know why I didn't think about this to start with. I should have just picked you up. I'll follow you back to your place and you can leave your car there. I'll drive from there and take you back."

When I hesitated, he chuckled. "I don't have some nefarious plan. I just remembered that you have no tolerance for alcohol. I couldn't let you drive home."

Well, he was right about that. I could just about smell the cork from a wine bottle and have it go to my head. "Good thinking," I said.

He followed me back to my place, then pulled behind when I drove into my driveway, and I got into the SUV with him. I was still stunned that I had been so wrong. But finding out that he wasn't back with his ex hadn't magically changed things and put us back where we used to be. There were still a lot of unanswered questions, and it seemed more comfortable to talk about Timothy Clark, which was why I was there in the first place.

"So some unknown person had to be there while Timothy was having his evening cocktail. Find out who was there and find the killer," I said.

"That's probably what the cops think, too," Mason said.

"And if they figure the scarf is mine, it's not a stretch for them to think it was me," I said with dismay.

We pulled into the parking lot of a warehouse store that had a huge selection of alcohol. Mason had checked, and they had the crème de noyaux we needed.

"It's not going to come to that, but I could absolutely

rip that evidence to sheds," Mason said reassuringly. Then he distracted me with weird facts about the liqueur we were after. "It turns out that the apricot kernels crème de noyaux is made with have some natural cyanide in them or something your body metabolizes into cyanide. It's colored red artificially now, but the nineteenth-century version was made from apricot kernels, cherry pits, and other botanicals. The color came from red cochineal." He wrinkled his nose. "They're bugs."

He grabbed the bottle off the bare-bones shelving and showed it to me. It was bright red, almost too red.

"That's where the pink comes from." We headed to the front of the store and he paid for the bottle.

He gave me some background on Timothy Clark as we drove to his house. Timothy had picked up the habit of drinking pink squirrels when he was on *Bradley V, P.I.*, since it had been his character's cocktail of choice. The irony was that while it had been the trademark drink of Binkie MacPherson, the drinks on the show were all fake. But Timothy had gotten curious about what the real drink tasted like, and once he'd had one, he'd become hooked.

"I heard he had quite the sweet tooth," I said. It was getting late, and even Ventura Boulevard was quiet as we headed to Encino.

"Even though he was really more of a second lead, a lot of people thought he'd stolen the show. I suppose he thought he'd get another series when the show ended. He probably held out for a while and then realized it wasn't going to happen soon and started taking some small parts to pay the bills, though it had to be a blow to his ego. He did some speaking engagements and somehow became an acting coach. He gained credibility when a couple of his students did well. One got a super-successful commercial. Another woman is a regular now on a sitcom called *Ethnic Smethnic*.

"I don't know how he segued into the workshop business, but I'm sure he used the success of his two coaching clients, along with his own credits, to attract students. Word is that he was just about to increase the number of workshops he put on."

Mason let out a breath as he turned onto his street. "And that's the end of what I found out so far," he said. He left the SUV in his driveway instead of pulling into the garage, since he'd be driving me home later.

"You don't sound like you think much of him," I said. It wasn't the words he'd used as much as the tone.

"It's not fair of me to judge, because I don't know for sure, but I'm sure it was a sketchy operation. It's not hard to play on people's dreams. It's fine for the two people who got something big, but I'm sure there are others who just kept paying him and getting nowhere."

"Actually, I just met his current group of students. They're definitely an emotional bunch."

"And probably at least one of them was involved romantically with him." Mason beeped the lock, looked at me, and saw I was surprised by his comment. "You have no idea what fantasies they probably draped on him. He knew their dream from the inside and could somehow magically make it happen for them—something like that."

"You could be right. Adele was all aflutter at the idea that Timothy had discovered her and seen that her true talent was to be a 'personality.' She thought she was special to him. Who knows what she would have done if she was single."

Spike started barking from inside Mason's house. The toy fox terrier clearly knew who was outside the door because they were barks of joy, not warning.

Though for the most part Mason lived alone, his house was huge. The outside of the ranch-style house was all dark wood that at night seemed to blend and become barely visible. The window with a lamp in it seemed to be floating in space.

As soon as the door was open, Spike danced around Mason's feet until he picked up the tiny dog. Spike looked over Mason's arm to check me out. He started to bark at me, then realized who I was. I reached over and gave his head a soft pat, and he licked my hand.

We passed by the living room and followed a hall to the back of the house. A huge den faced the backyard and pool and was the living center. It looked just as I remembered it. The furniture was leather and comfortable. A big-screen TV sat against one wall. A doorway on the other end led to the kitchen. Mason pulled the bottle of red liqueur out of the bag and set it on a bar cart against the wall.

"Take off your coat and make yourself comfortable," he said.

I looked around for evidence of his daughter Brooklyn. The last time I'd seen him, she had been living at the house while she went to law school. It seemed that whenever I came over, she'd had her work spread out in the den and glared at me for intruding.

There were no papers or law books sitting around. Other than Spike, the house seemed deathly quiet.

"See, I told you. I'm living alone now," he said. "And as you can see, no interior decorator has touched the place."

But there was something else he wasn't telling me. If Jaimee was out of the picture, why was he acting nice, but distant?

He went into the kitchen and came back with a bowl of ice and some cream in a small pitcher. "Let's see what I can come up with."

He began measuring and pouring the ingredients into a shaker and added some ice. The cubes banged against the metal as he made a production about shaking the drink.

"And now we strain out the ice," he said, putting some gadget over the top of the open shaker and pouring the frothy pink drink into two cocktail glasses. I started to reach for one. "Wait. This is the most important part." He dropped a maraschino cherry into each glass, which immediately sank below the surface of the creamy drink.

"To research," he said as we clinked classes.

As I lifted my glass, I got a whiff of the almond scent, and it reminded me of the Bobaccino. I considered sharing how Barry had snatched my drink. But it seemed awkward somehow, so I just took a sip. "Wow," I said. "This must have a million calories, but it certainly tastes good."

I lifted my glass to drink some more, but Mason put his hand on my arm. "Slow down. It's pretty light in the alcohol department, but it will still pack a wallop for you. Why don't we sit down?" he said, pointing to the cushiony couch.

I agreed and then took another sip of the drink. I was already feeling a buzz. I suppose it gave me the push to say what was on my mind.

"So, what happened? Are you seeing someone new?"

"Huh?" he said with a puzzled expression.

"I'm just wondering why you never called."

He took a sip of the drink and made a face. "Clark must have liked them, but this is too girly a drink for me." He set the glass on the coffee table and went in the kitchen to get a beer.

"You broke up with me, remember?" he said when he returned. "And I did try to call, but you never picked up or returned my messages." He set the beer bottle on the table. "You broke my heart." I looked to see if he was joking, but his face was dead serious.

"I'm sorry. I had no idea. I thought stuff just rolled off of you."

He seemed surprised. "Geez, you make me sound like some lounge lizard. I have feelings, and they were hurt. I have the empty whiskey bottles and worn-out Adele CD to prove it." For a moment his expression lightened. "Yes, I still play CDs." I took another sip and put the drink down, too. The buzz had intensified, and it was beginning to feel like my brain was stuffed with velvet.

"Maybe now you understand why I had been trying to keep my family away from my social life in the first place. Even with Jaimee out of here, I know that unless she marries again, issues with her will keep coming up. You can end a marriage but you can't erase a relationship."

My mind seemed to be moving in slow motion. I wanted to say something about where all this left us, but before I could form the words, he continued. "But the wound healed, and frankly, I never, ever want to feel that bad again. Besides which, I don't think the Adele CD could take it. So I went back to my old ways. Casual, fun, and no strings."

"Then, you met someone?" I said, finally able to put some words together.

He had the teasing grin I remembered as he said, "A gentleman never kisses and tells." He checked for my reaction, but the truth was, the few sips of the drink had made me immobile. I was such a cheap date.

When I didn't say anything, he shook his head and reached for the glass. "I told you to go slow. It went right to your head, didn't it?"

I nodded, and he picked up the other glass and took both of them to the kitchen. He came back a moment later with a cup of steaming coffee. "Maybe this will help," he said as he handed it to me. "And you've obviously met someone. The voice at your house. Who is he? Someone special?"

"You mean Leo?" I said with a laugh. "Hardly. He's Rhoda's husband's brother, and somehow I've ended up doing some sort of Pygmalion thing with him. He's a widower and clueless about dating or the world. Can you believe he's never even had Chinese food?"

"That's the way it starts, but then you turn him into the perfect man for you and fall into each other's arms."

"You haven't met Leo or you wouldn't say that." Now that I knew the truth about Mason's situation, I didn't want to talk about relationships anymore. There was a moment of dead air. "We really ought to get back to why I'm here," I said, maybe too abruptly. "What about his family?"

It took Mason a moment to catch up to my thoughts and realize I was talking about Timothy Clark. I think he was as relieved as I was to let the whole other line of conversation go, too. "In a totally not unique story, his wife dumped him when his show got canceled. She took their daughter and moved to New York. I'm sure the cops are talking to her, but my source said there seemed to be peace between them. There were no problems with custody or alimony. It appeared that she got what she could from him and moved on."

"That's too bad," I said. "Spouses are usually such good suspects."

"The cops will probably take a while before they come to the conclusion that she's not involved. By the way, I gather that Clark having a pink squirrel to end the day was common knowledge."

"So pretty much anyone who knew him could have planned it," I said, and he agreed. "If only I hadn't gone with Adele and Elise, I wouldn't be in this mess," I said with a sigh. "Sorry, I guess that sounds kind of cold. But you know what I mean. I wouldn't be personally involved." By now, whatever effect I'd felt from the alcohol had worn off completely.

Mason leaned forward. "I would never think you were

cold. And I get it. Who wants to be a possible suspect in a murder of someone they don't even know?" He touched my hand briefly. "Anything I can do to help, just call my cell anytime." I got up to leave. "And if you need backup, getting bailed out of jail, picked up if you're stranded, anything at all—just call. I mean that as your attorney and your friend."

I laughed as we walked to the door. "See, I would have been fine to drive myself home."

"But only because I took the drink away. As your lawyer, I couldn't take a chance on you getting a DUI."

I got it. When he had said he was my lawyer and my friend, he'd been giving me the limits of our relationship. I'd certainly made a fine mess of things, and I guessed there was no way to ask for a do-over.

* * *

I felt like I was in the song about raining men. Mason had barely dropped me off—no, he didn't walk me to the door and there was just a friendly pat on the shoulder as he bid me good-night—when my landline rang. It was Barry wanting to know if he could speak to me for a few minutes.

When I opened the door to let him in, he was already on the front porch. Since the doorbell hadn't rung, Cosmo and Felix didn't realize someone had come in. At first anyway. But then both dogs started to bark until they recognized Barry.

Barry was doing his best to be all serious cop while the

dogs jumped at him, wanting attention. Keeping a somber expression, he bent down and gave both of them a few pats.

When he straightened, he didn't make a move toward the living room.

"So, you were with Mason," he said. "Is that on again?"

"He's my lawyer," I said, not wanting to get into any details about whether Mason and I were in any sort of relationship.

"Your lawyer?" Barry said with interest. "Now why would you need a lawyer?"

"Oh, you know it's always good to have a lawyer. You never know when some question will come up about whether your neighbor's fence is encroaching on your property."

"That would be a real estate attorney. Last I heard, Mason was defending criminals."

"Whatever," I said lightly. "Now, what was it you wanted to talk about?"

"I'm sorry my taking your Bobaccino upset you. It wasn't about your figure." He blew out a breath, and I could tell he felt awkward. "I'm sure you must realize I always thought you were perfect just the way you are." He stopped and seemed to be measuring his words. "I thought the drink was tainted. That's why I took it."

I felt heat rising to my face as I put the pieces together. Of course, Barry knew Timothy's pink squirrel had been laced with cyanide. Even without me admitting anything, he knew I was probably looking for the killer. I swallowed hard, thinking about what would have happened if I'd drunk it. What was it Mason had said about cyanide being an awful way to go? Detective that he was, Barry was excellent at reading facial expressions. He put his hand out and touched my arm.

"It was just almond flavoring, but there was a note attached to the bottom." I waited for him to hand it to me, but instead he took out his phone. "It's evidence now," he said as the screen lit up. The note said, BUTT OUT OR NEXT TIME YOU WON'T BE SO LUCKY.

I stared at it until the screen went dark. "So, now do you want to talk?" he asked.

Well, actually I did. I wanted to thank him for the earlier compliment and for looking out for me, but I also knew that any acknowledgment of the drink and the note would give him an opening, and I was afraid he would get me to unravel the whole story. So I just looked up at him and said no.

He blew out his breath in consternation. "At least will you be careful?" he said as he went out.

"I always am," I said with far more confidence than I felt as I shut the door behind him.

Chapter Eleven

"Tell me everything," Dinah said. I had Saturday off and we'd met for brunch, and for once neither of us was in a hurry. Commander was busy at the Mail It Quick center that he owned, and my mother and the girls were practicing at my house. The rain had ended and the whole weekend was supposed to be dry. It was warm enough for us to take an outside table at the restaurant that looked out on Los Encinos Park, though we did choose a table with a heat lamp nearby. We'd brought the baby blankets we were working on. The deadline was approaching quickly and we tried to work on them every spare moment we had.

As our hooks moved through the cotton yarn, I told her about the previous day. Her mouth was open by the end. "How do you pack so much in one day?" she asked. "Barry, Leo, Mason, and then Barry again."

"I feel kind of bad, giving Barry such a hard time. He did sort of save my life . . . well, if the drink had been tainted."

"And he said you were perfect the way you are," she added.

"But Mason told me not to say anything." I looked at Dinah, and her expression grew sympathetic at the mention of Mason's name. "I was an idiot to assume he'd gotten back with Jaimee. What can I say?" I shrugged sadly. "Who could blame him for going back to his superficial dating?" The server brought our food, and we put down our hooks. "I really need to concentrate on who left the drink and the note, anyway." I had already filled Dinah in on cyanide being the murder weapon, so she understood the meaning of the almond scent in the drink left for me. "It could be a shortcut to finding the killer, don't you think? I've obviously got them worried. It would be great to wrap this up quickly."

"You should talk to Bob and see if he remembers who ordered the drink."

"I already did. The drinks are super-popular, and he had no idea who ordered what. The only thing I know for sure is that he didn't add almond flavoring to any drinks."

"Who was in the bookstore?" she asked, and I laughed.

"A lot of people." I mentioned that more girls had come in and seemed excited about the bookstore.

Dinah's face lit up. "Teenagers excited about a bookstore and physical books? Maybe there's hope for them yet. I wish that influencer would fall in love with dictionaries."

"Lara-Ann did say that a woman came in looking for me but didn't leave a name." I thought it over for a moment. "That could be anybody."

With no leads to go on at the moment, we returned our focus to our food and our crocheting.

* * *

Sunday I was back at work at the bookstore. I grilled Bob about the drink again, but he had nothing new to add, and in the end I had no more to go on.

Monday I was busy with bookstore chores. There were new books to put out, displays to be straightened, and customers to help. Before I knew it, the afternoon was fading and it was almost time for our group gathering.

I was just finishing putting out a stack of flyers for upcoming events on the information booth counter when Lara-Ann came up with a customer in tow.

"Molly, maybe you can help her. She's looking for someone named Lydia. She says she works here."

As soon as I saw her straw hat, I recognized her as one of the women from the workshop. She glommed on to me right away. "I remember you from the other night. You're the detective person Lydia said is working on finding out who killed Timothy. We met the other night." She held out her hand and said, "I'm Deana Lewis."

"Right," I said, and took her hand. Then I turned to Lara-Ann and whispered, "Was she the one from the other day?"

Lara-Ann just shrugged and said, "Maybe," before she walked away. Deana was wearing a white coat with her name embroidered on it and, below it, WILGREN PHARMACEUTICALS. She noticed me looking at the coat.

"I didn't realize I still had this on." She slid it off as she talked. "I work in research. But I'll probably have to quit if I get the drug commercial. They're a competitor." She let out a sigh. "It's not the kind of job I really want, but it's acting and it would pay the bills."

Just then, Adele came out of the children's department and saw me talking to Deana. Adele went into crisis mode and rushed up to join us and then to pull us off to the side as she saw some of the Hookers coming in the door.

"Lydia, I sent you an email, but there was no response. I didn't have any other way to reach you. I was hoping you might know something. It seemed like you had some inside information about what happened to Tim."

Deana looked at me when she said the last part. Adele was biting her lip, no doubt to remind herself to be quiet even though she was probably dying to share that she'd been to Timothy's house. Finally, Adele shrugged.

"Have the police talked to you yet?" Deana asked. I heard Adele suck in a mouthful of air. "Well, they found me," she said in an annoyed voice. "Tim was pretty careless with the records he kept, but there was a list of the people in the workshop somewhere with contact information. I'm guessing the cops found it."

"What did they ask you?" Adele said.

"How did I know him? Did he have any enemies?" She stepped closer to Adele. "It's not like I lied or anything to the cops, but you know Tim and I had sort of a thing and I didn't mention it. I'd appreciate it if you wouldn't either."

Adele's expression sharpened. "Deal, but you can't tell them I work here either, okay?"

"Sure. Why do the cops' job for them?" She glanced around the bookstore and watched as Sheila came in and went to the back of the store. "From what the detective said to me, I'm guessing they think someone in the workshop might have killed him. He kept asking me if I'd actually gotten some tangible benefits from the workshop—in other words, work."

I wanted to ask her if the detective she had talked to was Barry, but I also didn't want to admit I'd had anything to do with anything, so I kept quiet. "Lucky for me, I got a callback on the play this morning, so I could tell the detective about that. Timothy would be so pleased. I'm the second lead in *Trending*. It's the work of a new playwright at an equity waiver theater in North Hollywood." She checked my expression to see if I understood.

"I know what equity waiver theaters are." They have ninety-nine seats or less and, since they're nonunion, are a great place for both new writing and new acting talent to get a shot. I mentioned that my late husband had had a public relations firm and that I had often helped out. She suddenly viewed me with new interest, but when she asked if I still had any of his connections, I changed the subject.

"What about the others? Do you think they were happy with what they got out of the workshops?"

Adele opened her mouth to answer, but Deana held on to the floor.

"It depends what their expectations were. Tim told me from the start that I was a born actress and he could help with the fine-tuning and tweaking of my talent, so I was all about getting work. But for some of them, well, it was the one day a week when somebody took them seriously as an actor."

"Tim saw my talent, too," Adele interjected. "He was

helping me fine-tune how to best present my personality. He mentioned that I dressed to show off who I was." She gestured toward her outfit with a flourish. Her loose-fitting jeans had white doilies sewn on at the knees. Her black top had a row of small white doilies attached near the neckline, so it looked almost like she was wearing a necklace. To finish it off, she wore a hot-pink beanie with a floppy white flower. I had to wonder if Timothy had meant that as a compliment or merely an observation. "If only I'd asked him to give me the details about our upcoming meeting," Adele added.

Deana barely seemed to be listening and was muttering about trying to get the right people to see her upcoming play. "Maybe Alexandra can help me," Deana said, speaking mostly to herself. Meanwhile, she had been watching the trail of people heading to the back of the store. "Isn't that CeeCee Collins?" she said as our lead Hooker arrived at the table. "I'd sure like to meet her. I bet she has a ton of connections."

Deana took a step toward the yarn department, but Adele blocked her way.

"No, you can't go back there. It's for Hookers only," Adele said in a firm voice. Deana did a double take at the Hooker name until Adele explained the crochet connection.

Deana leaned around Adele for another look. "Maybe I could join them. I'm sure I could pick up crochet. I already know how to knit."

Adele's eyes grew stormy, and I was sure it had more to do with Deana saying that she knitted than her persistence in trying to connect with CeeCee.

Adele looped her arm through her workshop mate's and walked her to the front. I didn't hear what Adele said to her, but I noticed that my fellow Hooker stood there until Deana was completely out the door. Then she caught up with me as I headed to join the group.

They had already started and there was a debate going on. Rhoda had brought a sample of another baby blanket pattern and was offering it as an alternative to the one CeeCee had handed out.

"Dear, I appreciate your effort," CeeCee began. She had such a happy tinkling sound to her voice that it totally covered up the fact that she was overruling Rhoda's suggestion. "I showed this one to the captain at the fire station, and he said it was perfect because of how stretchy and substantial it is. It offers a layer of protection to such fragile infants." CeeCee held up a cream-colored one she'd made and was in the middle of showing how it stretched when she looked up and stopped what she was doing. "Elise! At last you've come. I was so—"

"I saw Logan on the news," Rhoda interrupted. "How terrible that he was the one to find Timothy Clark."

The name hung in the air. They all must have remembered my warning about Adele's reaction, and they turned toward her.

Instead of having some kind of meltdown, Adele just stared back at them all. "What? Is something wrong?"

"It's nothing, dear," CeeCee said quickly, before looking at me with a question in her eyes. I just shrugged. I never knew with Adele. As I heard her let out her breath in a rush,

I realized she might have learned more about acting from Timothy than I'd thought.

"He must have told you more about it," Rhoda said. "How did it happen? Wasn't Timothy Clark in a TV show a while ago? Something about a silly detective?"

Elise took center stage. "Logan is still recovering from the shock. Of course, I don't know anything about what the place looks like, but I think he had gone downstairs to a den or something, and he saw this man, and then it turned out he was dead."

"We're just glad you're back," Adele said. "I'm sure it's all very upsetting for you and you don't want to talk about it." She said *don't want to talk about it* in a different voice full of meaning.

"Adele, you're absolutely right," Elise said, sinking into a chair. Sheila explained what the group was doing, handed Elise a sheet with the instructions, and told her to pick some yarn from the pile on the table. Elise seemed relieved to pull out a hook and start crocheting.

"I'm certainly glad it didn't turn out for me the way it did for Timothy Clark," CeeCee said. "I wasn't talking about the dead part, though I'm glad about that, too. I was thinking more along the lines of his career. When *Bradley V, P.I.*, ended, it doesn't seem like he got much work." She let out a burst of her tinkly laugh. "When I think of that character he played, I always laugh." The bright expression drained from her face. "I know what it's like. I faced a similar situation when *The CeeCee Collins Show* ended. But I hung in there, tossed aside my ego, and gladly took secondary roles and even small parts. The reality show got me in the public eye again and, well, playing the part of Ophelia in *Caught by a Kiss* got me an Oscar nomination."

"Enough about murder. It's so depressing," Rhoda said. "Molly, you're a big hit with Leo. He told me that you were going to take him shopping and introduce him to exotic foods. He hasn't seemed this upbeat in a long time. Thank you so much."

"It sounds like he has a crush on Molly," Eduardo said, his handsome face lit by a teasing smile.

"It's nothing like that," I said. "He just needs a little help getting back on track."

Dinah threw me a concerned look. "You don't want him to get too dependent on you."

"I see your point," I said. Hadn't Leo said that his wife had handled everything? It wouldn't do if he just put me in that same position. "Don't worry, I'll figure out a way to push him out of the nest so he can see that his wings work on their own."

When the meeting ended and everyone was gathering their things, Adele pulled me to the side. "I have an idea how we can do it."

"Do what?" I asked, sensing trouble.

"Get back inside Tim's house," Adele said, watching as Elise put her hooks in her canvas bag. "Remember I talked to you about it?"

"And remember I said no?" I said.

"Pink, we have to do this. We have to get back in there. After talking to Alexandra, I'm sure the details of my meeting are probably on some calendar in his house."

"I'm not going back there," I said. "I got in enough trouble the first time."

"There won't be any trouble this time. And you could look around for clues about what happened to him. It seems like a win-win to me." She looked at me with pleading eyes. "Let me ask Elise to get us in."

Figuring there was no way Elise would agree, I said yes.

She rushed from my side and went to snag Elise. Meanwhile, I cleared off the table and saw that someone had left their hook holder. It was blue metal and looked like a giant hook, only it was hollow with space to hold a set of normal-size hooks. I looked over the table for the plug that closed the end of it, but it seemed to be missing. I stuck it in the pocket of the long cardigan I'd pulled on.

I was surprised when, a moment later, Adele rejoined me. "I worked it all out," Adele said with a pleased smile.

Uh-oh.

Chapter Twelve

"I didn't mean now," I said to Adele as she urged me to get my things. "We can't just leave the bookstore."

"Elise said it has to be now. She said the house has been released by the police. Logan had a special crime scene cleanup crew take care of stuff, and the house is officially back on the market, or will be tomorrow. There's been a drop in the price because of what happened, and she said Logan is anxious to sell the house quickly. She thinks he might be bringing someone over to see it tomorrow." Adele looked at me with a triumphant smile. "I didn't even have a chance to ask her about looking at the house; she brought it up first." Elise was going to be one dynamite real estate agent. After everything, she was still trying to sell Adele the house.

"C'mon. Elise is waiting outside." Adele waited while I left the cardigan on the chair in the information booth and grabbed my rain jacket before she led the way to the front of the store.

Even with her rushing me, I took a moment to think

about who knew what. All these secrets were exhausting. Elise didn't know that Adele had any connection to Timothy Clark. And Adele didn't know about my dropped scarf or that Barry had been dogging me. She also didn't know that Timothy had been sitting in the den the first time we'd been there.

As we went to the front, I called Lara-Ann over. "We're just going out to run an errand. Can you keep an eye on things?" I mentioned that Rayaad was manning the checkout and Mr. Royal was in the office if she needed anything.

"No problem," she said. She put down the copy of *The Mysterious Case of Mr. Jingles* she'd been reading and went to the information booth to hang out.

Elise's car was at the curb with the motor running when we came outside. The weekend respite of dry weather had ended, and it was raining lightly. The cars going by made a sloshing noise as they drove down Ventura Boulevard and the street was black and shiny, reflecting the lights from the stores.

With no discussion, Adele rode shotgun, and I squeezed into the back seat. Again. I was expecting Elise to begin a real estate pitch on the house, but she seemed nervous.

"It will have to be a quick look," she said to both of us.

The side windows of the car were covered with raindrops and slightly foggy, so I couldn't track where we were until Elise pulled over. As we got out, I saw that the rain had lightened into a mist and that she had driven past the house and parked around the curve. "I didn't want to park in front and make it obvious that someone was here looking at the house," she said. "Logan still can't know that we were here."

The three of us walked up the curving narrow street and stopped in front of the house. It was easy to find with the FOR SALE sign out front. In the darkness, the place seemed rather desolate, and I felt a little shiver as Elise did her magic with the lockbox and got the door open.

"Keep your coats on this time," she ordered. "Shoes, too. Just wipe them on the mat."

Elise went ahead and turned on the recessed lights in the vaulted ceiling. The large space was airy and pleasant, but I was drawn to the sliding-glass door and the view beyond. The water on the window blurred the view, and I slid it open and went outside. The view was mesmerizing. I looked down to the flat area at the very bottom of the hill and, looking across, could see the dots of light from the houses on the opposite hillside. The patio ran the length of the house, and a stairway led down to a twin patio that ran along the lower floor. It ended in a stairway that must have led to some sort of walkway at the base of the house. From there it was all sheer hillside down to the street below.

"C'mon, Pink. We don't have time to admire the view." Adele waited until I'd come inside and shut the glass door before leaning in close. "Where do you think Timothy would have kept all his stuff about the workshop?"

We looked around the open space of the upper floor while Elise pointed out the features of the kitchen.

I gestured toward the lower floor. "He probably had a room he used for an office."

Elise was in full real estate mode and paying no attention to what we said. "This is a chance of a lifetime for you. I think the price drop is going to be substantial," Elise said as we followed her down the staircase.

The lower floor felt stuffier somehow, and there was a faint smell of bleach and carpet shampoo. While the upper floor was all open, the lower floor had a central hallway with rooms angling off of it. Elise took us directly to the master bedroom and bath. It was clear from the furnishings that it had been used solely as a place to sleep rather than partly as an office. There were also two smaller bedrooms. The first was furnished with typical bedroom furniture, but the second one had a couple of chairs and a table along with a trunk. Elise walked in and looked around. "You could probably turn this into a craft room. Logan said that it had been used for making videos or something."

I noticed what looked like a giant shade with a pull cord hanging on one of the walls. Curious, I gave the cord a tug, and it began to unroll. I was surprised that it was all green.

"It's called a green screen," Adele said. "They're used in filming. You can fill the green background with anything you like in post-production." She stood in front of it and made moves like she was skiing. "Just a little editing and it could look like I was shooshing down a snow-covered mountain in the Alps," Adele said.

Elise looked at her with surprise. and I had to choke back a laugh. Adele's outfit with the floppy flower on her hat and the jeans decorated with the doilies along with her ample build did not say "skier," no matter what kind of background you put behind her.

"How did you know all that?" Elise said.

Adele hemmed and hawed for a moment, and then I jumped in to save her. "That's pretty much common knowledge now," I said nonchalantly.

Elise furrowed her brow. "Well, I didn't know about it." She looked at the wall again. "I suppose I should make note of it in case I come across it again in a house."

"The man who was living here probably used this room to film things for his students who were willing to pay extra," Adele said. Elise wasn't really paying attention, but I remembered Adele going on about Timothy making a reel for her, filmed on his phone in the yarn department. I guess she had gone for the bargain version.

"Let's not waste any more time in here. I'm sure whatever it was used for is irrelevant to you. Let me show you the room for Mother Humphries."

The hall ended in a doorway, and I could see the back of a black leather couch and, beyond that, a big-screen TV. I shuddered, realizing that must have been where Timothy had been sitting when we'd come the first time. I also wondered how Elise had missed seeing him.

"You didn't come in this room when we were here before?" I asked.

Elise seemed flustered by the question. "When I got to the bottom of the stairs, I turned the other way. I think I went into the master, and then I got Logan's text." She glared at me. "I really don't want to think about it."

She walked around the room, pointing out the features. I glanced down at the light carpet in front of the couch and noted that it was spotless. The crime scene cleaners had done a good job of removing any telltale signs of the murder. I took in the whole room in a glance, and Elise was right. It could easily be made into a separate living area. There was a bathroom and a closet along with a large bar area that could be turned into a kitchenette.

But, of course, that's wasn't why Adele and I were really there. While the rest of the house looked staged to sell, this room felt lived in. Was there anything in the room that could provide a clue as to who had killed Timothy? Elise wanted to hurry us along, but Adele gave her the story that she needed to spend some time in the room, imagining it for Mother Humphries. Elise begrudgingly agreed. She started to lean against the back of the sofa, gazing at the hallway, and then must have remembered that this was where Timothy had been sitting and jumped away. She said she'd be sitting in the room with the green screen.

As soon as we were alone in the room, Adele started checking out all the photographs of Timothy on the wall and the painting of him as Binkie MacPherson, until she saw me go to the writing desk in the corner. The top was spread with papers and things, and I started flipping through everything.

Timothy was certainly a paper guy. Adele found a notebook marked WORKSHOP. She thumbed through it quickly, noting that it contained a list of students and records of when they had paid him.

"Thank heavens," she said with relief in her voice as she shoved the notebook in front of me and pointed out the listing for Lydia Fairchild. "See, I paid in cash and gave him a junk email address, so there's no way there's any connection to the real me."

I was more interested in the calendar and grabbed it before she had a chance to. I began to go through the pages, looking for the previous week's listings. Alexandra had been right: Timothy was obsessed with Post-it notes. Instead of writing things in the spaces provided on the pages, he had stuck the sticky notes on the pages. I found the column for the previous Monday and went through the scribbles on the squares of paper. In the spot designated for five o'clock, a turquoise paper said simply, MAKE AN OFFER THAT CAN'T BE REFUSED.

"Let me look," Adele said, impatiently trying to flip the pages ahead.

I was going to commiserate with Adele about Timothy's note-taking when Elise came in and waved to get our attention, then put her fingers to her lips and cocked her head. The noise was unmistakable. Someone was fussing with the door.

Elise froze and then began to whisper, "It's probably Logan. He must have told one of his clients about the price reduction." She turned to Adele. "They could make an offer and buy it right from under you. Unless you want to make an offer now."

"I can't make an offer under this kind of duress," Adele whispered back.

"In that case, we have to get out of here, now," Elise said, panicking. We all looked back toward the stairway as we heard the front door open and close.

I was glad that I had checked out the patio when we'd first come in because the two of them were going in circles, looking for an escape. I grabbed each of their hands and took them through the sliding-glass door that led onto the lower-level patio.

I quietly slid the glass door closed behind us, and we flattened ourselves against the wall. "Now what?" Elise said, choking on the words.

I pointed out the stairway going down and, crouching low, led the way. They were on my tail as we rushed down the steep stairs that ended at a vine-covered gate. Even in the dark I recognized it as a bougainvillea and knew that beneath the showy fuchsia-colored blossoms, there were torturous thorns, and I carefully reached for the gate release. There was a strip of sidewalk at the bottom that led to the side of the house. I saw a railing and hoped that meant there was a stairway that went up to the street. I told them to stay put while I went to investigate.

I was right about the stairway, but I could hear voices and knew we definitely did not want to run into whoever was up there.

"Change of plans," I whispered when I rejoined them. "We have to go down the hill," I said. The three of us looked down the steep embankment that was almost vertical and ended in the street below.

"We can't go down that," Elise said nervously. "But we can't stay here either."

I offered to go first and acted quickly before I thought it through enough to talk myself out of. I tried to dig my feet into the muddy earth and took a step and then another before losing my balance and landing on my butt. I did the only thing I could do. I pushed off and went bumping down the hill. It was like sledding but without the sled and with mud instead of snow. I heard shrieks coming from behind me before I ended my descent and rolled off the dirt onto the street. A few moments later, Elise and Adele landed next to me.

Confident that we were invisible, I stood up and looked back up at the house. A figure stood on the lower balcony where we'd been standing just a few minutes before. The light behind him illuminated his shape, and I realized that I recognized it.

What was Barry doing there?

The three of us held on to each other as we walked up the street we'd landed on. At the top of the hill, it twisted back and eventually went past Timothy's house. Thank heavens Elise had left her car facing downhill a distance from the house.

We crouched down and, trying to be as quiet as possible, opened the car doors. I tried unsuccessfully not to get mud all over as I fell into the back seat. Adele and Elise got into the front seat and closed the doors silently.

"Don't turn on the headlights," I said as she started the

motor. She took her foot off the brake ever so slightly, and the car moved slowly down the street. I looked back and saw Barry's Crown Vic parked in front of the house along with several cruisers.

"Step on the gas," Adele yelled. Elise must have listened, because the car abruptly picked up speed and lurched around the curve and down the hill. When we reached the flat street at the bottom, we all let our breath out. We were home free.

* * *

Elise barely stopped the car as she pulled up in front of the bookstore. Adele and I got out and she roared off. She wanted to rush home and change out of her muddy clothes before Logan got there.

"What happened to you?" Lara-Ann asked as I tried to unobtrusively enter the bookstore. I had knocked off as much mud as I could, but my cloth slip-ons were still encased in the stuff. I was glad I couldn't see the back of my camel-colored pants, but I could feel the cold wetness from the layer of mud I was sure covered them. Lara-Ann handed me a tissue and pointed to my face. I wiped something off and looked at the tissue and the glob of dirt that had come off.

I made some vague excuse about slipping in the mud. It was the truth; I had just left out how and where. It was probably better that Adele had gone straight home, deciding that her setup for the next day's story time could wait. It would have been much harder to explain why two of us had arrived encased in wet dirt.

I thanked Lara-Ann for taking care of the place while I was gone and then went to the storage room to hopefully find something to change into. I found a gauzy skirt in a colorful print. It looked a little odd with the black V-neck sweater I was wearing over a point-collared white shirt, but there weren't any other options. I finished off the look with a pair of sandals I'd left at the store the previous summer.

My next stop was the ladies' room. I saw a hint of mud still on my cheek, and I wiped it away and put on some lipstick, as if that would make everything okay. I let out a sigh as I came out of the short hallway that led to the restrooms and practically walked into Barry.

"Oh, you're here," he said.

I shrugged and smiled. "Of course. Where else would I be?"

He gave me the once-over and cocked an eyebrow. "It's a new look for you—sort of a gypsy librarian," he said. He pointed at my feet. "That's an interesting concept—sandals on a rainy night." I saw him looking over the top of my head. He had the advantage, since he was taller. I began to pat my hair and suddenly came away with a glob of mud.

"There must be a leak somewhere," I said, peeling away the dirt.

"That must be it," he said. "And that person I saw on my last call just happened to look like you."

"That must be it. It couldn't have been me." I tried to appear casual. "What was your last call?" I asked.

"There was a problem at Timothy Clark's house." He

looked at me intently. "We got a call from Logan Belmont. It seems that the neighbors saw three women going into the Clark house and thought it seemed suspicious after what had happened, and they called Logan since his name was on the sign out front. When he went to check it out, he saw that there were lights on and he heard noise from inside. He was concerned because he hadn't given the okay for the house to be shown again, so he called us." Barry shrugged his shoulders. "Hearing that there were unauthorized people wandering around a house where there's been a murder always gets our attention."

"And so it should," I said, keeping a serious expression. "Did these unauthorized people break in?" I asked.

Barry's eyes narrowed. "No, there was a lockbox for real estate people to have access."

"Maybe someone was looking at the house," I said. "So, there was no crime committed."

I quickly made a move to change the subject. "Did you come here for a reason? Can I help you find a book?" I asked innocently.

Barry had his frustration hidden behind his cop face, but I knew it was there. "You know, I heard from Jeffrey, and when he heard that I had been neglecting Cosmo in his absence, my son got very upset. To make it up to him, I promised to stop by on a regular basis to give him a run in the yard. I hope that's all right."

Of course it wasn't, but I couldn't say so. The last thing I wanted was to have Barry popping up at my place whenever the whim hit him. "You don't have to do that. I'll give him all the yard runs he needs," I said.

"Oh, but I insist. I promised Jeffrey."

"Well, then, can we at least agree on certain times and days?" I said.

"I wish we could," he said, "but you know my schedule. I never know when I'm going to have an hour. It's lucky I have Jeffrey's key to your place. I won't bother you, I promise."

Right. As if that was going to happen.

Chapter Thirteen

I was just getting ready to leave the bookstore when Dinah called my cell. "I have a surprise and something you should see. Come over."

"Are you sure it's not too late? I don't want to stir up problems with Commander."

"I have it all worked out. Just come over."

Dinah's house was just a block from the bookstore parking lot, so I left my car where it was and walked to her place.

She opened the door as I walked up the steps that led to a small landing. She suppressed a giggle as she waved me in and whispered, "This is just like the old days." As I walked with her, she looked toward the short hall that led to the bedrooms. "I never realized what an early to bed, early to rise kind of guy he is. But it's not going to cramp my style anymore."

We'd used to gather in her living room and spread drinks and snacks on the coffee table in front of her chartreuse couch. But the couch had since been replaced by a more sedate-looking tan one, and Commander had hit his knee on the coffee table one too many times and it had been replaced by end tables.

She led me to a den that had been added on years before. She closed the sliding-glass doors behind us that separated it from the rest of the house. Before the den had been added, the doors had led to the yard.

"Welcome to my late-night paradise," she said. "I've been working on it for weeks and finished the last of it today."

I saw the papers she was grading spread on the coffee table that had once resided in the living room. The chartreuse couch was in there now, too. The TV was on, tuned to the news with the sound turned down to almost nothing. She was so excited to show off her lady cave, it took a moment for her to notice my attire.

"There has to be a story behind your clothes," she said, her face lit by a grin.

"I'll tell you in a minute." I looked around the room. "So this is the surprise?"

"There's something else, too. But first feast your eyes on this place. We can have late-night sessions here again—whenever we want—without troubling Commander." She showed me the wet bar that had a minifridge and a microwave. The cabinet above was stocked with tea, cookies, and chocolate. While I admired it, she took out her favorite teapot and put in some Constant Comment tea bags and then showed me the hot water spigot she'd had put in as she filled the pot with steaming water. Instantly, the air filled with the spicy orange scent. She pulled out a box of shortbread cookies, and we carried everything back to the coffee table and set it down.

As soon as we were settled, each with a cup of steaming tea, she asked about my clothes. She listened as I told her about my evening's adventure.

"I wish I could have been there. And really wish I'd been there when Barry showed up at the bookstore and saw you in that outfit." She checked the level in my cup and poured in some more tea.

"I can't believe that with all the sneaking around and rolling in the mud, Adele didn't get her answer and the closest thing I got to a clue was a note in his calendar on the day I think he drank his fatal pink squirrel that said something about making an offer someone couldn't refuse."

"The night isn't over," Dinah said. "I did a little sleuthing on my own." She went and got her cell phone. She reminded me that she'd missed happy hour because she'd agreed to take over a class for another instructor who was sick. "Her class met in a room that the extension program uses, and this was hanging on a bulletin board in the hall." She clicked on her phone and scrolled through her photos, then handed the phone to me. I had to enlarge the type and started to read it line by line, but Dinah stopped me.

"That's ridiculous. I have all the comforts here. Just wait." She took the phone back and fiddled with it, and a moment later, I heard the printer across the room come to life. She retrieved the sheet and handed it to me. "This ought to be better."

It said CANCELED across the top, and below was a class

description from the extension program. They were non-credit classes in all different subjects, like computer programs and belly dancing. One was called "How to Break into Acting." I glanced over the description, which said it was a fun class meant to offer the basics with lots of class participation. My eyes slid down to the instructor. I'd already figured it was going to be Timothy. There was a brief listing of his credits and a mention that two of his former students— Cauli Flower, the vegetable fairy, and Susan from *Ethnic Smethnic*—were going to be special guest speakers. The class had two 3-hour Saturday morning sessions that were scheduled for the following month.

"When I saw Timothy's name, I stopped by the extension office and grilled the woman who worked there," she said with a mischievous smile. "I found out that he was a guest speaker about a year ago at a one-day conference they'd put on about careers in the entertainment industry. She said they'd been thrilled when he contacted them a few months ago and suggested the class, though they knew he had an ulterior motive. They'd been around the block a few times with professionals giving extension classes on things like composing commercial jingles, sitcom writing, and standup comedy and learned that what they were really after was students for their private workshops. She said they'd made sure he knew he couldn't directly pitch his workshops during the class. He had seemed fine with it, and she was sure he was going to do what the others did to get around it. They always brought at least one of their private students with them and they worked the crowd during breaks and after the class. She said the administration let it slide because the classes were always super-popular."

"It makes perfect sense. I heard he was looking to do more workshops and he needed students. I bet I know who he would have brought along to work the crowd, too." I told Dinah about Timothy's assistant Alexandra.

"If we were playing our Sherlock Holmes games, I'd deduce that the note in his calendar could have been for a meeting with someone who worked for him who wanted to quit, but he didn't want them too. Like maybe somebody who helped him out with the class." Dinah set her cup down. "What do you think?"

"Well, Watson, Clark was also selling his house. Maybe the meeting was with Logan, and Logan was the one making the offer. He wouldn't be the first killer to arrange to have people with him when they found a body. But what I really deduce is that, no matter who did it, I better find them soon. Any day now, Barry is going to stop just showing up to ask me questions and get tough about the scarf and what happened tonight. Or he could get Detective Heather involved."

Dinah smiled. "I don't think so. I bet he's doing the Columbo act so he can keep coming by and seeing you."

"Well, he did say that he was going to be taking over Cosmo's care while Jeffrey is gone."

"No matter what either of you says, it's not over between you."

I started to argue, and she laughed. "What's that line—I think the lady doth protest too much."

I went to gather my things. It had been a long day, and I was ready to head home and take a hot bath. Dinah and I tiptoed to her front door, both trying not to laugh.

"This was fun," I said.

Dinah looked toward the bedrooms. "I knew I'd figure out a way to keep Commander's ridiculous schedule from cramping my style." She looked at my feet in the sandals. "It's kind of cold for those. How about I lend you some socks?"

* * *

"Late night for you," Samuel said when I came through my living room. If he noticed the strange skirt or sandals with socks, he didn't mention it. There had obviously been another rehearsal in my living room, and he was picking up some cups and plates that had been left around. He gave me a report on the animals and mentioned that there was food. "You know Pops; always better to get too much."

"How's it going?" I asked.

"You know Grandma, I mean Liza. She's a trouper. They're adding the new number this weekend and she and the girls want it to be perfect. You're going to come, aren't you?"

"Sure," I said before continuing to my area of the house.

All I could think of was that hot bath. As I pulled the bathroom door shut, I noticed that the door handle was loose and tightened the metal base on both sides of the door. I couldn't deal with even one more thing. I sank into the hot bath and let the day—and the mud—wash away.

Chapter Fourteen

When I arrived at the bookstore the next morning, I slipped the colorful skirt back into the storeroom and left a pair of sneakers instead of the sandals, just in case of any further wardrobe mishaps. Adele was busy with the kids' department all day, and I didn't see her until the Hookers gathered in the yarn department for happy hour.

The group was already around the table when I joined them. I was pleased to see a stack of completed baby blankets in the center of the table. Everybody's hooks were flying, as some of them were already working on a second blanket for the donation.

Elise looked up when I walked over, and our eyes met. "How's Logan?" I asked, thinking of the night before and all that had happened, along with my conversation with Dinah.

She rolled her eyes skyward as she rocked her head. "He's pretty upset. I guess there was a problem at a house he listed."

"No more dead bodies, I hope," Rhoda said.

Elise's eyes bugged out, and both she and I looked at Adele, who'd just come in. Thankfully, Adele seemed to have missed the comments and calmly took her seat at the end of the table.

Adele pulled out the blanket she was crocheting in a lime-green cotton yarn. She held it up. "This doesn't look right to me." She looked to CeeCee, who was sitting at the opposite end of the table. "Are you sure about this pattern?"

"Dear, you have to trust me," CeeCee said in her cheery voice. "It will all work out in the end, though you might have to do a little stretching to shape it." As if to demonstrate, she held up the blanket she was working on. At the present time, it was not a triangle or a square and certainly didn't look very promising, but as she tugged here and there to straighten it out, it looked better. "When you finish the square and put on the border, it will be fine." She glanced over the group gathered around the table. "Where's Dinah?" She spoke directly to me.

Dinah had called me that morning, a little embarrassed to admit that, after what she'd said the night before about not letting Commander cramp her style, he had volunteered her services to do the setup at the senior center, and she was going to have to miss our gathering that night.

Commander Blaine had gotten over the grief of his wife's death by helping others socialize. By now, organizing events at the senior center had become a regular part of his life, and, when they got married, he assumed that Dinah would just fall in with this plan.

"Commander had some plans for the evening," I said, purposely leaving it a little vague.

"So, she gave in," CeeCee said.

"Sort of," I said with a shrug.

Eduardo looked up from his crocheting and laughed. "That is why I'm not married. I don't want to deal with this idea of who should get their way. My girlfriend does her thing and I do mine, and we get together when it works for both of us."

"I'm just hoping that Leo has a girlfriend soon that he can make any kind of arrangements with," Rhoda said, and then she turned to me. "I don't know what you're doing, but he seems to have a spring in his step. How did you get him to agree to shopping and Chinese food?"

I cringed, realizing I'd forgotten all about my offer.

"It's probably because Molly is the one who asked him. She has a magic touch," Sheila said.

Everybody turned in surprise when she spoke. since she was usually quiet.

"There's no magic involved," I said. "He's just ready to change."

I really believed that it was all about timing rather than anything about me.

It was a relief when the conversation returned to crocheting and we compared our work on the baby blankets. When the group broke up, I stayed behind to straighten up. I was surprised to see Adele still hanging out by the table.

"It's Tuesday night," I said with a smile. "Don't you have to rush home for your special night with Eric?"

"It got called off. Mother Humphries didn't like the movie they're showing at the senior center." She stepped a little closer and dropped her voice. "About last night." She shook her head with regret. "If we'd been there just a few more minutes, I probably could have found out when the meeting is. I was thinking—"

"No. I'm not going back there again," I said.

"That's not what I was going to say, Pink. I was thinking that I could talk to your son. The one who's the TV agent. Once I explain the situation to him, I'm sure he could find out who Timothy and I were supposed to meet at the Craftee Channel. And since it's almost a done deal, he could step in and finish it up."

I took a moment to compose myself and try to find the right words. It seemed to me that at the very least, Timothy would have told her exactly when the meeting was if it was in fact real.

"So, do I call him or does he call me?" Adele said.

"How about neither. Let me call him first," I said. "This might not be his kind of thing. I'm not sure if he's involved with that kind of programming."

Adele put on her storm-cloud face, and I was glad when her cell phone rang. As she spoke, her gloomy expression morphed into a big smile.

"That was Eric. Mother Humphries changed her mind and the coast is clear."

With that, she took off without even a good-bye.

As it turned out, I didn't have to worry about calling Peter. He was rummaging around my garage when I got home. My older son didn't approve of me at all. He was upset that I was letting his brother live at home. He thought it was crazy that I had such a menagerie of pets. He didn't think I should let my mother keep using my living room as her rehearsal hall. He had not been happy when I broke up with Mason. The only thing he was happy about was that I was no longer seeing Barry.

He thought it was ridiculous that I kept my large house and was continually suggesting I downsize to a condo. But he was a bit shortsighted about that. He never seemed to put it together that if I moved to that small condo, as he wanted, there would be no room for his Jet Ski, kayak, bicycle, golf clubs, baseball bats, and assorted balls of all sizes.

Today, it was his golf clubs he was after, since he had a meeting/game the following morning. After he found them and loaded them in his car, he came back through the yard and walked in the kitchen door. He was dressed in his work clothes. He favored suits with whatever shirt was in fashion. It seemed the T-shirt look had died and it was back to the old standby of a dress shirt with no tie.

"So what's up?" he said, looking around the kitchen and then at me as I made myself a cup of tea.

I offered one to him, but he decided to rummage around in the refrigerator instead. I had been too tired the night before to see what leftovers remained from the rehearsal, and I'd left without breakfast that morning. I looked over his shoulder and saw a plate with a brown cake that I recognized as my mother's Mystery Cake.

Years ago my mother had found a folded piece of paper

with a handwritten recipe stuck in a book at a used bookstore. It seemed as if the previous owner of the book had used it as a bookmark. There was no name on the recipe; the paper was torn, taking with it part of the list of ingredients, and, of those still listed, one was illegible. There were vague directions on how to mix it and how long to bake it. The only reason my mother had figured it was a cake recipe was because it said to bake it in a tube pan. She decided to make it on a whim, and it had become a family favorite. She had figured out what the missing ingredients were and finally realized that the one that looked like *suet* was really *salt*.

"I see Grandmother was here again."

"Your brother calls her Liza now," I said, hoping he'd take the hint. My mother didn't mind being a grandmother; she just didn't like to be called one.

He shrugged it off. He handed me the cake plate and I took it to the counter. I was still thinking about his question regarding what was going on.

What about Adele's request? I knew what the answer would be, but I also figured he might have some information about Timothy Clark and his acting workshops. "What do you know about Timothy Clark?" I asked.

Peter's dark eyes narrowed. "I know that he's dead. Why do you want to know?"

I was sure he didn't really want to know the truth. He would have a fit if he knew about the whole fiasco of my scarf being found at Timothy Clark's house and that I might have been there when he was already dead. He'd be even more upset if he knew I was trying to find out who had killed Timothy before I got arrested for interfering with an investigation.

"I know somebody who was in his actor's workshop," I said by way of an excuse. I cut him a piece of cake and invited him to sit at the small built-in table in front of the big windows that looked out on the yard.

Peter poked at the cake and broke off a piece. "He used his Emmy nomination and the fact that he's a recognizable name to get students. He's not the first one. I've heard of comedy writers, scriptwriters, and even voice-over actors putting on workshops. It's a cash cow, since their work is spotty. But do all the lessons do any good?"

"There was that girl who played the vegetable fairy in that commercial and someone else who's in a sitcom. And he's gotten other students parts in things like equity waiver theaters."

Peter rolled his eyes. "Right, but they're probably the exception. In the meantime, I bet Clark nickel-and-dimed them with all kinds of fees. By the way, the vegetable fairy you mentioned was a client of our agency. I say *was* because she came in last week and lost it when she met with her agent. She threw a tantrum because the best he had done for her was get her a few lines on one episode of a sitcom, so she fired him."

I heard some noise from the entrance hall and figured Samuel had come in. If I was going to ask about Adele and her meeting, it was going to have to be now. "What if he told one of his students he had set up a meeting for them but he hadn't yet given them the details?"

Peter finished off the cake. "It depends on exactly what was said. But my guess is it was classic hanging out a carrot to keep someone coming and paying him."

Someone came into the room and I looked up, expecting my younger son. I gasped when I saw it was Barry. Peter saw him, too, and I heard him grunt with displeasure.

"Sorry if I'm interrupting," Barry said. He nodded a greeting at Peter and directed his comment at him. "My son is away and he didn't want me to neglect his dog."

As if on cue, Cosmo came skidding into the kitchen and put his paws up on Barry's knee. I thought back to what Peter and I had been saying and was relieved that, from the outside, it seemed pretty generic.

Barry busied himself giving Cosmo a treat and then, when Felix joined them, gave him one as well.

"Okay, let's play ball," Barry said, opening the kitchen door and letting the dogs run out.

The floodlights apparently illuminated the yard enough for the dogs to see the ball, because I heard them running back and forth and saw flashes of fur as they took turns bringing the ball back to Barry. Taking turns wasn't exactly accurate—it was more like whichever of them got to the ball first.

Peter watched through the window. "I can't believe that you let him have a key. Why doesn't he just take the dog to his place?" he asked.

I started to go through the whole story again, but Peter stopped me. "I know, you keep Cosmo because you think he gets better care here. Then why don't you just tell him possession is nine tenths of the law and that the dog is yours now?"

"I couldn't do that to Jeffrey." I looked out the window and saw the look on Barry's face as he played with the dogs. The expressionless cop face was gone and he was smiling. The dogs had managed to cut through his emotion control. "Or to Barry." I turned to my son. "I didn't realize it before, but the only time he lets go is when he's with those dogs."

"Mother, you're hopeless," Peter said. "You're too soft-hearted for your own good." He put his dish in the sink. "Tell Liza that her cake was great as always."

I cut him a piece to take with him and wrapped it up. He opened the door to leave just as the dogs ran in, followed by Barry.

"I hope all that talk about Timothy Clark doesn't mean you're in the middle of something," Peter said with a disapproving shake of his head as he passed Barry and went out the door.

I swallowed hard, sure that Barry had heard. He was looking away, but I imagined his eyes lighting up. He didn't say anything at first and just offered the two dogs another round of treats. And then he turned to face me. His face was morphing back into his usual blank cop expression. "What were you and Peter talking about?"

I needed to change the subject fast. "You're really lucky that I nixed us getting married," I said.

It was rather an abrupt change, and he looked stunned. "What brought that up?"

I noticed him looking at the cake sitting out on the counter. "You're not, by chance, hungry?" I asked and he closed his eyes as if trying to rein in his appetite, and then he let out his breath in a gush.

"I was ready to take some of Cosmo's kibble," he said.

"Is there even any food at your house with Jeffrey gone?"

"I need to go to the store," he said.

"So you're living on fast food?" I said.

"Yes." His shoulders dropped and his face relaxed into what I thought of as "Regular Barry." He suddenly looked weary and I heard his stomach growl.

I bypassed the leftovers from the rehearsal and began to pull things out of the refrigerator. "It's nothing fancy, but probably more healthy than what you've been eating," I said with a smile.

I quickly put together a salad made of kale and shredded broccoli and let the dressing blend in while I sprinkled grated cheese on a couple of flour tortillas. I added some sliced tomatoes and put my version of quesadillas into the microwave. I offered him some sparkling water to drink.

"So what prompted you to tell me I'm lucky we broke up?" he said.

"It's Dinah and Commander." I told him about Dinah and Commander's differing schedules. "It's not easy when two people who are used to doing things their own way get together," I said.

"That must mean that the two of you aren't wandering out late at night getting into trouble anymore," he said.

I was afraid where this line of conversation might go.

"And it's not easy for Adele either," I said quickly, and then regretted it. I couldn't tell him she had a whole secret life as Lydia Fairchild.

"Why? What's with Adele?"

I froze, trying to think of something else to say, but Barry beat me to it. "You mean having to live with her mother-in-law?" he said.

"Right, that's it. That's the only problem she has," I said. I probably sounded a little too forceful about it, and he gave me an odd look.

We sat down together at the table. "I'm doing pretty well on my own," he said. "You're probably right about us not being a good match. Though it is too bad we never took that trip to Hawaii that I planned."

"Imposed on me," I said, remembering how, without consulting me, he had arranged the whole thing and then been surprised that I was upset. Looking back, I realized I might have overreacted to what I'm sure he'd thought was a romantic gesture.

"It would have been nice." He looked at me and, for a moment, his gaze warmed. "I kept thinking about you when I saw all the couples there. They seemed to have something special going on, like it was a honeymoon for them no matter how long they'd been together." He laughed quietly. "It was a different trip with Jeffrey. All he wanted to do was check out where they filmed *Hawaii Five-0*." I hated to admit it, but I felt a little shiver when he described the couples, imagining what it would have been like for us. I quickly offered him some cake.

As expected, he accepted it and inhaled it as he had the rest of the food, and I started to think I'd managed to make him forget what he'd overheard.

I picked up the dishes and stuck them in the dishwasher as a hint that it was time for him to leave.

He got up and gave Cosmo's fur a ruffling. "Next time, I'm going to make sure to brush him."

"Sure, whatever," I said, walking him to the front door. Then he stopped. "What did Peter mean when he said he hoped you weren't in the middle of something regarding Timothy Clark? The man you insist that you didn't know," he said. He picked up on my stunned look. "You didn't really think your attempts to distract me were going to work."

I struggled for something to say. "My son is an agent and Timothy Clark was a well-known actor. You don't have to have known him to be curious about his death."

"Molly, I know you were there last night. I know finding your scarf there proves you were there before. Not to mention the note with the drink," he said in a stern tone. "And I know you knew Timothy Clark. What's going on? I can help you straighten it out if you just tell me what happened."

"Really? I know that's the kind of thing you say to suspects, implying all they have to do is spill their guts and you'll let them go."

Barry was silent and his lips were drawn into a tense expression. He knew I'd seen the truth of the matter.

"I didn't mean it that way for you," he said. I could tell he was frustrated that his usual line hadn't worked. "I just meant that I'd appreciate it if you told me whatever you know."

I debated what to tell him. Should I toss him the idea that Logan Belmont finding the body with some of his clients could have been a setup? That wasn't really admitting anything. But I still believed that silence was my best approach. I simply said nothing, and the dead air made him crazy.

"Did I tell you that we found footprints on the slope outside Clark's house? We just have to match them up to the right shoes."

I knew he was bluffing since the three of us had slid down the hill and might have left butt prints but not footprints.

"Good luck on finding whoever it was," I said, opening the door.

"Thanks. You know me. I never give up."

Chapter Fifteen

Finally alone, I settled into the room where I kept all my yarn and projects and was deep in thought about my attempts at a murder investigation, eating a piece of my mother's Mystery Cake, when the phone rang. I was embarrassed to admit that it made me jump. Maybe that drink and the note that went with it had left me more shaken than I wanted to admit.

"Molly?" Mason said when I answered. "What happened? I haven't heard any more from you about the Timothy Clark situation."

"Sorry. I thought no news was good news." I didn't add that the way he'd made it so clear that anything between us would be strictly platonic made me feel awkward.

"I was concerned, Molly. Has Barry been hounding you?" he asked.

I felt a twinge when he said my name. Before, he had always called me Sunshine. It had been his nickname for me because, he'd said, I always brightened his day.

"I wouldn't call it hounding. He just keeps showing

up." I realized I was still holding a fork with a piece of cake on the end, and I set it down on the plate. "There was another incident."

Mason knew me well enough to read into what I'd said and figure that it was a little more than an incident. "As your lawyer, you really should keep me in the loop." He sounded upset, as if he had something on his mind.

"I hate to trouble you with it now. It's late and certainly past your office hours. Maybe I should call you tomorrow." I was doing my best to keep my voice businesslike, but I knew some of my feeling came through.

"Remember I said you could call anytime," he said. "We might as well discuss it now." There was silence on his end for a moment, and then he began to talk. "I'm sorry, but I have to say this first." He took a deep breath and then let it out. "The problem is that you're still under my skin. I kept thinking that time would make it go away . . ."

"Sorry . . . I guess," I said, not sure how to react. There was more silence. Finally I spoke. "What is it you want me to do? Tell you about the incidents? Find another lawyer?"

"What I really want is to see you," he said. This time the silence was on my end. I wasn't sure what to say or, for that matter, do. I certainly didn't want to do anything rash like invite him over now.

He picked up on my hesitance and probably regretted sounding so direct. "I didn't mean this minute," he said. "Maybe tomorrow—during the day. I was going to work from home. We could meet for lunch somewhere."

"No, that won't work. I already promised Leo," I said.

"Leo, again? What's the status of that?" Mason said.

"I'm going to help him update his look and introduce him to exotic food."

Mason chuckled and suggested dinner, and we agreed to meet up after I finished at the bookstore.

"It will be kind of late, so our options will be limited," he said.

I suggested a sushi restaurant with late hours and he agreed. My head was still spinning from his about-face.

"You better tell me about the incidents now, though," he said.

I pictured him shaking his head with disbelief as I told him about our second trip to Timothy Clark's.

"Adele wanted to do it. She believes that he really set up a meeting for her, and she thought if she found the information, she could go to the meeting herself."

"And I'm guessing there was nothing," Mason said.

"Right . . . well, sort of. The man had a calendar filled with Post-it notes, and we didn't get to look through them all. She wanted Peter to look into it."

"Let me guess," Mason began. "He said no."

"I didn't exactly ask him, but I knew no would be the answer if I did."

"I'm sure you weren't there just to accompany Adele. Why did you go?" he asked.

"Now that I know what happened to Timothy Clark, I wanted to have a look around the room he died in, and I was hoping there might me some kind of notation of who had come over that night."

"Did you find anything?"

"I found a Post-it note with something for last Monday. There was no name. It just said something like 'Make an offer that can't be refused.'"

"Without hearing him say the words, it's hard to know what he meant. Was he trying to buy or sell something, or was he trying to settle something? Whatever it was, someone wasn't happy with it. And must have been expecting to not be happy with the offer, since they had to have brought the cyanide with them."

I had picked up the blue-baby blanket I was working on and was crocheting as we talked. I wished I could crochet as fast as the others. Most of them had whipped up several of the blankets already, and I was just hoping to finish this one. But it wasn't just the impending deadline that had made me grab my crochet. What Mason had said about wanting to see me had made me nervous, and crochet was always my antidote for that.

"You said Adele didn't get a chance to look through the calendar. Why?"

"We kind of had to leave in a hurry. Someone called the cops and we had to get out of there unseen." I described the position of the house on the hillside.

"What did you do, roll down the hillside?" he said.

"More like slid. It was muddy, which was good and bad. It made it easier to slide, but a whole lot messier."

Mason laughed uproariously at this. "I'm sorry for laughing, but the image of Adele with some crochet hat on coming down the hill is just too funny." He let out his breath. "My other clients are so dull in comparison."

"That's not quite the end of it," I said before telling him about seeing Barry there and his subsequent appearance at my house.

"You didn't say anything, did you?" he asked quickly.

"No, but he overheard something Peter said to me about Timothy Clark. It wasn't really anything, but enough to keep him chipping away at me. And he said again that he has proof that I knew Timothy Clark."

"Do you think he's bluffing?' Mason asked.

"I don't know. If he'd just said it once, I might believe he was, but he keeps saying it. I've racked my brain and haven't been able to come up with anything. I'll keep looking."

I realized I hadn't mentioned the Bobaccino with the note to Mason. I told him about it now as well as how I had tried unsuccessfully to find out who'd left it.

"You definitely must be stepping on somebody's toes. Maybe you should take a step back with the investigation and let me deal with Barry. We don't want anything to happen to you."

"I'll be okay. I'll just be more careful." I fell silent after that. There was nothing else to share about Timothy Clark, and I didn't want to go back to the personal stuff again since I was still processing what Mason had said.

I sensed Mason wanted to say something more, but finally he said, "See you tomorrow night," and we both hung up.

* * *

"I'm here for you to have your way with me," a male voice said. It was the next afternoon and I was at the information booth, helping a customer find a travel book on Vancouver. Both of our heads shot up as Leo stuck his hand in front of me and waved. I supposed I should feel some sense of achievement. He had already brightened up from the lost-puppy look he'd had when we had begun our "lessons" and had a big smile. The customer looked from him to me as she raised her eyebrows.

"We're just friends," I said to the woman. "He's been going through a tough time and I've been helping him."

"You betcha she has," Leo interjected. "She's instructing me in the romantic arts." He gazed at me. "And I can't wait for my next lesson. We're trying something exotic today."

I didn't dare look at the woman's face and just turned to Leo and suggested he wait for me in the café. As soon as he was gone, I felt a need to explain to her, or really overexplain. "He lost his wife, and he's clueless about everything. I don't know why his sister-in-law asked me. Well, except when my husband died, I had to start a new chapter. By the way, the exotic thing we're trying is Chinese food. You saw him—he has to be in his fifties and he's never had Chinese food. Can you believe it?"

She glanced in the direction Leo had gone. "I think you have your work cut out for you."

As soon as I finished with her and got my purse and jacket, I went to collect Leo. I found him looking at the wall we called the gallery. Every store and business in the LA area had one, featuring assorted photographs of celebrity customers. We had an assortment of professional headshots and candid photographs of the celebrities who had come in the store. CeeCee had managed to get a whole section up there of photographs of herself. My mother and her girl group had been caught in a moment in time as they performed their hit song. There were other local celebrities as well. Even Eduardo had a picture with Mr. Royal. Eduardo was dressed in his leather pants and billowy shirt from his cover model days. I was about to suggest we leave when Leo pointed to one of the candid shots. "Isn't that the guy from *Bradley V, P.I.*? My wife loved that show. I think he was called Binkie Macpherson."

I looked over his shoulder. I had somehow never noticed that photo before, but now I examined it closely. It was clearly some kind of special gathering at the bookstore. I could tell it had been taken in the event area and there was a crowd. Timothy was standing with Mr. Royal. I was in the background bringing in some chairs. And then it hit me. Barry must have seen the photograph. Detective that he was, he would have figured out it was an event, and he knew I arranged all the events for the bookstore. And, therefore, I had to know Timothy Clark.

I looked at the photograph again, trying to remember the situation. It was lost in the recesses of my mind, which seemed odd. I would certainly expect to have a strong memory of an event with someone that well-known. It began to come back to me, and now it all made perfect sense.

I'd have to talk to Joshua Royal and find out the details. But not now. I wanted to get Leo out of there before he had a chance to say anything to anyone else about his "lessons" that could be misconstrued.

We decided to start with shopping and then hit the Chinese restaurant. I figured Leo would feel too uncomfortable if I took him to some hip men's boutique, so I picked a large chain store. As soon as we walked in, Leo made a move to a rack of pants similar to the ones he was wearing.

"The point is to get something different," I said, standing in front of him and blocking the rack. "Let's see if we can get someone to help us." I glanced around the large store and saw a tall blondish man handing a customer a bag. I caught his eye as he looked up.

As he got nearer, he looked familiar, and I tried to place him. He must have caught the way I was staring at him and figured out I was trying to remember where I'd seen him.

"I was with your associate Lydia Fairchild. Brett Williamson at your service," he said with a mock bow. "She let our workshop people meet at Shedd & Royal so we could try to make sense of what happened." He shook his head with regret. "I still can't believe Tim's gone."

I nodded with understanding, but inside I was thinking that a golden opportunity had just fallen in my lap. While Leo was getting a new wardrobe, I could get some information.

I played it cool and first explained why we were there. Leo did a model twirl. "Everyone seems to think I need some new clothes."

"In a different style," I added. Brett stepped back and looked Leo up and down. The pleated beige pants and tucked-in long-sleeved plaid shirt made Leo practically blend in with the background.

"First we need to determine what you want to say about your appearance." He turned to me. "Actors know that how you dress, wear your hair, and carry yourself are all part of a role."

Leo seemed at a loss to explain what he wanted, so I took over and told Brett the situation.

"I get it. He wants to look good for the ladies," he said. "Let me see what I can do." He took Leo in the back and offered me a place to wait. "Who has approval?" Brett asked.

Leo pointed at me, but I shook my head. "It's really your decision."

Once Leo was in a dressing room with a selection of clothes, Brett came to stand with me.

"Ad—Lydia never said anything. What is your group going to do?" I asked.

"I don't know. Alexandra is trying to step in for Tim, but even though she sold a script and it's in pre-production, she doesn't have the know-how he did, or the connections. To be honest with you, I don't think she's worth the money. Timothy was great at picking out the direction each of us should take. He saw Lydia as a personality more than an actor, and he thought I should aim for second lead." Brett let out a sigh. "I lived for those Tuesday nights. When we got together and worked on scenes—well, it felt good to be recognized as an actor."

"He was helping me get anything I could so I would have something to put on a reel. I was 'man standing at counter' in an episode of *L.A. Medical*, and 'man in elevator' on an episode of *Boys' Night Out*. Timothy had lots of connections, and I'm sure he was just waiting for the right time to make use of them for something big."

I knew that what he had called parts were really considered extra roles and didn't take any great pull to land. He mentioned that Timothy had directed a few scenes that they had put on his DVD that could serve as a sample of his range.

"I suppose he tried to help you all get work," I said. "Your workshop mate Deana came into the bookstore the other day and mentioned that she'd gotten a part in an equity waiver play. She seemed to think that Timothy would have been so pleased." The words were barely out of my mouth when he made a face.

"So, you talked to Miss Deana. Did she really think that cozying up to him was going to get her anything?" He stopped and considered what he'd said before shaking his head slowly. "But then, it probably did. If there was a choice of who to push for something, he probably went with her."

I nodded noncommittally, hoping he'd keep talking.

"We all sort of put Tim on a pedestal. He'd actually lived our dream. It meant so much that he was helping us get there. I heard he planned to add more workshops so he could help more actors."

I asked him about the nuts and bolts on the costs of the workshops.

"Well, there was the basic monthly fee. We all paid cash

or checks at the beginning of the month. Then there was a laundry list of extras that were optional."

"Like what?" I asked.

"Private lessons, putting your promotional pack together. That included getting headshots made and the reel that I talked about. To keep the costs down, he had made a mini studio at his house." I thought he must be finished, but the list went on. "There was a fee for setting up an audition, another if you wanted him to accompany you, a fee if he set up a meeting with an agent, casting director, or producer which included the charge for him coming along—I think that's it."

A question continued to nag at me. "Do you think Timothy ever led any of his students on? Maybe gave them hope to keep them coming?"

His expression dipped. "You mean Lydia? I'd like to think that he told her all that stuff about hosting a show because it seemed to mean so much to her."

"So then, you don't think he actually had set up a meeting for her?"

"Let me put it this way," he said. "Whenever Tim set anything up for me, he made sure I paid him as soon as it was arranged." He glanced toward the row of dressing rooms. "I better check on Leo."

I was glad to stay in the front while Brett gave Leo his opinion on the clothes. Brett came back to the front and got me. "I suggested that a haircut might add to his new look, but he wants to talk to you."

When I got to the back of the store, Leo stuck his head out of the dressing room. "Do you think I should get a haircut? I've always cut it myself."

I had to fight putting my head in my hands. He cut his own hair. No wonder it looked so chopped off. "Absolutely. Go with a professional," I said.

Brett offered to set something up in a hair salon a couple of doors down. With Brett's continued assistance, Leo picked out a suit and several outfits. Before he left for the haircut, Brett asked Leo if they could take some pictures of him before and then after he got the haircut and was wearing one of the new outfits.

"I'd like to show them to the manager and pitch the idea of doing makeovers," Brett said.

He might have been an actor at heart, but he knew his job there was paying his bills. Leo seemed to be enjoying the fuss made over him and agreed to let Brett take some before photos of him and was okay with Brett walking him to a hair stylist in the same mall. The plan was for me to get a cup of coffee and come back to the store for the big reveal in a little bit.

I got a text when they were ready to show off the new Leo. It figured that since Brett was an actor, he was into drama. He had me come to the back of the store for the unveiling.

I had expected a slightly fixed-up version of the Leo I'd walked in with. In other words, a slightly more stylish but still bland-looking guy. When Brett pulled aside the curtain in the dressing room and Leo stepped out, I actually gasped. The high-end jeans fit Leo's slim frame perfectly, and the inky black sweater brought out the color in his face. Gone was the dull, side-parted hair, replaced by tousled tresses shiny with gel. His old sneakers had been replaced by boots, and the look had been finished off with a black leather jacket.

Leo got a look at himself in the mirror, and I saw him do a double take. "Wow, I look like a real bad boy," he said, taking a tough stance while Brett used his phone to get more shots.

"I drew the line at coloring my hair," he confided to me as we left the store.

* * *

I'd chosen a local Chinese restaurant for Leo's first taste of food from the Orient. It had been in Tarzana forever. It was short on decor—there were no good-luck cats, pots of fake cherry blossoms, or dragons on the wall—but the food was good. I think Leo was a little disappointed that it looked so ordinary with the wood booth against the wall and the Formica tables in the middle. We took a booth by the window that looked out onto the parking lot.

After briefly consulting our menus, Leo shut his and looked at me. "Why don't you order for both of us?"

He was still getting used to his new look and I saw him actually shrink back when he caught a view of himself reflected in the window, as if he were looking at someone else. I explained to the waiter that it was Leo's first time trying Chinese food and asked for suggestions. A few moments later, he returned with soup for both of us.

Leo was about to try the hot-and-sour soup when he nudged me across the table. "Isn't that your friend from the other night?"

Barry had just walked into the restaurant with two similarly dressed men and one woman. I didn't have to look twice to know who she was. I always said if there was a detective Barbie doll, she would look like Detective Heather. I was the only one who called her that, and even then only in my head. "Is she his girlfriend?" Leo asked. "She's really hot."

"No," I said, just a little too quickly. "They just work together."

They did have some history together, but I was pretty sure it was just that, history. I sunk down in the booth, but it was too late.

"They're looking over here," Leo said, and he began to wave.

The other three sat down, but Barry came over to our booth. He nodded a greeting to me and then started checking out my companion in his bad-boy attire. I saw Barry's mouth tighten.

"You remember Leo," I said. "He was at my place the other night."

Barry's head spun back to Leo, and he peered at him more closely.

"You didn't recognize me, did you?" Leo said, all smiles. "Thanks to Molly, I have a whole new look. And hopefully a whole new outlook, too. Chinese food today, then maybe Mexican tomorrow. By the end of the week, who knows, I could be eating raw fish." The likelihood of which didn't seem high, since, when he said it, he made a face.

Barry seemed perturbed as he turned his attention back to me. "I don't mean to interrupt your cozy lunch, but Heather and I were discussing that scarf I found at a murder scene. You know that she knits and knows a lot about yarn. I just wanted to let you know that she thinks we can track down the owner through the yarn."

I tried not to show it, but he had rattled me. There was a chance that she might recognize that the yarn the flowers were made out of was unusual. But good luck tracking it down. It had been discontinued for years. I didn't even have any left.

"I don't know why you're telling me," I said, my eyes wide with innocence. "It sounds like Heather has it under control."

Barry's cop face gave way to frustration. "Maybe I could have a look at your yarn stash," he said.

"Be my guest," I answered.

Finally, he went off and sat down with the others.

"Why is he giving you such a rough time?" Leo asked. "If you want, I could be there when he comes to look at your yarn. I'd make sure he didn't try anything funny."

I had to swallow a laugh. Leo's bad-boy look seemed to have gone to his head.

* * *

I pulled the Greenmobile into a parking spot in the lot behind the bookstore. Leo was about to get out of the car when he pointed to something stuck under one of the wind-shield wipers.

"It's probably some ad," I said.

"I'll get it," he said, popping out of the car. He retrieved it and handed it to me. I unfolded it, expecting the usual offer for a psychic reader or an oil change. Instead I swallowed hard as I read the message. It was written in rubber-stamped words and said:

Roses are red
Violets are blue
Keep it up and you'll wind up dead too.

Leo wanted to know what the note said, but I crumpled it up before he could read it. I asked him when he'd first noticed it on the windshield, and he answered with a shrug.

I tried to look on the bright side. So far the notes were just empty threats. But how long would that last?

Chapter Sixteen

"What did you find out?" Adele said, leaning in close and dropping her usually loud voice to a whisper as I pulled out a chair and set the blue baby blanket I was making on the table.

The group was already gathered for happy hour and I was a latecomer, as usual. I had been dodging Adele all day, since I knew she was going to corner me about my son Peter helping her.

Nothing you want to hear, I thought, but I didn't say it. I fumbled around trying to think of something that wouldn't make her go crazy. "Just like I thought, Peter doesn't deal with the kind of programming you were talking about," I said finally. "So, there's nothing he could do to help you."

Adele let out a heavy sigh, and her mouth slumped into an unhappy expression. "How can I be so close to grabbing the brass ring and someone keeps getting in the way of me being able to grab it?"

After what Brett had told me, I was pretty sure that brass ring wasn't anywhere close for her to grab, but I didn't want to be the one to tell her that. It seemed that Timothy knew how to keep his students' hopes alive and, at the same time, just out of reach. I wondered what would have happened if Clark had lived. Would he have kept stalling Adele, never giving a date for this supposed meeting? How long would she have kept believing him?

I looked across the table at Elise. She was deep in thought as she crocheted. She hadn't pestered me for any updates in my investigation, which made me believe she just wanted the whole thing to go away. I had to remind myself that all of Adele's consternation was about her meeting; she still didn't know about my scarf, or that Timothy had probably been sitting there when we viewed the house the first time, or that there was a chance we could all end up in trouble . . . or in jail. I dreaded finally having to break the news to her.

CeeCee was holding up a blanket she'd made in a girly shade of rose. She folded it and added it to the pile in the center of the table and urged us all to keep working. "We don't want to have a stingy donation."

I knew that Adele was going to keep complaining about her lost chance at the brass ring and decided to change the subject. I took the opportunity to ask her about the photograph I'd seen of Timothy at the bookstore.

Adele's demeanor changed immediately and her face lit up. "That was when Timothy discovered me," she said. "Joshua Royal arranged the evening. He knew Timothy from somewhere."

So that was why I had no memory of arranging it. I hadn't. It was no surprise that Joshua Royal knew Timothy. He seemed to have been everywhere and knew all kinds of people. When I'd first started working at the bookstore, Mr. Royal had been a silent partner. While Mrs. Shedd ran the place, he was off traveling around and having adventures. He'd done interesting things like working his way across the Atlantic on a cruise ship. I'd imagined that he'd worked hauling stuff around, or maybe helped run the ship's engine, but it turned out he'd actually been a dance host. With his natural charm, I'm sure he had all the ladies breathlessly waiting for their turn to twirl around the floor. His job had been to dance with all the women and get entangled with none of them.

I wanted to ask Adele more about Mr. Royal's involvement, but she had taken the opening I had unknowingly given her and was off, recounting the evening. "He broke us up into small groups and gave us a situation, and we did improv sketches." Adele was holding herself tall again. "When my group finished, Timothy's assistant—you met her, Alexandra—came over and said that I had been a standout, and then she told me that Timothy had been wowed by my charisma and he thought his workshop could help me develop it."

Unfortunately, talking about Alexandra got Adele thinking about her own aspirations again. "I have to find a way to keep that meeting," she said.

"What are you two whispering about?" CeeCee said to us.

"Nothing," Adele said quickly.

Just then Dinah slid into the seat on the other side of me. She did a double take when she saw where Adele was sitting, since the crochet diva always took one end of the table. "I wanted to be here sooner," Dinah said to the group.

"Dear, you really must work things out with Commander," CeeCee said. "I'm afraid he's turning out to be one of those old-fashioned men who think their way is the way things should be."

"Well, I'm trying to educate him," Dinah countered. She slipped off her jacket and unwound her trademark long scarf and set them on the chair next to her. The damp weather had left her spiky short hair a little wilted, but not her personality. She seemed as bristling with energy as always.

"Speaking of educating," Rhoda said from across the table. "I didn't even recognize Leo when he came home yesterday." She turned to the others. "You should see him. Molly got him to go from dumpy to wow. I'm thinking of turning Hal over to her to see what she can do." She punctuated this with a laugh to make sure we knew she wasn't really serious about me giving her husband a makeover. "He said that Barry stopped by your table at the Chinese restaurant and that he seemed to be hassling you." Rhoda worked a stitch. "I thought it was kaput with you."

"He wasn't hassling me and, yes, we're done as a couple." As I said it, I caught sight of Dinah giving me a disbelieving shake of her head. But I knew it was over between us, no matter what she thought. "He's working on a case and wanted to ask me about something."

"Is he investigating Timothy Clark's death?" Rhoda asked.

Apparently, they'd all forgotten that I'd told them not to talk about him around Adele. It turned out not to matter because, once again, Adele didn't react at all at the mention of his name. I'm sure that was deliberate.

Elise had closed her eyes and seemed to be holding her breath.

"Yes, that's the case he's working on," I said. I hoped that might be the end of it, but Rhoda went on about how she'd enjoyed the show Timothy Clark had been in.

"It's funny that when that show went off the air, he wasn't in something else," Rhoda said. "What happened to him?"

CeeCee stepped in, as our resident show business expert. "There are actors who hit it big once and then that's it for them. The trouble is that they don't realize that's what's going to happen and they blow all their money instead of planning for the future. Didn't I hear that Timothy Clark was doing actors' workshops now? People think he knows the secret sauce recipe to make it happen."

"Well, he probably had lots of connections. You know, and if he found somebody with real talent, he could help them," Adele said.

"Maybe," CeeCee said.

"Well, I heard that he coached that girl in *Ethnic Smethnic* and then got her in front of the right people," Adele said.

"It's nice that it worked out for her, and I'm sure he used that as draw to get more students," our actress leader said.

"But he probably only took students who he thought had star potential," Adele said.

CeeCee let out a small laugh. "Well, I'm sure that's what he told them. But, dear, don't fool yourself, he was doing the coaching and putting on the workshops to make money. Unfortunately, there are a lot of people out there trading on people's dreams."

"And making promises and then stringing them along," I said. "Which could have led to his murder. What if someone realized he was just taking their money and all the promises were empty?" I said.

I couldn't help but think of what Brett had said in the midst of Leo's makeover. He had said that Timothy was waiting for the right time to set him up with auditions. The so-called parts Brett had gotten were really just playing an extra. Maybe Timothy had used these small roles as a way to give Brett hope and keep him coming to the workshops and paying Timothy to make his reel.

"Yes, dear," CeeCee said, "that is quite possible. Actors are an emotional lot. You never know what will set them off." She looked over the group. "I didn't hear anything about the cause of death. Did you?"

"I, er, heard his nightly cocktail was laced with cyanide," I said, hoping no one would ask how I knew or why I was so interested in this case.

"If it was poison, you can bet the killer was a woman," a voice said from behind me. I turned and saw Lara-Ann. "At least that's what Inspector Reddington said in *The Mysterious Case of the Chess Queen*. Sorry, I couldn't help but overhear what you were talking about."

"How interesting," Rhoda said. "I wonder how it got in his drink."

"In *The Death at Edgerton Manor*, Lillian Vanderverre had a ring with a secret compartment. She was known for gesturing a lot as she spoke, so as she was talking to Lord Snapner, she flipped the compartment open and waved her hand over the lord's evening sherry." She smiled at the group. "You might have figured I'm a mystery aficionado."

"A ring with a secret compartment!" Sheila said in an excited voice.

We all turned toward her, surprised. Not only was she usually quiet, since she tried to calm her nerves by losing herself in her crochet, but when she did speak, it was always in a subdued tone.

"We have some of those in the store. My boss got them from a local jewelry maker, and he showed me the secret compartment each of them has on the front. I thought they would be great for aromatherapy. You could put a tiny piece of cotton soaked in lavender oil in the compartment and then wave the ring near your nose when you needed to relax." She paused and shuddered. "Now I get why he called them poison rings."

"Wow, I had no idea they existed outside of novels," Lara-Ann said. "Which store are you talking about?"

"Luxe," Sheila said, vaguely gesturing in the direction of the shop. "We're the lifestyle store down the street." She smiled at my helper. "You should check it out. We have everything from the occasional piece of furniture to unusual clothing and handmade shoes. We also have special teas and homemade soap."

"Don't forget your creations," Eduardo said.

I knew Sheila was too modest to do her handiwork justice, so I took over and explained that she had a signature style of crocheted and knitted pieces using a combination of yarns such that the end result had the hazy coloring of an Impressionist painting.

"Sounds great. I'll have to check it out," Lara-Ann said.

"Back to those rings," Dinah interjected. "The important question is, have you sold any recently?"

Sheila got her meaning and swallowed loudly as she seemed to be visualizing something in her mind. "I know we got in three, but I only seem to remember seeing two in the display."

Elise seemed preoccupied and was the only one in the group who didn't suck in her breath as we realized what that could mean. Sheila quickly added that it must have been sold when she was out of the store.

Rhoda pulled out a chair and suggested that Lara-Ann join us, but she explained she couldn't because she was covering so that Adele and I could be there. "I came back here for a reason," she said with a smile. "Someone named Mason called for you, Molly. He said you weren't picking up your cell and he wanted to make sure you knew he'd be waiting outside when the bookstore closed."

The whole table turned toward me. "Mason?" Rhoda said. "I thought you two were kaput, too."

I was struggling to come up with an answer when Eduardo saved me by rising to leave. "It's been fun as usual," he said. "Happy hooking." He gave us a wave and walked away. CeeCee's eyes bugged out, and she looked around to see if anyone had heard.

"I have so much to think about my brain feels like it's on overload," I said to Dinah as I walked her to the front of the store.

"I wish I could stay and we could talk it over," my friend said. "But Commander is making dinner. He goes to bed so early that unless we eat right after he gets home, it's like a bedtime snack for him. By the way, he apologized for volunteering my time and said he wouldn't do it again. Cooking dinner is his way of making up for it." She was almost out the door when she looked back. "You're seeing Mason? It doesn't sound like a meeting with your lawyer. Call me later with details."

As I walked back through the store, I glanced into the office and saw that Mr. Royal was behind his desk. The bookstore was quiet, and it seemed as good a time as any to talk to him about Timothy.

He was on the phone when I walked in, and he gestured with his hand to indicate that he was almost finished and then pointed to a chair. I could tell from his side of the conversation that he was planning another adventure, and I assumed, now that they were married, that Pamela Shedd would be going along too.

"What's up?" he said when he clicked off the cordless phone.

I had always found that it was good to make small talk to ease into any attempt to get information. So, I asked what he was planning. He seemed happy to tell me it was just a day's outing to Catalina. He was planning to entice Mrs. Shedd into zip-lining.

"You have to bring back photos," I said, imagining the sixty-something woman, whose dark blonde hair never had a strand out of place, flying over the island terrain.

Joshua Royal was one of those men who never seemed to age. He had a wiry build and moved with ease. He wore his thick hair long, and the streaks of gray running through it only served to give him character. With all the things he'd done and places he'd been, I always thought of him as the world's most interesting man. He never took being the boss very seriously and was more likely to be working alongside the employees than telling anyone what to do. Mrs. Shedd got the job of being the bad cop whenever there was a problem.

"I was looking at the gallery of photographs today, and I noticed one of Timothy Clark," I said, segueing into why I was there. "It's too bad about what happened to him. I'd forgotten that we had an event with him until I saw the picture. I was just wondering who set up the event. I know it wasn't me."

"Guilty," Joshua said, holding up his hand. "I should have handed it over to you, but it seemed easier to put it together myself since Timothy approached me directly."

"Then you knew him?" I asked, trying not to sound too eager.

"We weren't exactly friends, but yes, I did know him." Joshua leaned back in his chair and stared upward as if recalling something. "You probably don't know this, but I had a walk-on part on *Bradley V, P.I.* I even had a line. It was one of the things on my bucket list—to be on a TV show. I actually bought it at a charity auction, so I got my wish and the charity got a hunk of money. They were shooting on location at a house not far from here. The production had rented one of the neighbor's front yards to use for food service. When we broke for lunch, I didn't know there were two food lines—one for the principles and one for the extras and people like me with a line or two. I simply picked the first line, which was the wrong one, and a production assistant came along and rather rudely told me to move. Timothy was right behind me and told the guy I was with him. Then we ended up eating together. I'd see him occasionally around the area or if he came into the store, so when he had an idea for an event, he came directly to me. I knew that he would be a draw even without the free improv class. I figured he would pull in a lot of customers."

"That he did. I seem to remember a big crowd."

"That was the problem. It was really too big a crowd to manage, and a lot of them seemed to like our merchandise but then skipped the part about paying for it. So it was definitely not something I wanted to repeat."

Mr. Royal shook his head. "I never got a straight story about what happened to him. I wonder if it was natural causes."

"It was murder," I said.

Chapter Seventeen

As closing time approached, I began to get nervous about seeing Mason, wondering how it was going to go. We couldn't act as if nothing had happened. Where did that leave us, and where did I want it to leave us?

February was turning out to be a rain-soaked month, which was a good thing after the years of drought we'd gone through, though I might otherwise have wished for more sunny days. It had started raining again, and the large front window of the bookstore was splashed with lines of droplets. Before I even walked outside, I knew it was a steady persistent rain that would probably continue for hours. Mason was standing by the doorway with a big black umbrella, and he stepped forward to shield me from the wet as soon as I came outside.

There was an awkward moment of how to greet each other, particularly since our last meeting had been a purely professional one and further complicated by the fact that he was holding an umbrella. Finally, he offered me a spot close to him and took my arm.

"Well, here we are," he said in a cheerful tone.

"Yes, here we are," I said, repeating his words.

"The car is over there." He pointed to the black Mercedes SUV at the curb.

I was glad the ride to the restaurant was short because all we seemed to be able to talk about was the rain. Most of the restaurant was taken up by the sushi bar, but Mason got us a table by the window that looked out on a small courtyard, where we had a view of the raindrops hitting a fountain.

"Did we really just talk about the weather all the way here?" Mason asked, shaking his head. "Seriously, did we ever do that before?"

"No, but then I don't think we were both ever looking for an easy topic before," I countered. The server dropped off a paper sushi menu, which we ignored as we just sat looking at each other. I couldn't speak for him, but I felt awkward, and it seemed like the best thing to do was clear the air. "I want you to know that I'm really sorry for breaking things off the way I did and not answering your calls," I said.

"If only I'd known what you thought," he said as his mouth eased into a grin. "I would have had a pizza delivered with a note telling you that you were wrong stuck in the cheese." The grin faded. "Promise me you'll never shut me out like that again."

"Okay," I said. "Now what?" I was referring to us, but Mason grabbed the menu.

"We order food," he said.

"You do know I didn't mean what was next on our

evening's agenda," I said. I let out a nervous laugh and he smiled.

"Of course, but we need some sustenance before we get into that conversation." He handed me a pen and the sushi menu, but I pushed it back on him and suggested he order.

The restaurant had gotten louder as some people at the sushi bar toasted the sushi chef with small cups of sake. I heard one of them call out for another round.

Our food came and we both filled up our small plates with an assortment of the rolls Mason ordered. "So?" I said, picking up a translucent slice of ginger with my chopsticks.

"I don't think there's any way we can just pick up where we left off," he said.

"I'm with you on that. So, then, what do we do, start fresh?"

"We can't quite do that either." He mixed some soy sauce with wasabi and dipped a piece of rainbow roll in it.

"You know, maybe you're right about keeping things light. The best times we had were when we were both in it with our arms open. You know, no ties to bind us or expectations. Fun without drama."

"Really?" he said. "You never cease to surprise me, and I mean that in a good way. You'd go for that?"

"Actually, with everything I have going on in my life, I'm not sure I could handle anything more," I said.

"You're that busy?" He sounded a little miffed. "Just to be clear—does that mean we're exclusive?"

"How about this," I offered. "We don't own each other's time."

"As a lawyer, that still sounds a little vague," he said.

"It means we're both free to do whatever when we're not together. No explanations needed. There'd be no need to come up with an alias or a bogus yoga class to cover up what either of us is doing. You wouldn't commit my time to doing something, and I wouldn't commit yours."

Mason's brows were knitted together. "That sounds even more casual than my idea of it. How would I introduce you? 'This is Molly, my special someone for now,' or 'my fun mate'?"

I batted his arm good-naturedly. "You'd never say that. You said you were my lawyer and my friend. How about upping it a notch to my really good friend?" He shook his head and I offered more possible titles. "How about 'important companion'? Or you could call me your gal."

He laughed. "That sounds like one of your mother's songs."

The noise at the sushi bar had gotten even louder as the sake drinkers had clearly had a few too many. Mason threw them a dirty look, which they didn't notice. "This was just a hasty get-together," Mason said. "I insist on a do-over of our first date the second time around. It should be something befitting our reunion. How's that for a fancy phrase?"

I laughed at his word choice and agreed to a second first date. He paid the check and we huddled under the umbrella and hurried to the SUV. It was a short drive to the bookstore parking lot, and the Greenmobile sat all by itself in the pool of a streetlight. He pulled next to it and cut the motor. I started to button my raincoat and get ready to get out.

"I think we got through the hard part," I said. "I can't speak for you, but I feel a lot less tense now."

"Me too," he said. He saw me preparing to open the door. "Any new thoughts on your Timothy Clark investigation?"

I let go of the door handle and turned back to face him. "Are you trying to prolong our evening?" I said with a laugh.

"You caught me, but really, I am interested."

"Well, I think I might have figured out a motive and a method."

"I'm all ears," he said.

"I think Timothy Clark had a scam going with his acting workshops. Maybe scam is a little too harsh. More like he was milking people's dreams to make a living," I said.

"That's the Sunshine I missed," Mason said with a happy smile. "Tell me more."

I told him all about what I'd found out. It was fine until I started talking about Brett and how I'd talked to him at the men's store where he worked.

"What were you doing at a men's store?" Mason asked, leaning toward me.

"Shopping, of course," I said with a laugh. "It doesn't matter why I was there; it's about what Brett said."

"Who were you shopping for?" Mason said. Even in the dark car, I could see his brows were slightly furrowed.

"It was more like shopping with. I was there with Leo. Remember I told you about helping him update his look? Well, it turned into a makeover. You should see him now. He looks like a different person."

"You better watch out," Mason said. "Next he'll be

making a move on you." He said it in a joking tone, but his expression made me think he was really concerned.

I laughed it off. "Leo make a move on me? I don't think so. I don't think he would even know how. His wife did everything for him. Rhoda will probably have to play matchmaker." Mason relaxed a little, and I went back to talking about Brett. "It was pretty clear that Timothy was more like an acting coach for him. I got the feeling he paid Timothy a lot of money for the workshops, head shots, and a reel, all with the hope that Timothy would help launch his career when the time was supposedly right. What if he began to see through it and figured out that the time was never going to be right? He could have thought that people think of poison as a woman's weapon and figured using cyanide would keep suspicion away from him."

"Certainly a possibility. Didn't you say something about method?" Mason said.

"The cyanide could have been dropped in the pink squirrel from a ring with a secret compartment," I said excitedly. "That would make it seem even more like it was a woman."

Mason appeared a little puzzled, and then I told him about the happy-hour gathering and how we'd been talking about Timothy's death. "I kept it pretty general, as if I was just curious but not personally involved. I mentioned that I'd heard he was poisoned. Somehow we started talking about poison rings, and Sheila said they had some for sale at Luxe. It's kind of a stretch, but it could have been how the killer got the poison in his drink."

It was raining with such a vengeance that the droplets

were actually bouncing off the asphalt. "I hadn't thought about it before, but I wonder where the killer got the cyanide."

"We could continue this discussion at my place," Mason offered. "With a flick of my wrist, I could turn on the fireplace. We could have a sleepover."

"Sounds nice, but I have to go. I don't know what's waiting for me at home, and I have an early day." I had my hand on the door handle again.

"Now that we're special friends, don't I get a good-night kiss?"

"Sorry, of course," I stammered. "I'm still getting used to our new status." I leaned toward him as he did toward me. SUVs weren't made for romance, so making contact was a little awkward, but then we worked it out. It felt like old times, and it turned into an epic kiss that lasted a long time until we both noticed the center divider was poking us in the ribs and pulled away.

"The sleepover offer is still good," he said, caressing my hand.

With a hasty good-night, I got out of the SUV and into my car before I changed my mind.

Chapter Eighteen

I saw the black Crown Vic parked in front of my house when I pulled into my driveway. My mind was still on Mason. I was so glad that it seemed as if we'd worked things out.

I was sure Barry was ready to do his Columbo impression again, asking me just one more thing. I wondered if I should walk up to the car and tap on his window or play the game of going inside and letting him call me.

Why make it easy for him? Besides, it was raining too hard. I pulled into the garage and ran across the back patio, trying to dodge raindrops. Still, when I walked through the kitchen door, I was dripping wet. As usual, Cosmo and Felix were waiting to greet me. They stuck their noses out the open door and both immediately backtracked inside—it was too much rain even for them. The cats figured it out beforehand and didn't even bother coming to the door to try to slip out. I took off my rain jacket and hung it in the bathroom off the laundry area to dry. The house was dark and

I went around turning on lights, knowing the phone would ring at any moment.

Just as I flipped on the porch light, I heard it. I answered as if I didn't know who it was.

I had to hold in a laugh as he said exactly what I expected. "This is Detective Greenberg," he announced, and I rolled my eyes. *Really?* He couldn't just say Barry? "Something's come up and I wanted to ask you about it."

So maybe it wasn't exactly the Columbo line, but the point was the same. He was trying to wear me down until I made a mistake and admitted something he could use to get me to talk. I could have saved him the run through the rain. No way was that going to happen.

I opened the door just as he got to the porch. The raindrops were glistening in his short dark hair. He'd thrown a raincoat on, but still there were splotches of water on his white shirt and dark suit.

"If I didn't know better, I'd think you were stalking me," I said as he came inside.

Felix and Cosmo heard voices and ran to the door, giving off warning barks as they did. As soon as they saw who it was, they danced around his feet in anticipation of some treats.

"Do you mind?" he asked, glancing in the direction of the kitchen.

"Be my guest," I said, stepping out of the way.

"Good decision, because there would be no peace if they didn't get their doggy delights." I followed him into the kitchen as he fetched the treats. "You were out late." It was a comment, but the way he said it, it begged for an answer.

"Is that what you came to ask me about?"

Barry turned toward me. "No. I was just making conversation." He looked around the kitchen carefully. I shook my head, knowing exactly what he was doing. Mr. Detective was looking for evidence of whether I'd had dinner at home or not. It was a dead giveaway that the kitchen looked too orderly and I had put a water-soaked white paper bag with my leftover sushi on the counter.

"I suppose you and Dinah went out somewhere for a girls' night," he said.

"Nope, she was off with Commander."

"So maybe you just worked late and were going to eat when you got home." He picked up the paper bag and looked inside. "And you brought in takeout."

"What are you—the dinner detective? Not doing a good job if you are." I took out the small white container from the wet bag. "If I was bringing in food, it would be more than this."

"I was just going to say it looked like leftovers," he said. He sniffed the air in the vicinity of the container. "It smells like sushi rice."

"Good detective nose," I said, flipping the top open and showing him the six pieces of vegetable roll.

"Was it that Leo again?" Barry seemed perturbed.

"No," I said, trying to look serious. I couldn't help but

find Barry's apparent jealousy amusing. "I was just going to make some tea. Would you like some?"

"I wasn't planning on being here that long, but a hot cup of something would be good on a night like this." I told him to sit in the living room and I would bring it in.

A few moments later I set a steaming mug of Earl Grey in front of him along with a plate of butter cookies. He was sitting on one of the couches, and I took a seat across from him.

"Don't think this means I'm going to go easy on you."

He had on his blank cop face, but I saw it soften as the scent of the oil of bergamot in the tea and the buttery sweet smell of the cookies wafted toward him.

"So what did you want to ask me?" I said. "Are you still working on that case of that actor that got killed?"

He was not happy with me taking control of the situation, and he half closed his eyes with frustration. "You know that's why I'm here," he said.

"I don't know why you think I can help you." I was doing my best to appear as if I didn't know anything. I let my face brighten. "But then maybe I do know something. We were all talking about what happened to Timothy Clark today when the Hookers got together. Someone said that he was poisoned. I guess that means you're looking for a woman, because poison is supposed to be their weapon of choice," I said.

Barry's face broke. "Sherlock Holmes said that. He's a fictional detective. Everybody uses poison, and since far more men commit murder than women, more of them use poison than women." He rocked his head back. "Why did I just say that? I'm not here to discuss what your yarn friends think." He put down the cup of tea and glared at me. "After the situation at Clark's house the other night, the CSI team went back through the place, and they found a bunch of fingerprints and said that it seemed some stuff on the desk had been messed up. I was wondering if you'd mind giving me a sample of yours?"

"Why would I do that?" I said, trying to sound like it was an absurd request. I hadn't thought about us leaving fingerprints when we went looking at Clark's calendar.

"It looks kind of suspicious if you won't give them," he said. "Of course, I could always arrest you and then you'd have to give your fingerprints."

"Arrest me for what?" I said.

"For being difficult," he said, then caught himself. "Obstruction of justice, interfering with an investigation, and probably something else."

"Fine, then take me in," I said, standing up and holding out my hands. He stood and stepped in front of me.

"You know I'm not going to do that," he said. "Just tell me what's going on. Why were you at Clark's house? I know you didn't kill him, but you probably have information that could be useful in finding out who did."

He kept looking at me and then turning away. There was some kind of vibe going on with him, like there was an electric current in the air. Finally he leveled his eyes at me.

"Molly, we can't keep going on like this."

He held my gaze a little too long, and I felt my face growing hot. Was it my imagination that we'd both stepped closer, almost as if there was some kind of magnetic pull between us?

Then he abruptly turned away. "If you're not going to talk, I have to go," he said, heading to the door. I followed him and got there just as the door closed.

I heard him let out his breath with relief as he whispered to himself, "Are you nuts? Get a grip."

Chapter Nineteen

"I know I said I would call last night," I said to Dinah as we walked into the bookstore café. She had walked over to the bookstore to meet me for my morning break. "But it was just too late and, no matter what you said, I worried about upsetting Commander."

I got a red eye and she got a café au lait, and we found a table in a corner where we could talk.

"It would have been okay. I think I worked it out. I keep my cell on vibrate so he doesn't hear it ring." She set her mug of half coffee, half steamed milk on the table. "Now tell me everything about Mason," she said.

"It was a little awkward at first, but I think we worked it out. We're going to go back to where we should have stayed, companionship with no drama." I reached in my pocket for a tissue, and a crumpled piece of paper came out with it. As I started to smooth it out, I realized it was the note that had been on my windshield.

"Oh, dear," Dinah said after she'd read it. "Are you going to show it to Barry?"

"Are you kidding?" I said. "Actually, I forgot all about it until now. I don't think the threats are serious. Besides, there's no way to show it to him and at the same time keep stonewalling." I took a sip of my strong brew. "By the way, Barry was waiting for me when I got home. He was back doing his Columbo act."

I stopped and wondered if I should mention the rest. In the morning light, I had rethought it and had come to the conclusion that I might have just imagined what he'd said.

"He told me that thing about women and poison wasn't true."

"Was that all you talked about? Women and poison? Give me the juice. Was there anything personal?"

"Well, maybe. He seemed ultraconcerned about where I'd been, and then he brought up Leo."

"I'm telling you it isn't over between you two," she said. "The Columbo act is just an excuse."

I finally told her about the end of the evening. "But I'm not sure that's what he said, and that warm feeling I had might have just been an allergic reaction to something I ate."

"Or it was a reaction to someone you were looking at."

"This is too confusing. I don't want to talk about it anymore. I'm more interested in finding out about the poison rings that Luxe is selling."

Dinah took out the baby blanket she was working on and set it on the table. "No problem. I can work on this later. As soon as we finish our coffee, we can check them out."

It was great to have my sidekick again, and we drank

our coffees in record time before heading down the street to the lifestyle store.

As soon as we walked in, I took in the wonderful fragrance of the place. Most of it came from the handmade soaps that were scented with rose, lavender, and other essential oils. Sheila was behind a glass counter in the center of the store, waiting on a customer. She looked up and nodded a greeting. Dinah and I wandered around, checking out the merchandise as she finished up with the woman.

Sheila called us over as the woman left the store. "What can I help you with?"

"We were wondering about the poison rings you talked about," I said.

"They're right here." Sheila looked down inside the glass case, then opened the back door and took out a velvet tray. "There are only two," she said as she set the tray on top of the counter. "So I was right—we did sell one."

Dinah and I leaned close, and I picked up one of the rings. It had a thick silver band with a silver piece on the front with a design etched into it. Sheila gave the front piece a tug and it flipped open, revealing a small space. Dinah took it and, after closing the compartment, tried it on. She grabbed a cocktail glass off one of the shelves and waved her hand over it.

"I think you'd have to loosen the top," she said, demonstrating how to open the cover and then leave it so it didn't click all the way back in place. She pretended to be handing me the glass as her other hand passed over it briefly and the top opened up. "That's sure easy," she said.

I noticed the two rings they had in stock looked similar and asked about the missing one.

"It looked about the same as these two. They're hardly very feminine. I guess the look is supposed to be unisex."

I knew there was no guarantee that this was how the cyanide had ended up in Timothy's drink, but I was definitely curious about who had purchased the missing ring and asked Sheila if she knew anything.

"I know that I didn't sell it," Sheila said with a small smile. Her chin-length dark hair slid forward as she leaned toward the counter, and she instinctively reached up and tucked one side behind her ear so it didn't obstruct her sight.

"Don't you keep some kind of records?" I asked.

"Good thinking," she said. "We're still old-fashioned and write up receipts by hand. We keep a copy for inventory."

She asked us to keep an eye on things while she went in the back to look through the receipts.

"Any new suspects?" Dinah said when we were alone.

"The most obvious are people connected with his workshop. I've met all of them but only talked to a couple of them. Deana Lewis came in to talk to Adele—or Lydia, as she knows her. Apparently she was pretty cozy with Timothy, and it seemed calculated, as if it would give her an edge with him. She seemed very full of herself and also seemed convinced she was Timothy's star student."

"She sounds charming," Dinah said sarcastically.

"I met Brett Williamson when I took Leo shopping." I explained that he sold men's clothing and had helped with Leo's makeover. Dinah wanted all the details and got a good chuckle when she heard we'd run into Barry. "I miss all the good stuff," she said.

I circled back to talking about Brett as a suspect. "He appeared to put Timothy on a pedestal. He bought into the idea that he was honing his craft in the workshops, and it sounded like he was dropping a lot of money into Timothy's pocket for extras." I shrugged. "He even seemed to accept the fact that so far all he'd gotten were a couple of spots as an extra. Somehow Timothy kept him believing that his shot at stardom was just around the bend."

"You've got to remember you're dealing with actors," Dinah said.

"Good point. Maybe it was all an act and inside Brett was seething that after all the time and money he had spent, his career was still going nowhere fast."

"He certainly sounds like a possibility," my friend said.

"There are a couple others I haven't talked to. Alexandra Davinsky is the one who recruited Adele for the workshop. She was Timothy's assistant. She clearly sees herself as a head above the rest of the group. Apparently, she wrote a script that's in pre-production. All I know about Sonia Pierson is that the group used to meet at her house, but, now that Timothy's gone, so is the offer to use her house. And then there's Mikey Fitzpatrick. All I know about him is that he wants to be in a movie made from a comic book."

"I think the correct title is graphic novel," Dinah said. "I had no idea someone recruited Adele."

I rolled my eyes, thinking of what Adele had said about the bookstore event. I brought Dinah up to speed on the free improv class and what Mr. Royal had said regarding the evening. "It sounds like it was a rehearsal for what Timothy had planned for the community college extension class. From what Adele told me, Timothy's assistant laid it on pretty thick and said Timothy had pointed Adele out after she'd done her skit as someone with special talent."

"Maybe the special talent was writing checks."

"In Adele's case, I think it was cash, since she didn't want anyone to know who she really was." I stopped to think for a moment. "It's also how she's escaped being questioned by the cops. They're looking for Lydia Fairchild." We both laughed at the name.

"Oh, and I finally found out what probably made Barry so sure I knew Timothy Clark." I detailed the photograph from the event at the bookstore. "I'm carrying a chair behind Mr. Royal and Timothy, and since Barry knows I arrange the events, he figured I had set up that one."

Sheila made her way back to us. "Sorry for taking so long. We're a little disorganized, but I found the receipt."

She held it out for me to see. She wasn't joking about it being old-fashioned. It was the kind that came on a pad and made a carbon copy. Other than the date, the top part appeared empty.

"We try to get customer names and addresses so we can put them on our mailing list, but this buyer must have objected. There's not even a first name. And it was a cash sale, so there isn't even a credit card record."

It wasn't really a surprise, but I slumped with disappointment anyway.

"Wait a second," Dinah said. "Do you know who sold it?"

"It must have been one of our part-time people. Maybe her." She pointed out an arty-looking young woman who was helping a customer. Luxe offered old-fashioned service, and the customer was sitting in a chair while the salesperson brought things out to show her.

"That's Jennifer Page," Dinah said. "She was in my freshmen English class last year."

A lot of the community college students had part-time jobs in the area, and Dinah was always running into current and former students. Jennifer must have sensed we were looking at her and turned toward us. She recognized Dinah and waved. "She was a joy to have in my class," Dinah said.

The customer finally left empty-handed, and Jennifer came over. "Mrs. Lyons, it's so nice to see you. Can I help you find something?"

"As a matter of fact . . ." Dinah said with a twinkle in her eye, then asked her about the poison ring.

"Yes, I was the one who sold it," she said. "I wanted to demonstrate how it could be used for aromatherapy, but she wasn't interested. I tried to get her information, but frankly, she seemed a little paranoid that I was asking for it. She paid cash and didn't even take her copy of the receipt."

"Do you remember anything about her?" I asked.

"She was pretty brusque. She just tried it on and said she would take it. I mentioned that it seemed too big and we could get it sized for her, but she wasn't interested. I thought maybe she was buying it for someone else with bigger fingers. Then she paid for it and was gone. I wrote the receipt up after she left."

I asked what the woman looked like, but Jennifer seemed at a loss to describe her. I tried being more specific and asked about her hair color.

Jennifer shrugged. "I couldn't really tell because she was wearing a straw hat."

"The straw hat rings a bell. One of the women in the workshop had one on both times I saw her," I said as Dinah and I stood outside Luxe.

"Ooh, the plot thickens," my friend said, then looked at her watch. "I wish I could help you follow that clue, but I have to get back for office hours. One of the freshmen boys wants to discuss why I wouldn't accept his paper." She put up her hands in exasperation. "I couldn't read his handwriting. He's trying to say it's my fault because I wouldn't let him use a computer." She promised to come to the happy hour later in the day to get an update.

Midmorning was always quiet at the bookstore. When I walked in, Mrs. Shedd and Lara-Ann were hovering over a display table. They were a striking pair. Mrs. Shedd's honey-blonde hair didn't have a strand of gray, whereas Lara-Ann's hair was all gray, but the gorgeous kind that cascaded in waves down to her shoulders. She was somewhere in her forties, so the gray was definitely premature. Curious, I stopped by on my way to the information booth that was my quasi-office.

"Lara-Ann had some wonderful ideas for this table," Mrs. Shedd said. "She suggested we put some boxes of chocolates with the mysteries, and this crossword puzzle magazine that's mystery related. It's such a wonderful way to gently steer our customers to items they might otherwise miss." Mrs. Shedd was determined to keep the bookstore afloat and was always looking for new ways to add to the sales. She turned to our new hire and took her hand. "You are an excellent addition to the Shedd & Royal family."

Lara-Ann blushed and bowed her head in a self-effacing manner. "You know I do love working here," she said.

I too was certainly glad she'd joined the "family," as Mrs. Shedd called it. Now that Mrs. Shedd and Mr. Royal were married, they seemed to be away from the bookstore more often and more distracted when they were there. Lara-Ann made it a lot easier for me.

Mrs. Shedd gave a last look at the table and told Lara-Ann she was free to add anything else to the table she wanted. "We do want our customers to browse and buy," she said cheerily before announcing that she and Joshua were going out for an early lunch.

I was glad that Mrs. Shedd was happy with Lara-Ann, but I didn't want her to be too happy. Call it sibling rivalry in the Shedd & Royal family. I stopped Mrs. Shedd before she walked away and said we ought to include the Sherlock Holmes jigsaw puzzle and a book of Miss Marple's knitting patterns. Oh no, was I turning into Adele? Then I felt bad and, after Mrs. Shedd left, tried to be extra friendly to Lara-Ann. "It seems like you might be right about a ring being used to poison Timothy Clark." I told her about what

I'd found out at Luxe. "It sounds like the woman who bought it was acting suspicious."

"Really?" Lara-Ann said. "I can't believe that something I read turned out to be useful in a real-life mystery. Do you think I should tell the police about the ring?"

I shook my head. The last thing I wanted was for anyone remotely connected to me to volunteer information to the cops. "I'm sure they'll figure it out."

I continued my mission to be friendly by asking about her daughter.

I was amazed at how Lara-Ann's face lit up. "Thank you for asking. I won't bore you with the details, but we're hanging in there."

"Dealing with grown kids is never easy," I said sympathetically, thinking of my recent visit with Peter.

"Isn't that the truth?" She let out a sigh.

Seemingly out of nowhere, Elise came up and grabbed my arm. She looked to Lara-Ann. "I'm sorry for interrupting." She was already pulling me away. "I really have to talk to Molly now."

It still amazed me how such a wispy-looking woman could be so physically strong and so mentally determined. We stopped in an alcove between bookcases of reference books.

"Tell me, please, that you have things almost wrapped up. Barry Greenberg has been by to talk to Logan several times, and he kept giving me funny looks. I'm afraid that he saw me at the Clark house the other night. I'm so worried that he might bring it up to Logan. I'm fine as long as nobody asks me a direct question," she said. "If Barry asks me if I was at the house, I'd have to tell the truth." Her face collapsed. "If Logan finds out what I did, he'll never let me work with him. He's always going on about his pristine reputation." I wished she'd lighten up a little and maybe get a sense of humor. She was right up there with Adele in the drama department. As she continued on about Logan, I noticed she kept gesturing toward the café. I finally asked her if he was there.

"Yes. He loves the Bobaccinos your barista makes." She looked around frantically. "I told him I was coming in here for some yarn."

I assured her I was working hard to settle the case. What she'd said had added even more incentive. All of her worries were about Logan finding out she'd shown the house, but if Barry did ask her any straight questions and she spilled the beans, all of us would be in trouble. I reminded her that I had wanted to talk to Logan all along.

"Be my guest," she said. "Maybe he'll tell you more than he told me. He said he wanted to protect me from the horror of it all. Remember, don't say anything that would give away that you've seen that house."

"You seem pretty tense. Why don't you sit down at the table in the yarn department and crochet for a few minutes to calm yourself?" My suggestion, though thoughtful, was also self-serving. I didn't want to have to worry about her rushing into the café and interrupting while I was talking to Logan.

I had never said anything to Elise, but I still wondered

if it was sheer coincidence that Logan and his clients had found the body. Or had it been a setup?

Everybody in the café seemed to be in a similar pose—sipping on a drink and staring at some sort of screen. I had no trouble picking Logan out from the crowd. He was on the short side and wiry and would have been ordinary looking if it weren't for his hair. There was nothing out of the ordinary about the light-brown color or the texture; it was how it sat on his head. His hairline was almost a circle far back on his head, making him look like he was wearing a hair hat. As I approached the small round table by the window, I saw he'd already gone through half his Bobaccino and was staring at his cell phone.

"Hey, Logan," I said, trying to appear casual. I focused on his drink "How do you like your Bobaccino? I haven't tried one yet, though someone tried to give me one." I looked to see his reaction.

He let go of the straw and smiled. "You absolutely should try one. I like to customize mine. I have Bob throw in a couple of shots of espresso to the vanilla. The sugar and caffeine are a perfect mix for a pick-me-up," he said. He didn't miss a beat. "Are you finally ready to sell your house? What do you need such a big place for? We could get a good price for it and settle you into something more manageable, leaving you with a nice nest egg in the bank."

"Has my son Peter been talking to you?" I asked with a joking smile. "And, about not needing such a big place, I really do need the space with my other son living with me, all my pets, and my mother using it for a rehearsal hall."

He seemed surprised but not daunted. "Then maybe you need a bigger place. We could sell your place and find you a new place a little farther out."

I had to give him credit for being single-minded. I chuckled inwardly, imagining what he meant by a little farther out—like maybe in another state? But I wasn't there to talk about my house. "I'm really interested in Timothy Clark's place," I said.

He instantly sat up straighter. "I can get you a real deal on that place. They just dropped the price."

"Sorry, I didn't mean buy it." I cringed, realizing my mistake in phrasing. "I heard you were the one who found him."

Logan's enthusiasm disappeared and he sagged a little.

I was still standing and leaned against the table. "I saw you on the news. It must have been pretty unnerving to find a dead body." I gave it a moment to see if he was going to say anything, but when he seemed to have gone silent, I kept on. "I suppose you told the cops a lot more than what was on the news," I said.

"Yes," he said. I saw that he was going to leave it at that, so I kept prodding.

"I only heard a little of what you said to the reporter. Something about you were showing the house . . ." I let it hang, a suggestion I'd picked up from *The Average Joe's Guide to Criminal Investigations*, which was my favorite reference book, and it finally got him talking.

"It's always good if you can make a house special, and tying it to a celebrity adds to a house's cache, so I'd mentioned to my clients that it belonged to Timothy Clark. The couple were big fans of his show, and they seemed excited that he owned the house. As we headed down the hall on the lower floor, I was surprised to see him sitting on the couch in the den, since I thought no one was home. He had his back to us, and I thought it would make even more of an impression on the couple if I could introduce them to him."

He stopped and closed his eyes as if he was trying to shut out the memory. "I didn't realize at first. His head was down as if he was looking at something. When he didn't respond, I thought he might be asleep, and I tapped him on the shoulder." Logan suddenly looked a little green. "He just fell over on his side, and I got a look at his face and the mess on the rug in front of him. It wasn't pretty. But I guess cyanide can do horrible things."

I thought it was interesting that he knew the cause of death, considering it hadn't been common knowledge and I'd found it out from Mason. I asked him who had told him, and he seemed uncomfortable.

"It must have been something the police said." He paused and then spoke. "I know what it was now. The detective I spoke to asked me if I knew where you could buy cyanide, and that's when I figured it must have been the cause of Clark's death."

"So, do you know where you can buy cyanide?"

"Online, just like you can find all kinds of other stuff," he said.

I wondered if he had told the police that or if he had realized it might seem rather incriminating. Now that he had started talking, he went on, ruminating on how hard it was going to be to sell the house.

"You have to disclose if someone has died in a house and if it was a murder. Even with all the attention the place has gotten, it's going to be a tough sale. And the seller wants to sell it quick." He looked up at me. "You don't know anybody who wants to buy it, do you? It's a real bargain now."

I was still stuck on what he'd just said about "the seller." "I thought it was Timothy Clark's house," I said.

"It was. He bought it when he was on the TV show. But then it ended. I suppose he figured he'd get another series." Logan shrugged. "Foolish actors. He started pulling money out of the house with home equity loans, and then, when the cash ran out, he had to sell it."

"Who owns it now?" I asked.

"Why do you want to know?" I noticed a subtle change in Logan's composure. He seemed to be drawing himself inward.

I had to think fast and come up with a reason. Finally I said, "Just curious. It can't be a secret."

"It's a group of investors," he said. I noticed that he'd begun playing nervously with a pen on the table and was glancing around the café as if to avoid my eye.

What was he so nervous about? Then the obvious hit me. "Are you one of the investors?" I asked.

I remembered that Elise had said she had to tell the truth when asked a direct question, and I hoped the same held true for Logan.

He stopped fidgeting and seemed to deflate as if I'd stuck a pin in a beach ball. "You can't tell Elise." He leaned a little closer for emphasis. "It was a can't-fail plan," he said. "I met him by chance when I was handing out promotional stuff in the area. Clark needed a quick sale, and he agreed to a price below market value. I have a group of friends and we all pooled our money." He seemed suddenly stricken. "I took money out of our retirement account. The deal was we'd rent it back to him for a year and then we'd put it up for sale. And that's what happened. We put it on the market for a third more than we paid, and—" He stopped and let out a sigh. "It would have sold easily. But now . . ." He shook his head with dismay and bit his lip. "How did you get me to tell you that?"

Inside, I was shaking my head in disbelief at all the secrets these married couples had from each other. It made me glad that Mason and I had agreed to keep things light between us. I pretended to shrug off what he'd told me, but he was truly upset now.

"It wasn't like I didn't try to help him. I called 911 and then we just waited there. Not there, there. I took my clients upstairs. On top of everything else, the air-conditioning was blasting on the lower floor and the place was like an icebox. I heard later it was a way to confuse the time of death."

But had he really heard it, or was he the one who'd done it?

Chapter Twenty

"You can't give up now," Rhoda said in a cajoling voice. "He's almost there, but before I try to fix him up again with someone from the sisterhood, I want to be sure it's not going to be another disaster. Just do one dinner with him."

Rhoda had arrived early for our happy-hour gathering, and I was talking to her as I straightened up the yarn department before joining her at the table. I debated about her request. I wanted to be done with Leo, but it also seemed unfinished to leave it hanging.

"Okay, I'll do it," I said finally. "There is one more area I want to talk to him about."

"Sex?" Rhoda said with a bright look. "Good, because I'm sure he needs some updated information."

"Not sex. He'll have to figure that out on his own. It's just a little tweak he needs."

"You might want to mention romance. My sister-in-law was the blunt, boiled-beef type. She thought flowers just died and candy just gave you cavities." She had her cell phone

226

out. "I'll just call him and set it up for tonight. Maybe you can go to one of those romantic spots that Mason took you to. He and Rebecca almost never ate out, and when they did, it was a place with fluorescent lights and bare table-tops," she said. "I can't thank you enough for what you've done already. Hal is so relieved that Leo has stopped sitting around moaning and groaning."

Most of the rest of the group arrived en masse and took seats around the table. CeeCee went to the head of the table but didn't sit. She pulled out a stack of baby blankets and put them on the table. "Let's see how you're all doing."

"Here's mine," Eduardo said, holding up the blanket he was making to show that it was almost done. He had fin-ished the square and now was adding a border. He had chosen a neutral shade of tan for the blanket and was using a darker shade of the same color for the edging.

Dinah rushed in and skidded to her chair. "What did I miss?"

"We're showing off our baby blankets." CeeCee waited until Dinah took out the sunny-orange one she was working on. Like Eduardo's, it was close to done. "That's such a happy color," she said with a smile. "Related to all this, I have some exciting news. My publicist has arranged for some press coverage of our donation. They're going to meet us at the Tarzana Fire Station. Everybody is hungry for some happy news these days."

I saw Adele's eyes light up. "I should really be the liaison with the media, since we are coheads of the group. What kind of press are we talking about?"

Adele seemed serious, but it was hard for the rest of to take her seriously given what she was wearing. She had never changed out of her story time outfit. She had read the book *Ladies on the Loose*, a book about women having varied careers. She had been demonstrating being a doctor and wore a white coat with DR. ADELE embroidered on it. She had a kids' stethoscope sticking out of her pocket. And she had topped it all off with a lot of makeup.

I saw CeeCee roll her eyes a few times. "Someone from Channel 3 and a reporter from the *Times*. And thank you for your kind offer of help, but it is best if I deal with them."

No surprise, Adele pouted at this news. Then everyone's hooks began to fly as we rushed to finish our blankets. Dinah and I had our heads together the whole time as I told her about my visit with Logan. She cringed when I told her about his customized Bobaccino. But then she looked at her watch and gathered up her things.

"I have to go," she said to me, then repeated it to the group. "Commander and I are going out for a fun evening; no senior center tonight. It's just the two of us," she said with a smile. "He runs out of steam early." She gave me a knowing nod.

When the rest of the group broke up, CeeCee wished everyone a happy, pleasant evening and reminded us that all our blankets needed to be completely finished before the presentation. Rhoda went to the front of the store to wait for Hal to drop off Leo, and I snagged Adele.

I had spent the afternoon thinking over the three women in her workshop group. "I need to talk to you," I said, following Adele back to the kids' department. It was deserted at this time of night.

I told her about Dinah's and my trip to Luxe and the news about the poison ring before I got to the point. "The woman who bought it was wearing a straw hat," I said finally.

Before I could ask the question, Adele spoke. "That's Deana the Diva. She wanted that straw hat to be like her trademark."

"Do you understand that if she was the one who bought the poison ring, she could have been the one to kill Timothy?" I said, since Adele didn't seem to be focusing.

"Why would she want to kill him? You heard her say that she was his star student and he was her boyfriend."

Was Adele really that naive? "I think she was having an affair with him," I began. "But I don't think he was her boyfriend. More like she thought it would get her some kind of edge with him."

Adele seemed annoyed with the idea. "I guess she thought it was like the old days with the casting couch and all. We women don't have to do that kind of stuff anymore. I certainly didn't, and he still saw what a major talent I am."

"What about that woman who discovered you? Alexandra something-or-other." I tried not to choke on the word *discovered*.

"Why do you want to know?" She'd barely asked the question when her face lit with understanding. "You're trying to find out who killed Timothy. Why? Leave it alone. I thought the whole point was for you, me, and Elise to stay as far as possible from the whole thing so it would never come out that we were there."

"There's something I have to tell you," I began. I had been dreading this, but it was time for Adele to know just how much trouble we could be in. I began by bringing up the timing of our being there and Logan's arrival. "And he's the one who discovered Timothy."

Slowly a look of horror came over Adele's face. "Then, you mean, he was there when we were there?" I nodded and she came unglued. She seemed upset enough, so I didn't mention the charges that could be brought against us. "There's something else." I took a deep breath and told her about the scarf.

"OMG, we're screwed," she yelped.

"Not necessarily." I told her how I'd been stonewalling Barry. "The plan was to try to wrap it up while I was still stalling him."

"Pink, you have to do it." She was close to hysteria. "The cops can't find out we were there. It would all come out then. Cutchykins can't find out about my secret life or that I'm implicated in a murder." She had her head in her hands. "There has to be a way I can get the details of my meeting."

I chose to ignore her last statement and instead asked her about Alexandra again.

"I don't know everything, but I heard they met when Timothy was a guest speaker at an all-day workshop at Beasley Community College. I'm not sure exactly how it happened, but I think he met the girl who got the part in the sitcom and the one who's in the vegetable commercial through the extension class, too."

"It sounds like Alexandra was almost like his partner," I said, and Adele nodded noncommittally. "I wonder how he felt about her starting her own workshops."

Adele suddenly straightened. "She was?" Then she shrugged it off and sounded upset that she'd been out of the loop. "I don't know how Timothy felt about her. All I do know is that now she's looking to take over our workshop."

"What about Mikey Fitzpatrick?" I asked.

"What about him?" Adele asked.

"He seemed to be happy with whatever Timothy had done for him. What exactly did he do for Mikey?"

"All I know is that he made a reel for him that made him look like a real superhero. If you want to talk to him, he's going to be a special guest at story time tomorrow."

Adele's expression brightened as she looked up toward the entrance of the kids' department. "Here comes Cutchykins," she said, getting out of her chair. Then her smile faded. "And his mother, too."

She rushed off to meet them as I wondered if she realized she was still dressed as Dr. Adele.

* * *

Rhoda found me and said that Leo was waiting out front. I gathered up my things and said good-bye to Mrs. Shedd and Mr. Royal before I left.

It was already dark outside, and since there hadn't been

any rain all day, the street and sidewalk were dry, but the air had a bite. Leo came toward me as I walked out the door. He was wearing another of the outfits we'd gotten. He'd come a long way from the parka and faded pants. And I felt a wave of pride. I was sure he'd do better with the ladies now. There was just a little bit more he needed to know.

"Hi, good evening. Where are we going? Rhoda said you had someplace special in mind." He was all smiles, and the gloomy-looking guy he'd been was hard to even remember now.

As soon as Rhoda had suggested I take him someplace that Mason had taken me, I knew where to go and had called ahead to make a reservation. I was about to give him a rundown on the place when my cell phone rang—well, actually, my watch vibrated and lit up with the call. I usually didn't answer calls in the car, but since we weren't moving, I hit ACCEPT, still feeling like I was Dick Tracy talking to my wrist.

"You answered your cell," Mason said, his voice full of surprise.

"I even answered it on my watch," I said. "Thank you again for it." I switched over to my phone and put it to my ear.

"My pleasure," he said. "I thought we could get dinner. It wouldn't be our grand second first date. That's still in the works."

I was a little taken aback. A day or two ago we'd been estranged, and now he was assuming we'd get dinner. I had gotten used to being on my own again, not having to check in with anyone if I made plans. He started to go into his plans for after-dinner delights when I cut him off abruptly. "I'm in the car," I said, "and I'm not alone."

Mason's tone became wary. "Who's with you?"

"Leo," I said brightly. I didn't want to hurt Leo's feelings by implying it was an imposition to be going to dinner with him. "This is kind of his graduation," I said.

"What does that mean?" Mason said. His voice was loud enough for Leo to hear.

"Molly is going to give me a heads-up on romance. She's taking me to a restaurant at the beach that has Mediterranean food," Leo said, smiling and nodding at me.

"What does a heads-up on romance entail?" Mason didn't sound happy.

"I'm not giving away my secrets," I said.

Mason got hold of himself. "Maybe we could get together later. After your dinner?"

I told Mason I'd have to call him. Leo seemed relieved when I got off the phone and we got going.

"The ride there is a nice start to a romantic evening," I said, as I steered the Greenmobile off of Ventura onto Topanga Canyon Boulevard.

In no time, we had left the Valley behind and the rustic landscape was lost in the darkness as I navigated the curves of the canyon. Leo was enthralled with the small shops and restaurants as we passed through the town of Topanga and then undertook the most rugged part of the ride. In the darkness, it was hard to see the mountains, but I knew they loomed above us, jagged and empty of civilization. When we got to the stoplight at Pacific Coast Highway, I couldn't tell where the ocean ended and the sky began. It was all just midnight blue now.

"When you go on a date, it's about more than just getting food. Where you go is important. We're going to a restaurant with atmosphere," I announced. As we drove the rest of the way, I gave him a rundown on what the Mediterranean dishes were like. "It sets a mood when you share food," I said. "When we get there, you are going to do the ordering for both of us," I said, and he looked panic-stricken.

"How do I do that? My wife always handled anything to do with food," he said. I promised to help him, and he relaxed a little.

The Seaside Taverna was in a white stucco building that had a traditional terra-cotta roof. Inside, the lights were low and flattering. Mason and I had been there numerous times. I told Leo it was known as an in spot with the people from the entertainment industry and that we might even see some celebrities.

The place was packed, and I was glad I'd made a reservation. We were led to a table in the corner where we had a view of the whole place. Leo was busy looking around at the decor and all the people. It still stunned me that a man in his fifties had missed out on so many experiences that seemed so ordinary to me.

As he started to sit down, I stopped him. "It's really

old-fashioned, but women still like it when you pull out their chair for them."

He nodded and dutifully pulled out my chair and then pushed me up too close to the table. I had to tell him that the last part wasn't necessary.

He started to sit across from me, but I suggested that it would work better if he sat next to his future date.

We looked over the menus together, and he was overwhelmed by so many dishes he'd never heard of, let alone tried. I helped him decide what to order and reminded him about sharing them. When the server came to take the order, Leo kept looking at me for acceptance.

When we were alone again, I got ready to give him my pitch. "There's something important I need to tell you about dating. It seems like your wife handled everything, but if you're going to be the picker rather than the pickee, you need to take charge of things. Like, not wait for someone to find you—you find the person you'd like to go out with." I looked at him to see if he understood.

"That's really outside my comfort zone. I don't know if I can do that," he said as his brow furrowed.

"Of course, it's up to you," I said. "I'm just saying that it would be better if you learned how to make the first move and then follow up." I struggled with what I was going to say, but I thought it was important to his future happiness. "For example, don't wait for her to kiss you," I said.

He got all flummoxed. "I don't know how to do that."

I pointed to his leather jacket on the back of the chair.

"You've got the look down; now you need to add the confidence to go with it." He seemed uncertain, but I assured him he probably had more confidence than he realized. "Don't let Rhoda pick out a date for you. You go yourself and meet all the women in her sisterhood group. You'll see; one of them will stand out to you and you'll find the confidence to make a move on her."

I remembered what Rhoda had said about his wife's view of flowers and candy. "And you can never go wrong sending her some flowers," I said.

I dropped the lecture and took the opportunity to glance around the restaurant to see if there was anyone famous to point out to Leo. I did recognize someone, but not from the movies or TV. Brett Williamson and a nerdy-looking guy were sitting with Alexandra Davinsky. The two men seemed to be hanging on her every word, and she was gesturing broadly as she spoke. I wished I could hear what she was saying.

Leo noticed that I was basically staring at another table. "What's going on?" he said. "Do you know those people?"

"We both kind of know him." I discreetly pointed out Brett and reminded Leo that he had sold him the outfit he was wearing.

"Should I go up and tell him how much I like the clothes?" Leo asked.

"No," I said, a little too quickly, and Leo seemed startled.

"I'd really like to hear what they're talking about," I said.

Now he was watching them, too. "It's about your detective stuff, isn't it?" he said, and I nodded.

I had an idea and asked Leo if he was up for a little adventure.

He struck his attempt at a confident pose. "In these clothes, I'm ready for anything."

I called the server over and said there was a draft at our table and asked if we could move. I pointed to a table near the group, but in the shadows. The server agreed, and we slipped along the side of the room and went to the table. The slipping around was more for our benefit. The three of them seemed too wrapped up in their own world to even notice us as we took the table near them.

"Timothy meant well, but he was yesterday's news. My script is in pre-production right now," Alexandra was saying.

She had her hair back in a loose bun with perfectly calculated tendrils falling free. Her outfit was the kind that looked either really trendy or really stupid, depending on the current style. I thought back to the brief moment when anklets paired with heels had been "the look." Her voice definitely carried, and I'm sure that was no accident; she wanted everyone around her to know that she had a movie in the works.

The nerdy-looking guy didn't seem to know her very well and asked what the story line of the movie was.

"It's Jason Bourne meets the old beach-blanket movies," she said. "Chuck Norris plays the senior life guard slash undercover spy."

The nerdy guy was savvy enough to have a few questions about when and where the movie would be released.

"Actually, we're making it for the Flix channel," she said. "They're producing a lot of original content. We're already working on a deal for the sequel and another script I have an idea for. It takes place at a women's prison, and they all put aside their differences to put on a musical."

Leo was listening with rapt interest, while I was having a hard time not laughing. She segued into talking about her workshops.

"I really need a commitment from you two soon, as space is filling up." She glanced around the restaurant and suddenly pointed to someone and then waved with a smile. The two men were too busy looking at her, but I followed her gaze to see who she was waving at. I recognized Steve Bohannon, who'd played a suave detective on a long-running TV show and had later done movies playing similar characters. He never looked up from his conversation or reacted to her greeting. It was all just a ruse to impress her tablemates.

She was even more aggressive than I'd imagined.

"Tim had all kinds of connections, and we all know what he did for the girl in *Ethnic Smethnic* and the one who plays the vegetable fairy. Why should we think you could do the same?" Brett said.

I heard Leo gasp. "The vegetable fairy—that was Rebecca's favorite commercial. I loved it too. The way she ran through the broccoli forest." He was so excited that his voice was loud. I saw that the three of them react and begin to look around. It was more reflex than reason, but I didn't want them to see us. I couldn't think of anything else to do, so I grabbed Leo's shoulders and pulled him toward me before kissing him.

"Excuse me for interrupting," an angry male voice said. I stole a look around Leo's head and saw that Mason was standing next to the table, staring down at us.

"This is awkward," I said with a sheepish smile. I noticed that Mason was blocking the other table's view of us, and I let go of Leo's shoulders and leaned back in my seat. Leo looked like he'd just been struck by lightning and was speechless.

"I know who you are," Alexandra said, looking at Mason. She got up and stood next to him, sticking out her hand. "You're Mason Fields, the famous attorney to the stars." Mason turned toward her and thanked her for the compliment. He clearly wanted to leave it at that, but now that she had her foot in the door, she pushed it in. "I'm Alexandra Davinsky. You might have heard about my movie *Beach Blanket Undercover*."

Mason was all polite smiles as he tried to dismiss her, finally pointing out that the server was standing next to her table. She pushed her card on Mason before she sat down. The server was delivering the bill, or should I say bills—they each had a separate check.

I was about to ask Mason how he happened to be at the Seaside Taverna, but he answered before I had a chance. "What a coincidence running into you two," he said with just the slightest edge to his voice. "When you said you were busy, I arranged to meet a client here."

I looked around the restaurant, not believing what he was saying for a moment. Leo had given him enough information about the place, and I was sure he had figured it out. I wasn't sure how I felt about it.

He followed my glance and said, "I'm early. He's not here yet."

What a great save, I thought, thinking how well Mason thought on his feet, but then he was a criminal lawyer.

"I might as well sit with you until he gets here." He pulled out a chair and sat on the other side of me.

"So, what's new?" Mason said, glancing back and forth between Leo and myself.

Leo was still stunned by everything that had just happened and was staring down at the table.

I felt the need to explain. "That woman you just talked to is trying to take Timothy Clark's place with the acting workshops. I wanted to hear their conversation but not be seen by them. When they turned our way, I had to do something."

Leo had found his voice by now. "I was confused since you were telling me I should make the first move on a date. And then you did. Now I get it. It was because I got so excited when that woman started talking about the vegetable fairy," he said.

To get off the subject of the kiss, I grabbed at the lifeline Leo had tossed my way. "Isn't it funny how everybody calls her the vegetable fairy? I'm sure she has a real name."

But I'm not sure either of them even heard me anyway.

On the Hook

Leo had taken my suggestion of ordering food too far and had offered to handle ordering for Mason as well. Mason, meanwhile, seemed to take it as if he'd just been challenged to a duel. Why couldn't they all just get along?

Chapter
Twenty-One

Shedd & Royal was usually quiet when I came to work in the morning. But Adele had planned a special story time, and when I came into the store the next morning, there was already a buzz of excitement. The café was busy with groups of mostly women huddled around the tables. That was where they all congregated after dropping their kids off in Adeleville, as Adele had renamed the children's department.

Mason had ended up ordering his own food and insisted on picking out the dessert for all of us. As expected, his "client" never showed up. I drove Leo home with Mason on my tail. When we got to Rhoda's, I gave Leo a hug and told him he was on his own now and that I was sure he would do fine. He thanked me profusely and then gave Mason's car a dirty look.

Even Mason was wiped out by then and gave up on his after-dinner plans. He followed me back to my place and, when he was sure I was safely in, went home. Barry must have been taking a night off from his Columbo duty, to my great relief. I fell asleep with my clothes on and overslept enough that I had to hurry to get to the bookstore on time.

Adele was standing at the entrance greeting arrivals. As with everything Adele did, dropping kids off for story time was not a simple affair. She had lists and membership cards and who knew what else. But she was bringing business into the bookstore, so Mrs. Shedd maintained a hands-off policy.

I almost choked when I saw her outfit that morning. She was wearing a one-piece pink body suit that covered both her hands and feet under a fuchsia one-piece swimsuit. Across the front, she had attached a homemade banner that read Ms. MAGNIFICO, who I gathered was a female superhero, though I wasn't sure if she existed outside Adele's imagination. Apparently being a superhero didn't mean you didn't wear makeup. Adele had gone even heavier than usual.

I heard talking and laughing coming from inside her area as the kids fidgeted around waiting for story time to start.

"Here he comes," Adele said, turning toward her charges.

The kids, mostly around four years old, rushed to her side and looked out into the store. I felt a blast of air as the front door opened and Wonder Man walked in. He wore an electric blue bodysuit with orange boxer-style shorts over it. There was a decal on the front of his outfit of the silhouette of Wonder Man holding up the world. His head was exposed, and I recognized Mikey Fitzpatrick, even though he was clearly in character. He managed to convey power as he walked through the bookstore. He turned and bowed his head in greeting to anyone he passed. His expression was serious and he had a hawklike gaze, as if he was looking for trouble to take care of.

The kids squealed with delight as he entered the children's department.

I wondered how much of his performance skills Mikey had learned in the workshops. I sure bought that he was a superhero and, as he gave me a nod, I was ready to hand him my troubles to fix.

Everything quieted down once story time began, and I went back to the yarn department and did some straightening. It was chilly in the store that morning, and I pulled on the cardigan I kept in the bookstore for times like this. I was surprised to find the hook holder still in the pocket. I had left it in the pocket to keep it handy for when I hopefully found its missing piece.

The rise in the noise level was a clue that story time had ended. I moved to the information desk and looked up to see kids running in circles next to their mothers as they headed to the front of the store. It seemed as if most of them usually ended up at the cashier line. Despite all her craziness, Adele certainly did seem to help the bookstore's bottom line.

"Another successful story time," Lara-Ann said, stopping at the information booth as the stream of kids finally stopped and the last person in line checked out. "I offered to help Adele since she had such a crowd." She put her hands up in a helpless expression.

"Don't feel bad, she never wants anyone's help. She is the queen of the kids' department."

Mikey came out of the kids' department as Adele gave him a theatrical hug.

"Is he a kids' author?" Lara-Ann asked.

"No. More like a special guest. He's an actor that Adele knows. I think he did it as a favor to Adele. And he probably gave out his card to the mothers. I bet he does parties."

As he approached, I noticed that, out of character, he had lost a little of the power in his step and his expression had returned to that of a mere mortal rather than a superhero. If anything, he looked a little worn out. I really wanted to talk to him about Timothy Clark. And now seemed like the best chance I was going to get.

"Since he worked for free, I think the least the bookstore could do is get him a Bobaccino," I said to Lara-Ann. "Could you keep an eye on things for a few minutes?"

She agreed, and Mikey seemed to perk up at the idea of a sweet drink.

The café had emptied and Mikey and I both went up to the counter. Bob immediately recognized Mikey's character and acted slightly awed, as if the man standing in front of him really was Wonder Man. The power of the costume fascinated me, and even I had a hard time calling him Mikey when he was dressed like that. Mikey slipped Bob a business card before he ordered a cherry almond Bobaccino.

"Sorry, but we just have plain cherry," Bob said.

"Give it a slug of that," Mikey said, pointing to bottle of almond-flavored syrup in a row of bottles on the counter.

"Or I could do it myself," he said, noting that there was easy access.

Bob insisted he'd take care of it and turned to me. "I'll take a red eye." I stifled a yawn, still recovering from the night before.

Bob sent us to sit and said he'd bring the drinks. I suppose it was special service for a superhero. I wasn't sure how I was going to break the ice with Mikey and turn the conversation to Timothy Clark, but the superhero across the table turned out to be easy to talk to. All I had to do was ask him how he'd gotten his start playing Wonder Man. Then I merely waited until he got to talking about the workshops and Timothy.

"It's too bad what happened to him," I said.

"It's really too bad for me," Mikey said. Bob had just brought the drinks, and Mikey dipped into his right away. "Hey, man, this is really great," he said, holding up his glass in a toast of thanks to Bob.

I looked at the drink in all its pinkness and with its almond flavoring and couldn't help but think of Timothy's pink squirrel habit and the drink that someone had left me.

"Tim was all about timing and keeping us going until the right thing came along. I have to thank him for this. It's not exactly *acting* acting, but I get to play a great role and I'm paying the rent. Just today I probably booked three or four birthday party appearances. I do fairs and some street work too. Timothy was going to help me get a regular gig at Universal near the studio tour."

"I suppose hearing what he'd done for others was what kept your hope alive," I said.

"You mean the girl in *Ethnic Smethnic* and the vegetable fairy?" he said in a tired tone. "He had them come and speak to the workshop once a while back."

"They must have actual names," I said.

"You're right, but frankly I don't remember either one of them. It's kind of like how the people who hire me never call me Mikey. Even when they call to set it up, they call me Wonder Man."

"I understand that someone in your group is taking over the workshops," I said, trying to sound nonchalant.

Mikey almost choked on his drink. "You mean Alexandra?" He shook his head in dismissal. "She thinks she's such hot stuff, but she doesn't have any connections. Big deal—so she has a movie in production."

I almost corrected him and said pre-production but managed to stop myself, realizing it would seem odd that I knew so much about it. He didn't seem to notice and continued on.

"Between this other woman in the workshop named Deana and Alexandra, it was almost a catfight every week. It was always about who was more important to Timothy. I mean, c'mon, they had different positions in his life. Alexandra was his assistant, almost like his pimp. She always hung out at any free events trying to get new students for him. The big score was if she landed him an acting coach gig. And Deana, well, we all knew they were going home together."

"Do you have any idea who would have wanted to kill him?"

"The cops asked me the same thing."

"What did you tell them?" I asked, trying to sound casual.

"It's not for me to point the finger at anyone and sic the cops on them, so I told them I didn't have any idea and that as far as I knew, everybody loved Timothy."

"But I'm guessing they didn't," I said, hoping that he wouldn't notice that I seemed to be a little too interested for a person not involved.

"Thank you for this drink. I really needed something. It takes a lot out of me to even pretend to be a superhero for an hour." He drank down the last few swallows as he considered my question. "I wasn't in the fantasy world the rest of them were, thinking that Timothy believed we were all so talented. He was doing what he had to to keep his head above water while he tried to get his own acting work. And he said what he had to say to keep everyone coming back. I'm not so sure the others would take that news as well as I have. Take Deana. I'm pretty sure she was only in a relationship with him because she thought he would give her special preference. In her dreams. I know he thought she was very limited. Basically all she could play was a neurotic wannabe artist—in other words, herself."

"So you're saying she could have found out what he really thought about her and killed him?"

He put his hands up. "I'm not saying anything, but I can't stop you from you drawing your own conclusions."

"Hey, Molly," Bob said, coming up to our table.

He held up his hand as a shield and pointed his finger behind it toward the door. I glanced casually and saw Barry and Detective Heather standing in the doorway staring at me and Wonder Man. They both seemed to be fighting back grins.

Mikey took one look at them and, muttering under his breath that talking to them once was enough, got up and headed out of the store, still in his superhero attire.

"You certainly keep interesting company," Barry said as he came up to my table while Detective Heather continued to the counter to place her order. "Isn't he a little young for you?"

I let out my breath, relieved that Barry hadn't seen beyond the Wonder Man suit.

I thought I was in the clear, but then I noticed that Mikey had left a card on the table, which Barry picked up and read. Suddenly his eyes opened wider and he stared at me.

"Why were you having coffee with Mikey Fitzpatrick?"

"Do you know him?" I asked innocently, and Barry half closed his eyes and blew out his breath.

"Molly, you are playing with fire here. I'm not the only detective working on this case. Somebody else is going to connect the dots between you and that scarf, and I won't be able to do anything about it. Your best bet is to come clean with me." He slipped into the chair and looked across the table at me just a little too long. "I know what you're up to. You think you can catch the killer before you're in over your head. I'm telling you now, you're already in over your head."

Detective Heather came up to the table and gave me a piercing look, then turned back to Barry. "I got you a coffee," she said, holding out the paper tray containing two large cups. "I had an interesting conversation with the barista. Do you know who Wonder Man really is?"

"Yes, I know, he's Mikey Fitzpatrick," Barry said in a world-weary voice.

He got up and stood at the table for a moment while Detective Heather walked to the door. Barry held up two fingers and pointed them at her and then pointed them at me. I got it—she was watching me.

Lara-Ann walked into the café and glanced at the two detectives as they walked out.

"Someone is looking for a copy of *Marjorie Morningstar*. The computer says we have it, but I can't seem to find it. Can you help?"

I got up, tossed my cup, and followed her into the main part of the store.

"That man you were talking to—I 've seen him in here before. He looks like a cop," she said.

"It figures you would notice that, with your love of mysteries," I said, putting on a pleasant expression before explaining that he was my ex.

"Is he stalking you? I remember that in *The Cop Who Cropped*, the heroine was being stalked by her ex. They'd met in a scrapbooking group. Even when they broke up, he kept coming to the scrapbooking group, and then he'd follow her home and sit outside her house."

"It's nothing like that. He's just working on a case he thinks I know something about."

"Well, do you?" she asked, sounding interested.

I wasn't sure how much to say. "You remember the Hookers were talking about an actor who was killed?"

"Sure. We all started talking about poison rings," she said.

"That's the case," I said.

"Then you have some inside dope. Did the police find one of those rings?"

"I don't know," I said with a shrug. "I'm more concerned about finding out who did it. It's the only way I'm going to get him off my back."

"How interesting," she said. "You're really in the midst of it, while I only read about it. Though Mrs. Shedd and I were talking about hosting a mystery event at the bookstore."

"Really?" I said. "I'm the one who arranges most of the events." I smiled, trying to cover the edge in my voice. Lara-Ann was a great addition to the staff, and I was sure she was just trying to be helpful. At least I hoped that was all. I really needed to make an effort to get to know her better.

Still, I was grateful to have Lara-Ann as it got to be time for the Hookers' happy-hour gathering. I could join the group and let myself get lost in crocheting instead of constantly glancing around the bookstore, worried that a customer might need help.

"Tomorrow we do the presentation. I hope you can all come. We've got someone from the newspaper, and Channel 3 is sending Kimberly Wang Diaz. So, dears, remember to be ready for your closeup," CeeCee said as she added another baby blanket to the stack. "But these days, with all the cell phone cameras, I guess we all have to be always ready for our closeup."

CeeCee certainly was. Of course, she had a stylist who oversaw her appearance. By keeping the classic style of her chestnut-brown hair the same since the days of *The CeeCee Collins Show*, she had managed to appear unchanged. Her makeup was perfect and never overdone, and her black slacks and turquoise linen shirt had a timeless look of casual elegance.

The rest of us all surveyed ourselves with concern. Everyone, that is, except Eduardo. He had long since given up the leather pants of his cover model days and, now that he owned The Apothecary, generally wore well-cut designer jeans and a blazer. The only leftover from his days as a model and celebrity personality was his luxuriant long black hair, which he wore pulled back in a ponytail.

And then, of course, there was Adele. "I know just what to wear," she said brightly as we all rolled our eyes. Adele didn't know the meaning of the word *subtle*.

Rhoda fastened off the yarn on the toast-colored baby blanket she'd been making. "Leo couldn't stop talking about last night," she said, looking at me. "He said you kissed him."

"What?" Dinah said.

"It wasn't like that," I said, turning to my friend then I

spoke to the whole group. "I looked at the evening as his graduation." Then I realized how that sounded. "This kiss had nothing to do with it. It was for camouflage." I dropped my voice and spoke to Dinah, telling her about the people sitting next to us.

Rhoda interrupted. "Leo wondered about Mason, but I explained he was your attorney."

"What do you need an attorney for?" CeeCee asked.

Adele and Elise both stopped what they were doing and shook their heads as they stared at me.

"It's always good to have an attorney around, just in case," I said.

* * *

By the time I got home, I was looking forward to a quick dinner and a hot bath. But I knew from the cars parked in front of my house that my mother and the girls must be rehearsing. I pulled into the driveway and crossed the yard. When I opened the kitchen door, I heard singing and hand clapping. Cosmo and Felix were waiting by the door and ran out as soon as I opened it. I quickly shut the door behind them, keeping the cats in.

The upside of the rehearsal was that my mother had made another Mystery Cake and it was sitting on the counter along with a bunch of white containers. I knew by the smell that tonight's takeout was Italian. I'd have a plate of food and then it was crochet time to finish my baby blanket so I could add it to the bunch in the morning. But first a nice bath.

As I passed through the living room, my mother and the girls were practicing some choreography I'd never seen before. The song wasn't from their usual repertoire either. Samuel was accompanying them on the keyboard, and my father was watching from the couch. My mother would always be a star as far as he was concerned, and he was a proud grandfather to Samuel. He barely flinched as the three women had a bit of a misstep and my son cut off the music.

"Thank you again," my mother said when she saw me. "I want you to know the girls and I really appreciate you letting us practice here. It's really essential now that we're adding the Diana and the Dinettes hit to our show *Bop Biddity Do Boob Boob*." She turned to Lana and Bunny. "Let's show her what we've got."

Samuel played the intro, and the three women started gyrating with amazing flexibility while clapping their hands. They got a little further into the routine before they fell out of step and my mother called a halt. "Let's try again," she said.

"I'll catch you later," I said, thinking of the nice bath that awaited me.

Blondie was sitting in her chair and looked up when I came into my bedroom. I gave her the little bit of petting she would tolerate and then headed to the bathroom.

As I closed the door, the handle came loose again and actually came off in my hand, but luckily before I had shut the door completely. I really needed to find a handyman. I put the handle back in and tightened the plates around the base. Still, to be on the safe side, I left the door slightly ajar, then turned on the water. The tub looked out over a small enclosed area that I had planted with flowers. A cascading fountain sat against the wall. It was completely private, so there was no need to cover the windows.

I always found the bathtub a good place to think. That night, I rethought everything Mikey had said. It was funny that a man in a superhero suit had seemed the most realistic about Timothy, or was that merely a cover? Mikey had seemed way too familiar with how to add almond flavoring to a Bobaccino. But then I thought about what he'd said about Deana and Alexandra being at odds with each other, and suddenly I had an idea. By the time I'd gotten out of the tub, it had turned into a plan.

Chapter
Twenty-Two

CeeCee had told the Hookers to meet in front of the bookstore and then we'd carpool to the three spots where we were presenting the baby blankets. I had managed to finish mine just in time. When I got to the bookstore, only Elise was standing out there.

"Where is everybody?" she asked.

"Dinah couldn't make it—she has a class this morning—but I don't know about the others."

It seemed that the rain was done for a while. The wind had changed, bringing in warmer air and making my tan suede blazer appropriate for the day. I had added a rust-colored cowl to jazz up the all-black I had on underneath.

Now that Elise had dropped the vampire look, her so-called professional outfits were pretty blah. I guessed that was the point. She wore a casual pantsuit in a color that would probably be called wheat with a white shell. The only excitement in her outfit was the nubby shawl in shades of earthy browns she wore over the suit.

She glanced around and then at me. "As long as we're

alone—what did you tell Logan when you talked to him the other day? You seemed to be talking for a long time," Elise said. Her birdlike voice sounded a little frantic.

I had to think back; the conversation with Logan already seemed like a long time ago. I realized I hadn't told him anything because he had been too busy telling me about his deal with the Clark house and how he hadn't told Elise anything about it. I tried to figure out what I could say without divulging any of his secrets, but Elise was too impatient.

"You didn't say anything about going to that house, did you?" She swallowed a few times before continuing. "It was bad enough when I was just worried about him finding out I'd shown the place, but for us to have been there with a dead person who had been murdered . . ." Her voice warbled as she said *murdered.* "I'm still trying to figure how I missed seeing him," she said.

"You went right to the master suite when you went to the lower floor, and then you got Logan's text."

"And I got all crazy," she said with a sigh.

Adele had just come out of Shedd & Royal. She'd put her own spin on CeeCee's suggestion that we dress up for the newspeople. Adele had made a black cardigan and then covered it with small crocheted squares done in different colors and different stitches. She looked like a walking afghan. She hadn't stopped there and had also added a black crocheted headband she'd covered in different-colored crocheted flowers. She seemed pleased with her appearance and made a point of standing near the door where anyone going into the bookstore would be sure to notice her.

Elise glanced in Adele's direction. "Between you and me, I don't know why she'd want that house now. Unless she likes the idea of sticking her mother-in-law in a room where someone was murdered."

We agreed that seemed too much, even for Adele. I was just glad that Elise had forgotten that she'd asked me about my conversation with Logan.

CeeCee joined us, glancing around in dismay. "I was hoping more of the group would show up. Particularly Eduardo. He shows that we aren't just a women's group, and he photographs so well."

I mentioned that Dinah had a class and couldn't come. Adele gave up her position by the door and came to join us.

"We have to go," CeeCee said.

There was some wrangling about who would drive, and Adele won out. CeeCee rode shotgun in the front seat of the Matrix, while Elise and I got in the back. At least her car had four doors.

"Remember, ladies, the newspeople are meeting us at our first stop, so everyone be on your best behavior," CeeCee said. She was staring straight ahead out the windshield, but the back seat crowd all knew who her comment was meant for.

The fire station was located on Ventura Boulevard between a plant nursery and a mattress store, about a half mile from Shedd & Royal. Adele pulled up to the curb, and I noted that the large garage door was open and the shiny red trucks stood ready to zoom out if there was an emergency. A knot of men in midnight-blue uniforms hung around the front as Kimberly Wang Diaz checked her makeup in a small mirror while her cameraman set up. Another man who looked to be in his late twenties was hanging out nearby. I guessed he was from the newspaper and, by the way he was shifting his weight from foot to foot with an annoyed twist to his mouth, not so happy to be there. But then, covering a bunch of yarn-loving women donating baby blankets was a pretty light assignment. An older man standing near him had a camera bag on his shoulder and was grabbing shots of the fire station.

The whole group looked in our direction as we got out of the car and made our way toward them. "I'll introduce everyone," CeeCee said, but Adele objected.

"We should each do our own introduction," Adele said. There was no time to argue, so CeeCee took the path of least resistance and agreed, though she insisted on speaking first since she had arranged the presentation.

CeeCee turned on the charm and greeted the group of men. "I'm CeeCee Collins," she began. They all recognized her and the reporter moved in closer, beginning to scribble in a notebook. His photographer started shooting photos of us. Kimberly Wang Diaz held out her microphone as her cameraman got it on tape.

CeeCee was about to say more, but Adele moved in front of her and did a twirl to display her showy sweater as she began to rap. "I'm Adele and I'm here to say, that I'm also known as the Queen of Crochet."

At that, she began to pull scarves out of the tote bag she'd been holding behind her back and skip around the group, keeping a beat as she rapped, "We're here to give blankets for babes away. Hey, crochet. Give crochet a yay."

The assembled group seemed stunned, then chuckled as she began to hang the scarves around the necks of the firefighters. When she tossed a wild pink scarf made out of fluffy yarn around the neck of one of the men, he began to vamp.

"Let me hear you now," Adele called as she moved on. "Give crochet a yay." She kept at it until she had everyone calling "Yay!" back to her. She swirled a striped yellow-and-white scarf around another firefighter's neck. He began to dance along with Adele, putting his hands in the air as he called "Yay!" back to her. She pranced up to the newspaper reporter, who had joined in with the chanting, rocking back and forth with the rhythm she was creating as she threw a scarf made of multicolored granny squares around his neck. All the while she was playing to Kimberly's cameraman.

Finally, CeeCee stepped in front of Adele and put her hands up to end her rap. Adele did a last "Say yay for crochet" and then winked at the camera. "Got you hooked, huh? Stick with us; there's more to come."

"Thank you, Adele, for your colorful . . ." CeeCee was at a loss to describe what Adele had done. I wasn't sure what to call it either, other than typical Adele.

CeeCee did her best to take charge and held out one of the baby blankets as she spoke to Kimberly. "I'm sure you know that parents or persons with lawful custody can surrender an infant in the first seventy-two hours after their birth to a fire station, hospital, or some other locations with no questions asked. We want to make sure the fire station has some lovingly crocheted blankets ready to wrap around any surrendered newborns."

Adele behaved herself as CeeCee made the actual presentation of the blankets to the fire captain, though she made sure she was in the shot. Then she collected the scarves she'd distributed, and we were just about to wrap up when Adele spoke to Kimberly and the newspaper reporter.

"Too bad you can't come with us. You never know what I have up my sleeve." At that, she pulled out one of the giant metal hooks that was really a hook holder. She had somehow managed to use it to crochet, and there was a row of chunky work hanging off of it. Everyone but our group was surprised and laughed.

Kimberly conferred with her cameraman and then turned to Adele. "Maybe we will follow you to your next stop." Adele mentioned Tarzana Hospital, and Kimberly started toward the news van. The reporter overheard and nodded to his photographer, and they rushed off to a Prius.

"When you've got it, you've got it," Adele said to herself, after saying good-bye to the firemen. Then she led the way to the Matrix.

Elise and I traded glances when we were in the back seat of the car. "I guess we're just the extras," she said. CeeCee overheard and apologized for us not being introduced. She promised to do it at the next stop. I'd believe it when I saw it.

The news van was already parked at the curb when we got to our next stop. The reporter and his photographer were hanging around near the entrance. Tarzana Hospital was small and had been built in such a way that if it ever flopped as a medical establishment, it could morph into a hotel. An overhang sheltered the main entrance and, in keeping with the Tarzan theme, there were topiary bushes in the shape of lions on either side.

Adele was still on a high from her performance at the fire station, and she giggled as she rushed ahead to the cluster of people standing just outside the sliding doors.

Making sure that Kimberly and her cameraman were ready to catch it, Adele began her performance in front of a woman in a severe business suit, who was no doubt a hospital administrator, along with a group of men and women in scrubs I took to be doctors and nurses from the ER.

"I'm a Hooker and oh so proud. I say it often and I say it loud. Come crochet today; say yay crochet!"

As expected, the Hooker line got a laugh, and as Adele kept repeating her "Say yay crochet," she finally got the group to say "Yay!" along with her. Not satisfied, she yelled out, "Say it loud, say it proud: Yay crochet!"

She kept that up until they were yelling back to her. She had the tote bag and pulled out a long red scarf and waved it like a banner. People going in and out of the hospital stopped to watch.

"There's single and double and half double, too. Good way to ease tension for you and you," Adele rapped, pointing at different people in the group. "If you want to learn to crochet, just stop by the bookstore and say way-hey." The reporter and his photographer had moved in close as Adele began rocking back and forth. "That's Shedd & Royal

Books and More. Just come down the street, then c'mon in the door." She finished off by draping some of the scarves around the necks of the hospital employees before pointing to CeeCee. "Hey, say, we're here today, to give you blankets; now say hooray!"

CeeCee took her cue and stepped up to the hospital group. Inspired by Adele's show, CeeCee's spiel about the surrendered newborns and the transfer of love from the handmade blankets was longer and more emotional. At the end, the whole group applauded, barely noticing that Adele was retrieving the scarves as she'd done at the fire station.

Adele was so juiced from being in front of a crowd and their reaction that, if I didn't know her better, I would have thought she was on drugs. CeeCee was caught up in it now, too.

"I'm not sure that I approve of your methods, dear, but it's great that the newspeople are sticking with us. They'll give us much more coverage now." She turned to Adele as we were driving to the next stop. "It was genius to keep doing something new instead of repeating the same rap lines and using the same scarves."

If Adele was high from the performance before, CeeCee's words pushed her to a new level. Her head was too far up in the clouds for her to drive, and CeeCee had taken over. I don't think Adele even knew where we were anymore when we got to the last stop. The car had barely rolled into the parking lot of the West Valley Police Station when Adele grabbed the tote bag, preparing to get out.

I heard her muttering, "I can't keep me from the world," as she took the lead.

CeeCee had made the arrangements for the presentation and probably had just said we'd be coming by to give them some baby blankets. The desk sergeant looked stunned as the four of us along with our press contingent came into the lobby and approached the glassed-in area.

CeeCee leaned close to the glass and introduced herself. She turned to us. "The officer is getting somebody for us to present the blankets to." Then she turned to Adele and suggested we keep the presentation simple.

But by now Adele was too fired up from the crowd's approval for CeeCee's words to register. As soon as the door to the secure area opened and some men and women in uniform came out, Adele began to rap. "We're here to give blankets for babies wee. We crocheted them by hand and they're something to see." She looked at the assembled group. "It's all about crochet. It's not knitting as some people think. Working with those needles could drive you to drink." Adele began to twirl and rock as she showed off her sweater. "See this beauty, I'll show you some more. To you and you and you coming in the door."

The commotion must have reached back into the station, because I noticed more people had come into the lobby for a better look. Barry was among them, and I saw him roll his eyes and try to hold in a smile as Adele gyrated around. Detective Heather was with him and she seemed to be scowling, but then maybe she'd heard Adele's dis of knitting, which was her yarn craft of choice.

I returned my gaze to Adele, who had moved on to her "Hey, crochet, give a yay for crochet" line. She was practically in a frenzy as she began tossing out the scarves as if she were on a Mardi Gras float throwing out beads. Then she began hanging scarves around assorted people's necks. All the while she played directly to Kimberly and her cameraman.

"This is just a taste. I can do much better when it isn't in haste. Oh, what the heck, call me, call me, you TV exec. That's Adele at the bookstore; remember it's called Shedd & Royal Books and More." She stretched out the syllables so that *more* worked with *bookstore*, though I think at this point she was more focused on the message than the rhyme. I was probably the only one who realized that she was making a last-ditch pitch for that elusive meeting that was going to make her a star.

Adele was so lost in her pitch, she had no sense of what was going on around her, and she didn't notice that someone was pushing through the crowd. It was hard to miss Eric Humphries with his tall stature and barrel chest. He was in his motor officer uniform and holding his helmet. He was wearing reflective sunglasses that hid his eyes, but there was no doubt where they were looking. Adele repeated the pitch and began a third time, but suddenly a loud authoritative voice cut through her chant like a knife.

"What's going on?"

Adele froze midstep just as she saw her husband approach. She turned to the crowd and did a quick curtsy before running off.

CeeCee, being the professional she was, had been responding to Adele's "additions" to the original plans for the blanket handoffs seamlessly, and she did it here once again, stepping into the spotlight as if nothing had happened and going right into her story about surrendered infants.

While she was talking, I moved through the group, retrieving the scarves. And then a female officer handed me one that made me stop in my tracks. I recognized the orange color and the simple design with the yellow flowers attached to it. It was the twin of the one I'd dropped at Clark's house and that the cops had. I hadn't considered where Adele had gotten all the scarves until that moment. She had borrowed the stash we'd been collecting for an upcoming charity sale. I'd liked the one I had made for myself so much, I'd made another one to donate.

I shoved it to the bottom of the stack on my arm and looked around at the assembled group. Barry and Heather seemed to be watching CeeCee. In all the commotion, they probably hadn't even noticed the scarf. I hoped.

Chapter
Twenty-Three

"He wasn't supposed to be there," Adele wailed. "He's supposed to be riding around giving tickets and saving people on the street." Her voice changed to pride. "You know motor officers are often the first responders." The uptick only lasted for one sentence, though, and then her storm-cloud face returned. "Cutchykins said things are different now that I'm a police wife and I have a responsibility to not do anything that would embarrass him."

She began to cry, and all I could think was that if Eric was so worried about someone making a ruckus, he had picked the wrong person to marry.

We had driven back to the bookstore parking lot and were sitting in the Matrix letting Adele collect herself before we all went our separate ways. So far it wasn't going well.

"So, then, he wasn't specifically upset about what you said?" I asked, trying to be vague, since I was the only one who knew what she had been trying to do and that Eric was clueless about her acting classes. I hoped he didn't have any aspirations to become a detective. Adele, taking a yoga class? He should have seen right through that.

Adele understood my question. "I covered that up. I said I hadn't gotten to the end of my rap and that it was about me doing story time."

And he bought that? I thought, but I didn't say it out loud, as it could have led to questions from CeeCee and Elise. I was the only one in the car who knew everybody's secrets, and the responsibility of keeping them all from everybody else was starting to wear on me. And now I had my own secrets as well. If I told them about the scarf, Adele and Elise would freak out. It was better to leave them in the dark. I was glad that I had set the plan I'd come up with in the bathtub into motion. It made me feel as if I was at least doing something instead of waiting for the mystery to solve itself.

It had occurred to me that if they didn't get along, Deana and Alexandra would be glad to dish dirt on each other, possibly pointing to one of them as the murderer. I had decided to start with Alexandra, since she wanted something from me and it would be easy to get her to come in.

Mason had given me the card she had handed him in the restaurant, and I had used it to contact her before we left for our big presentation. As soon as Alexandra had heard that I wanted to talk to her about possibly letting the workshop meet at the bookstore, she had wanted to come over right away. I'd had to push her off until the afternoon.

I was thinking about how I could direct the conversation while CeeCee continued trying to smooth things over with Adele. "Look at the upside," CeeCee said. "We got a lot of attention for our project and for the bookstore. I can't wait to see the footage on Channel 3 news. I think Kimberly is going to make quite a story out of it. You gave her a lot of color," CeeCee said, patting Adele's arm.

Adele's tears stopped and she sat up. "Yes, the news story." She turned toward the back seat and gave me a knowing look. "I'm sure that's going to get some results."

CeeCee opened the door to get out. "You seem better now, dear," she said to Adele, "and I have a meeting I have to get to. We're discussing a reboot of *The CeeCee Collins Show*."

CeeCee didn't see it, but at the word *meeting*, Adele began to pout again and got out of the car in a hurry. Elise got out of the back seat and took off, saying she was meeting Logan.

In her huff, Adele had left the tote bag of scarves, and I grabbed them as I got out of the car just before Adele turned back and beeped the lock.

Mrs. Shedd snagged me as I came into the bookstore. "You were gone longer than expected," she said. She looked toward the kids' department. "Adele rushed by without a word. Is everything okay?"

"You know Adele; she's always got a surprise up her sleeve. The good news is that she managed to get in a plug for the bookstore on the news."

"I'm glad you're both back. It seemed a bit much to leave Lara-Ann on her own. Joshua and I are going out for a long lunch. He said he has a surprise for me. He always thinks of the most exciting things I would never do on my own."

As she said it, Mr. Royal appeared from their office. They were an inspiration. Of the three couples that had gotten married in the triple ceremony at the bookstore, so far they seemed to have had the least difficulty adjusting to each other.

I had the tote bag hidden behind my back as if the whole world knew the orange scarf was in it.

"Mason Fields called for you," she added hastily before heading toward the door with Mr. Royal. "Well, we're off." She let out an excited giggle.

I knew I was being silly, but I wanted to distance myself from the scarves as quickly as possible. I'd stick them in the cabinet and then call Mason back. I was on my way back to the yarn department when, as I passed the information cubicle, the phone rang. I kept the tote bag sheltered from view as I reached over the counter and grabbed the phone.

"Molly, at last," Mason said after I'd done my official Shedd & Royal Books and More greeting. "If I didn't know better, I'd think you were avoiding me," he said before telling me that he'd left two messages with Mrs. Shedd.

"I just got to the bookstore and got your messages," I said.

"I tried your cell," he said. Given all the commotion, it was no wonder I'd missed it, even with the vibrations on my wrist.

"I tried your house," he said with a question in his tone.

"I wasn't home. It's a long story. I'll tell you about it later."

"Ah, that's just what I was calling about—later," he said brightly. "I found the place for our second first date. I thought we could do it tonight." Though it was a statement, his tone made it sound like a question.

"How about some details?" I said, and he chuckled.

"I'm not telling. It's more exciting to keep it a surprise."

I felt myself smiling. The idea of a fun evening with Mason seemed like just what I needed. "It sounds good to me. What's the dress code?"

"Anything you like."

We arranged a time for him to pick me up and signed off. I held the phone for a moment with a goofy smile, thinking of the evening ahead.

"Here she is," Lara-Ann said. I looked up and saw that she had Alexandra with her. I stood up straighter and prepared to deal with the scriptwriter/workshop leader.

I glanced down and saw the tote bag resting against my leg. The sooner those scarves were stashed, the better.

"We can talk in the yarn department," I said to Alexandra. I thanked Lara-Ann for bringing her to me, and she walked away.

Alexandra glanced around the area in the back of the store as if it were already hers to use. I began to put the scarves away and went into my planned speech. "Before we make a decision about letting the workshop meet here, I need some more information."

"Sure. Ask away," Alexandra said. She had pulled out a chair and begun poking through a container of assorted hooks and knitting needles we kept on the table for anyone who wanted to try out a yarn before they bought it. When I got to the orange scarf, I reconsidered what to do with it, remembering something I'd read in *The Average Joe's Guide to Criminal Investigations*. The section had talked about not leaving things to chance. I decided not to leave the scarf in the bookstore and instead stuffed it in my purse.

"I'm concerned about how much noise your workshop would make," I said. "Your group seems rather emotional, but then I suppose it's connected to the death of Timothy Clark. Everyone seems really worked up over it—well, except for the woman in the straw hat. I think her name is Deana. She stopped in here the other day, and I overheard her talking to Lydia. Something about not wanting the police to know she had a personal relationship with Clark. She seemed surprisingly unemotional considering that her lover had just been murdered."

I noticed Alexandra's eyes light up. "Deana put herself on a pedestal, and she was as cold as a statue standing on one. I don't know if she honestly cared about anyone. She looked down on the rest of the group as if she was the only real actor." I hoped Alexandra would say more about Deana, but she must have thought about her own behavior and how it might look. "I personally handled my grief by channeling it into a scene I was writing. Since I'm acting as the new leader of the group, it wouldn't do for me to be seen falling apart over what happened, but of course I'm devastated." She pulled out a set of silver double-pointed knitting needles from the container and began to examine them, testing the sharpness against her finger. "These things could be lethal." She reached for a ball of red yarn and tried stabbing it with one of the silver needles. I tried to explain that wasn't how they were used, but she looked at me with a glint in her eyes and said, "Who cares? This is so much fun."

She was probably going to ruin the yarn, but I didn't want to try to take it away.

"We writers are always working," she said with delight. "I just got a great idea for a horror flick. Some maniac uses these needles to make a human voodoo doll." She looked at me a little too long as she stabbed the ball of yarn a few more times.

I instantly saw a fault in her story line: if the human was the voodoo doll, who got the effect of the voodoo? I wasn't about to bring it up, though. I tried to steer her back to talking about Deana, but she seemed obsessed with her horror movie idea. All her gleeful stabbing was really starting to creep me out.

I was relieved when Lara-Ann interrupted and said somebody's credit card had been rejected and they were making a scene. Alexandra seemed perturbed at the interruption and said she couldn't wait around. She took the whole set of double-pointed needles and stabbed them in the ball of yarn all at once before she got up to leave. As she walked past me, she was muttering on about her horror movie plot. "Yes, the maniac gets upset when some nosy Natasha butts in where she shouldn't. The maniac could attack her in a parking lot late at night or maybe in her driveway."

Was it some kind of veiled threat?

By the time I got to the front of the store, the customer with the bad credit card had fled without their merchandise or the card, which had probably been stolen. It took me two red eyes to get through the rest of the afternoon. Since I had the evening off, I skipped happy hour and went home to get ready for "the date."

Judging by the cars in front of my house, my mother and the girls were having another rehearsal. Samuel was in the kitchen when I walked in the back door. "We're taking a dinner break," he said as he held up a plate of salads. "They decided to eat light."

"Liza could start a bakery," I said, noting that my mother had brought over a tray of her lemon bars as well.

Samuel gave me a look of surprise when I referred to my mother by her name.

"You call her Liza, so why shouldn't I?" I was edging out of the room as I spoke, anxious to get the orange scarf out of my bag before it fell out. I called out that I'd be going out again shortly as I left the kitchen.

The obvious place to put the scarf was in the room where I kept all my yarn. I looked around at all the bins that held my yarn and various partially done projects and the chest of drawers, but then I thought of something else. Why not hide it in plain sight? I had gotten a scarf holder at Ikea, and all the round openings were filled with scarves I'd made. I stuck the orange scarf through a hole that already held two others. With a sigh of relief, I followed the noise coming from my living room.

Everyone looked up and greeted me. They all seemed

to be having a good time. Having this second chance at a career was a boon to all of them. And the bonus of having everyone there all the time was that I didn't have to worry about the animals. Cosmo and Felix barely looked up as I passed through the large room. They were hanging around my mother, who was a real softy when it came to pets. I knew she was slipping them food off her plate. The two cats liked my father and were cuddled next to him. Blondie even made an appearance before following me back to her spot in the bedroom.

With all the commotion, I was grateful to shut the door on the hallway that lead to the master suite. I stopped in the closet to pick out something to wear. This was supposed to be a special evening, so I decided to dress up. I pulled out my favorite all-around black dress. It was silk and cut on the bias and was light as air. I would top it with a recently acquired long floral print jacket. Ballet flats would have to do as footwear.

As I went into the bathroom, I checked the handle and it was fine. Maybe I didn't need a handyman after all, I thought, pleased with my fixit job. Occupied with getting ready, I pushed away all thoughts connected with Timothy Clark's murder.

"Don't you look nice," my father said as I crossed the living room.

"Finally, some color," my mother added. She went on for a moment about how she'd been advising me to add some pizzazz to my wardrobe. If anyone knew about pizzazz, it was my mother. When she and the girls weren't in their sixties-style performance outfits, my mother had her own look. While living in Santa Fe, she had developed a love of silver and turquoise. She wore a lot of black, but it was mostly a backdrop for stunning jewelry and scarves in vibrant colors. And, of course, her signature group of silver bangle bracelets.

"Where are you off to?" she asked.

I had to keep from rolling my eyes. One thing was still the same as when I'd been a teenager—I wasn't about to discuss who I was dating with her. Even though I knew she heartily approved of Mason.

I was standing in the driveway when his black Mercedes SUV pulled in.

He did a wolf whistle as he clicked open the door and I got in. "You look gorgeous."

I thanked him for the compliment and returned the favor. He reached into the back seat and pulled out a bunch of flowers.

"I think this is appropriate behavior for a first date," he said with a grin. "You'll note that they are silk, so you don't have to worry about finding a vase, which was a good move on my part since you stopped me from coming to the door." He looked toward my house. "Who is it that I'm avoiding?"

I explained about the rehearsal.

"So you don't want me to see your parents?" he asked. "Why? I thought Liza and Irv liked me." He backed the large vehicle out of the driveway. "I get it. They think I broke your heart. You didn't tell them you broke mine, did you?"

He shook his head in a scolding manner as he put the car

into gear and we drove down the street. But when he turned to sneak a look at me, he had a teasing smile and I knew he wasn't serious.

The disarming thing about Mason was that he was comfortable in his skin. He wasn't racked with doubts about his life and actually seemed to enjoy it a lot. I loved his sense of fun.

As he steered onto the 101, I asked where we were going, and all he would say was, "You'll see. You're going to like it."

I had my doubts when he pulled into the parking structure under an apartment building. But when he led me through a doorway, the delicious aroma let me know we were in a restaurant. Ahead, a wall of windows looked out on the ocean.

"I picked this table especially for us," Mason said as he pulled out my chair.

I glanced up as I sat and could see why. We were in the corner of the large dining room with windows both in front of us and to the side. The water was all around us and it seemed as if we were on a boat. The sky was an inky black and merged with the water somewhere in the distance. A sliver of moon hung low in the sky and had a strange golden cast. When I looked back at the shore, I could trace the curve of Santa Monica Bay by the lights dotted along the sand.

"Wow, good choice," I said.

He took the chair adjacent to mine so we could both enjoy the view and be close enough to talk.

Mason and I liked to have appetizers as our meal. We

gave the waiter our selection, and then we were alone with the view.

"I was afraid you were going to bring Leo along," Mason teased. "He was a lot less nerdy than I expected."

"Well, that's because you saw him after the makeover. You wouldn't say that if you'd seen him in the parka."

"It doesn't matter. It's over with. He's not going to call you for a refresher course or anything, right?"

I laughed. "I thought we were keeping this casual. Neither of us telling the other what to do. Our time away from each other is our time."

"Actually, I think that was all you. I don't think I ever agreed to it, either. I can't believe I'm saying this, particularly after the speech I gave you about never ever wanting to feel hurt again, but I think the concept of casual dating may be bogus. It only works when you first meet someone or if you don't really like them that much."

"But you said you'd gone back to your old ways," I protested.

"I left out the part that it didn't work. I have no interest in nice but not very good. And if I feel more for someone—" Our eyes met and he held my gaze. "Then it just isn't enough."

I must have had a deer-in-the-headlights look. "Am I scaring you off?" he said with a laugh. "Relax. I'm not trying to corner you and say I want you to wear my class ring or anything. I just want to be part of your life—and not just when we're on a date."

"Like we're friends, but more?" I said.

"How about we forget titles and just let it be and see what happens?"

"I can live with that," I said.

"Enough with all this negotiating," he said as platters of appetizers were set in front of us. "Let's eat and then you can tell me what's happening in your investigation."

The whole thing with Alexandra had made me so uncomfortable I had blocked it from my mind, but now it came back with a vengeance. I told Mason about my hopes for the meeting and how it had turned out.

"I had hoped she'd tell me things about Deana, but all she did was defend herself before she got into taking about a plot for a horror movie that involved a nosy person becoming a human voodoo doll." I described the double-pointed needles she was fingering as she talked about it and how she had seemed to enjoy stabbing a ball of yarn. "I even thought it might be some kind of threat."

"That doesn't sound good. Do you think she could have been the one who left the drink and stuck the note on your car window?"

"Maybe," I said. Then I told him about my meeting with Mikey and how he'd been so familiar with how to add almond flavoring to a drink. "He seems like a nice guy, but who knows? He could have been the one who left the drink." I poked at a stuffed mushroom. "There's more. I told you about the line on the calendar about making someone an offer—"

Mason nodded.

"Well, after I tell you about my conversation with Logan, you'll see it has a whole new meaning." I explained the situation with the house.

"Clark could have wanted the house back or to keep them from selling it so he could keep living there. The note in the calendar might have been sarcastic. Maybe he had some information that would keep Logan and his friends from selling it? And Logan killed him to shut him up. I don't know about the others, but Logan had taken the money from his retirement account and planned to replace it without ever telling his wife what he'd done. I've always thought the way he was the one to find the body might have been a setup." I looked out at the darkness and noticed that the sliver of moon had slid down in the sky. "Not the most romantic topic for this beautiful setting," I said with a rueful smile.

Mason chuckled at the remark and urged me to continue.

"But then I keep coming back to Deana. She's a real diva, and I bet she thought she was going to be like the girl in the vegetable commercial or the one in the sitcom—the next student to strike it big." I stopped. "It is weird that Timothy only mentioned them by the parts they got and never by their names."

Mason had stopped eating and was giving me all his attention. "All that means is that he didn't care about them as people but only how they could bring him business—well, new students. If you want their names, I can find out," Mason said. He reached out and touched my hand. "I love being able to help you."

"Sure," I said. "But what beef could either of them have had with Timothy? They got their dreams. Deana could have thought having an affair with him was going to get her special treatment, and when it didn't, maybe she flipped out and wanted revenge. Who knows what power she thought he had? She works for a drug company; getting cyanide probably wouldn't be a problem for her, and the person who bought the ring was wearing a straw hat, which Adele says is Deana's thing."

Mason looked out at the dark sky. "Will you look where the moon is now? I've never seen anything quite like it. It looks like it's going to just drop into the ocean." He smiled at me warmly. "I wish I could say I had specially arranged this for us," he said with mock disappointment.

We'd abandoned our food and were mesmerized watching the moon slide lower in the sky.

"Look at it now," he said as he pushed his plate away.

The moon seemed to be dipping its toe in the ocean, and the golden glow reflected in the watery darkness. We both watched silently as the moon was swallowed up by the water and the sky became totally dark.

When the server came to collect our plates, I expected Mason to ask for the dessert menu, but he just asked for the check.

"No dessert?" I asked, sounding disappointed.

He smiled. "I thought we'd have it somewhere else."

"Where?" I asked as we left the restaurant.

"You know me. I love to make it a surprise."

He drove back to the freeway. By now the traffic had quieted and we flew down the road and between the dark mountains as the freeway went through the Sepulveda Pass.

Back in the Valley, Mason turned into an unassuming strip mall and I looked around.

"Okay, time for the big reveal," he said. "I thought we'd get ice cream and take it back to my place." He pointed to a small ice cream shop with a long line. "And it's not just your average strawberry and chocolate."

When we got inside the small shop, Mason leaned in close to me. "I call this millennial ice cream. You know how millennials are all about the experience?" He pointed to the flavors. They all had odd names and unusual ingredients. I mean, who thinks of black pepper in ice cream? I went for Globetrotter, which was made from vanilla beans from five different countries and mascarpone cheese. Mason got Smokey Road, containing high-end chocolate mixed with vanilla bean marshmallows, smoked almonds, and wood-smoked sea salt.

"Here or to go?" the hipster behind the counter asked, and Mason looked at me with a question.

"Your call," he said.

"To go, please," I answered.

Mason pulled into the garage, and we entered the house through his kitchen. Spike knew the sound of the garage door opener and was at the door waiting. He gave us both the royal welcome, though a little more so to Mason.

"The ice cream got a little soft on the way home. I'll put

it in the freezer," he said. "Go on in the den and make your-self at home."

I had always thought of the den as being the heart of his house. I found a comfortable spot on the leather couch and Spike jumped up to join me. Mason came in and turned on the fireplace. Flames danced around the logs that would never burn and gave off a cozy warmth.

A wall of windows and glass doors overlooked the yard. A rock waterfall sent water cascading into the dark-bottomed pool. The rest of the yard had an area of grass and lots of flowers, all of which was artfully illuminated.

"I'll get the ice cream when we're ready," Mason said, sitting down next to me on the couch.

There was no pretense of keeping a distance between us this time, and he leaned in next to me. It felt familiar and nice.

"I could give you a tour. I think you'd like what I've done to my bedroom."

"I don't know about seeing your bedroom. This is just our first date," I said in a Southern belle accent. "What kind of girl do you think I am?"

"I promise not to think less of you," he said, standing and reaching out to help me up.

"But our ice cream," I said.

"It'll keep," he said, nuzzling my cheek.

I began to feel a rumble on my wrist. I thought it was just an email and was going to ignore it, but the vibrating continued, and when I looked at the watch face I saw that it was a phone call and it was coming from my house.

"I have to take this," I said, sensing that something was wrong. I hit the ACCEPT button.

My mother's voice sounded tinny coming out of the watch. I didn't hear her at first, and she repeated the message.

"Come home now. The cops are here."

Chapter
Twenty-Four

Two cop cars and a black Crown Victoria were parked in front of my house. Mason had barely pulled into the driveway when I got out and ran across the front yard. I opened the front door and left it ajar for Mason.

My mother had somehow managed to keep them corralled and let out a sigh of relief when I came in. I screeched to a stop when I saw who was there. It wasn't so much the four uniformed officers as much as who was with them.

"Here's Molly. You can talk to her." My mother turned to me. "We put Felix and Cosmo outside, and the cats are hiding somewhere."

Detective Heather stepped forward and showed me some papers. "We have a warrant to search this property," she said in a total cop voice without the slightest hint that she knew me.

She looked exquisite as usual, dressed in a dark suit with a pencil skirt and fashionable shoes. Her hair was dark blonde now and done in a severe bun, which made her look more formidable than when she'd worn her hair loose around her shoulders. I glanced at her high heels, wondering what she'd do if I grabbed the papers and made a run for it.

By then, Mason had come in. He'd lost the Mr. Fun look and was all serious business as he introduced himself and demanded to see the search warrant.

Heather gave my outfit the once-over. "How convenient to be on a date with your lawyer."

She'd always had the hots for Barry and they had gone out for a while. I knew she somehow blamed me for them never having a happily-ever-after. I would have thought it might take a little heat off if she thought I was involved with someone else, but she still glared at me.

"You know what we're after. Why not make it easy on all of us and show us where it is?"

I did my best clueless impression and said I didn't know what she was talking about. But of course I did. She must have seen the scarf during Adele's rap at the police station, though I wasn't sure how she'd come here looking for it. And, honestly, had she really gotten a judge to give her a search warrant for a scarf?

"Have it your way. I have to warn you we're going to make a mess," she said as she took my purse and handed it to one of the uniforms and demanded to know if my car keys were in it. She sent one of the other officers to my bedroom.

"Wait," I said. "One of my dogs is in there. She's a terrier, but she won't bother you. Please don't bother her either."

The cop needed to be reassured a number of times before he finally followed Detective Heather's order. She took the two other officers down the hall that led to the three other bedrooms.

"Can't you stop them?" I said to Mason. "Some habeas corpus thing."

"I wish I could, but I can't. They have a warrant. But I'll help you clean up," Mason said, giving my arm a reassuring squeeze.

One of the uniforms hustled us into the living room. My father and Bunny were huddled on the couch. I was actually glad to see that Samuel wasn't there. Did I really want him to see his mother led out in handcuffs when Detective Heather found the offending scarf? Not that I wanted my parents to see it either.

Now I regretted my hiding-it-in-plain-sight idea, and I expected her to come in triumphantly waving it any moment. But when she didn't, I figured she was holding off until her searchers had made the biggest mess possible.

"What could they be looking for?" my mother said. "This has to be some kind of mistake."

"You're not a drug kingpin or something?" my father said as a joke. The uniform glared at all of us.

In the midst of my concerns about the date with Mason, I had forgotten all about the events of the morning and hadn't mentioned anything about the scarf, but he was intuitive enough to pick up on the fact that I knew what Detective Heather was looking for. He took my hand and told me not to worry.

The longer it took, the more my stomach churned. I

was almost relieved when Detective Heather and her crew finally came into the living room. I pushed my hands behind my back, as if it would make a difference.

"You're going down," she said. "Detective Greenberg might have looked the other way, but not me. I don't know what you did with that scarf. But I saw it today, and I might not crochet, but I knit and I know about yarn. You might have bamboozled Barry, telling him it was common yarn, but I know the yarn those flowers were made out of has been discontinued for years, making it not so common after all. If the fibers fit, we can convict. I know you were there and I'm going to prove it, and then—" She made a gesture like slapping on handcuffs.

My knees were ready to buckle by the time she left, but even so I rushed into the room where I kept all my yarn and looked at the scarf hanger I'd hung on the door. The scarf wasn't there.

Just then, I heard the kitchen door open. There was the sound of yipping dogs and voices calling out, "Pizza's here."

I went into the kitchen as Samuel and Lana were setting their stack of boxes down on the counter. My eye went right to my mother's singing partner's neck.

She saw me looking. "I hope you don't mind. It's cold out there and I had to protect my vocal cords. Your mother said it was okay. What a surprise when the flowers glowed in the dark." She took it off and handed it to my mother.

"I don't mind at all," I said. "In fact, you did me a huge favor."

My mother looked at the scarf in her hand. "That's

what the police were looking for?" Suddenly, she held it away from herself as if my creation might have committed a crime. "Why were they after it?" my mother asked.

"It looks like a scarf I dropped somewhere, and they're trying to prove it was mine."

"Oh, so they were going to match up fibers," my father said. The group looked at him with surprise. "Hey, I watched those CSI shows," he said.

"Sort of," I said. "No matter what Detective Heather said about matching up fibers, it's more likely they would try to infer the two scarves were made by the same person and, if nothing else, end my being able to stonewall about it."

"Spoken like a lawyer," Mason said. "But it's never going to come to that." He turned to Samuel and my parents. "Don't worry. I have everything under control." He opened the pizza box. "That smells great. Mind if I join you?"

"Thank you for changing the subject," I said.

I didn't feel like eating but took a piece to be polite. We all took our food in the living room. I pulled Mason aside and explained the whole scarf situation. Nobody felt like rehearsing anymore, so when Bunny and Lana finished their food, they called it a night. The rest of us tackled the mess the cops had left.

When we all met up in the living room, I remembered the news. I told Mason and we went into the den to watch while my parents and Samuel finished clearing up the food.

Of course the piece had been edited down. I barely even saw myself, but they'd left in enough of Adele's rap to show off that she really was the queen of crochet. Mason just rolled his eyes.

Afterward, I was going to thank my parents for their help and then walk them to the door, but my mother said, "Honey, I don't like the idea of you and Samuel here alone after what happened, so your father and I are staying over."

I knew she meant well, but it really made things more complicated. I had to give them my room, and I took the small guest room.

"You're welcome to come back to my place," Mason offered.

But after what had happened, I really didn't want to leave them there alone. We were all unnerved, to put it mildly. He sweetly offered to sleep on the couch and keep guard over all of us, but I thanked him and told him to go home to a real bed. We lingered in the doorway for a long time.

"This certainly isn't how I thought this evening would end," he said with a laugh. "But then it's always serendipity with you. I'm afraid you've ruined me for anyone else." He pulled me close to him. "But I wish I'd known about the scarf."

"I got so caught up in our date and Alexandra and her needles, I forgot about it."

"So then you liked our real first date?" he said, and I nodded.

"Does that mean you'll go out with me again?" he teased.

"Yes. Besides, I didn't get to eat my ice cream." He held me for a long time until the dogs started scratching at the front door and I was afraid they'd pull it open. With a sweet kiss, he bid me a good night and a good sleep.

It was a nice wish, but it certainly didn't come true. I was beset by all kinds of confused feelings. Had Barry really looked the other way? He had always put his job first. What was going on with him? Now that Detective Heather had taken over, she wouldn't give up until she got me to talk. Between all those thoughts and the small uncomfortable bed, it looked as if despite Mason's wishes, a good sleep wasn't in the cards.

Chapter
Twenty-Five

"I didn't do it, Pink," Adele said as her lip quivered. As soon as I came into the bookstore the next morning, I rushed right to the kids' department and confronted her. She was in her Heidi outfit—a blue pinafore with embroidery on the front over a white puffy-sleeved dress. She'd forced her brown hair into tiny braids that stuck straight out.

"I swear I didn't tell Detective Gilmore any scarf was at your house."

"Well, you must have told somebody something," I said.

"I was trying to smooth things over with Cutchykins, so when he asked me if Detective Gilmore could see the scarves I used in the rap, I said okay. It was after happy hour last night, and it was kind of awkward because Alexandra had come by looking for you. When I said you weren't here, she said she wanted to make me an offer. I had to tell her to hang out around the books while I talked to Detective Gilmore. I couldn't take the chance that Alexandra would call me Lydia."

Adele glanced at her watch and said something about the kids being there soon.

"I didn't even realize you'd brought all the scarves back." Adele stopped for a moment. "Did you see me on the news? It came off pretty good, didn't it? Not so good in the newspaper, though. The story was just about the baby blankets."

"You were talking about Detective Heath—I mean Gilmore," I prodded.

"I took her to the yarn department and showed her the cabinet where we keep the donations. She started asking about a scarf that wasn't there, that she'd noticed at the police station. As soon as she mentioned the flowers, I knew which one she was talking about. She asked me if we had the yarn the flowers were made out of." Adele began to whimper. "I thought she wanted to make one like it. I'd forgotten that was the scarf you dropped when we went to Timothy's house."

"So you told her that the yarn glowed in the dark and that the yarn was discontinued, didn't you?"

"I might have, but I never told her that you were the one who put the scarves back or that you might have taken it home with you. As soon as she left, Alexandra came back and started telling me how she wanted to expand on Timothy's idea and start a workshop for kids. She thought she could do a sample thing like Timothy did and then I could help her get students. She said I could be her assistant and that she'd give me a deal on our workshops."

"And what did you say?" I asked.

"I said it was okay with me but that I'd have to talk to

you about it. After yesterday, I'm sure I'll be hearing from the Craftee Channel and I won't need her workshops anyway. Besides, no matter what she says about her movie, she doesn't have the experience or connections Timothy did."

"How did she take it?"

"She just started talking about how she would run the workshop. She said that she wouldn't be like Timothy was, just making empty promises. She'd already talked to the producer of her movie and we'd all be guaranteed parts with at least one line. Then she started telling me dirt about the other people in my workshop. Apparently, Timothy had talked about all of us behind our backs."

"Really? What did he say?"

Adele seemed uncomfortable. "Stuff like that Mikey would never get past doing birthday parties and that Brett's best shot was to keep playing an extra. He had laid hope on thick for Sonia because he wanted to keep meeting at her house but said she couldn't act her way out of a paper bag. As for Deana, he said she had the diva thing down, but not much else." Adele's mouth began to quiver again. "Alexandra said she didn't believe that what he'd said about me was true." Adele's eyes began to tear. "She told me he said I had no talent except for making a fool of myself."

I'm not sure how it happened, but I ended up reassuring Adele that she did have talent and that we'd find a way to figure out when her meeting was. Then I lowered the boom.

"Detective Hea—I mean Gilmore—is going to hang on to this like a terrier. She will find a way to prove a connection between me and the scarf they have. We need to get together with Elise and figure something out," I said.

Adele didn't get it at first—until I explained that if they connected me with the scarf found at Timothy's, they'd want to know how I happened to be there.

Suddenly it sunk in and Adele appeared stricken. "Oh, no. You have to find the real killer, like right now."

We got Elise to come to the bookstore, and when Adele and I took a break, the three of us gathered around the table in the yarn department.

Adele looked at me. "You better tell her."

Elise sensed bad news and listened quietly. When I'd told her about having Detective Heather on my tail, she nodded resolutely.

"I figured you could handle Barry, but if she's involved, we're screwed. I guess I'll have to tell Logan I showed the house twice. And there goes my real estate career."

"It's more than that," I said. "We were there when Timothy was already dead. We could have moved around important items, and they could say we interfered with an investigation and tampered with evidence."

"But we didn't move anything around," Adele said. "Well, I lifted the shade, but that can't count."

I noticed that Elise looked a little green around the gills. "What if I moved something when I went downstairs? Remember I went to the master bedroom first?"

"Well, did you? Think back," Adele demanded. "We're all on the line."

"Pressuring me isn't going to help," Elise said, her voice faltering. I stepped in and suggested that Elise close her eyes and take a couple of deep breaths.

"Okay, I'm going to see if I can help you remember what you did. Try to go back to that evening." In my best calm voice, I described our arrival at the house. "We looked around upstairs, and you said you were going downstairs. Picture going down the stairs."

Her eyes suddenly flipped open. "I'm sorry, but I keep thinking of Logan's text and how my heart started racing."

"It was before that. Now close your eyes again and go back in time. Imagine going down the stairs." As I said it, I was going back in time, and suddenly I remembered something. "I heard you squeal when you were heading down the stairs."

"I did?" she said, surprised. Her eyes opened again and after a moment they got wide. "That's right. I almost tripped. There was something on the stairs." She began to talk faster in an excited tone. "That's why I went into the master. To put away what I tripped on."

"What was it?" Adele interjected.

"It was jewelry," Elise said triumphantly. "That why I wanted to put it away. I didn't want somebody to take it. A real estate agent is supposed take care of the seller's stuff."

Now I was excited. "Could it have been a ring?" I wasn't sure if Elise had been there during the group's discussion about the poison ring, so I filled her in.

Elise suddenly appeared stricken. "Yes, I think it was a ring. You mean that could have been the ring with a secret compartment the killer used? My fingerprints are on it and maybe my DNA. We have to go back there and wipe it clean and then put it back on the stairs."

"I'd rather figure out who left it there," I said. "It seems likely it was the one they sold at Luxe, and I know that the person who bought that ring was wearing a straw hat."

"Deana usually wears a straw hat," Adele said. Then she filled Elise in on Timothy's real thoughts about Deana, as relayed by Alexandra.

"Hearing that could have made her want to kill him," I said. "But suppose someone was wearing the hat as a disguise to try to look like Deana. Or she could have gotten the ring for someone else. The body was barely cold and Alexandra was already taking over his workshop. And what about the others—Mikey, Sonia, and Brett?"

Adele and I agreed any one of them could have been angry enough to want to kill Timothy. Elise had no idea who we were talking about. She still knew nothing about Adele's acting aspirations.

"Whatever," Elise said. "The point is, we have to move it back to where it was. Then I could make an anonymous call to the police so they'll find it."

Adele was deep in thought. "You're right," she said to me. "I bet the killer is someone from the workshop. I'm beginning to think that Timothy really didn't set up a meeting with the Craftee Channel. I have to say, it makes me very angry, and if he wasn't dead, I'd certainly like to tell him a thing or two. How could I have been so stupid?"

I took a moment to soothe Adele's feelings before moving

on. "Ladies, we're missing something important. Whoever killed Timothy has to know they lost the ring somewhere and want to find it before the cops do." I paused for breath. "How about we set up a sting?"

Adele appeared upset again. "I'm a law enforcement wife, so I should have thought of that."

"But maybe you can help," I said. "What if you called all five of them and acted like you're sharing some gossip? You could say that you know the real estate agent who was showing the house and that she found a ring on the floor and put it away somewhere, not realizing it might be evidence, and now she's going to put it back where it was and, when she's clear of the place, she's going to make an anonymous call to the cops."

Adele was really into it now. "Then all we have to do is wait to see who shows up. Or you two can wait. I can't possibly go there again. Cutchykins can never know about any of this now."

"I don't know how much real evidence will be left on the ring other than some residue of cyanide, but all that matters is that whoever it is *thinks* there's evidence. As soon as we see someone show up, we call the cops so they catch them with the ring," I said.

We went over assorted details. Adele would have to give her people a time frame when the ring would be moved. Elise suggested she say that the ring would be on the step for an hour before the cops would be tipped. We decided to do it after happy hour that night. Elise said we'd have to leave the lockbox open so the killer could get in. Once the killer showed up, we'd call the police so they could catch them in the act.

We went our separate ways and regrouped at happy hour.

"It's a go," Adele said under her breath. "I called them all."

I nudged Elise and gave her a thumbs-up. Then the conversation turned to the blanket presentation. Dinah kept looking across the table at me with a question in her eyes. I couldn't leave her in the dark, so I slipped over to the seat next to her and told her what was up.

"I could be the lookout," my friend whispered.

"I'm afraid that Elise will have a meltdown if there's any change in the plan. She's pretty close to the edge."

"Then be safe and promise that you'll come over later and tell all." She gave me a hug and showed me that her fingers were crossed for me.

The plan was that Elise and I would leave separately and meet outside. I didn't want to be too bundled up and just grabbed the cardigan I kept at the bookstore.

We took her car, since it was less obvious than mine, and parked down the street from the house but in full view of the door.

"I can't go in there again. You have to move the ring," Elise said, pressing herself back against the seat in a resistant move.

"Where did you put it?" I asked, and she shrugged and just said it was somewhere in the master bedroom. At least she gave me directions on how to open the lockbox and how to leave it open. I didn't feel that great about going into the house again either, but somebody had to do it.

I managed to follow her instructions and get inside.

I didn't turn on any lamps, but there was enough light coming in the windows for me to see the outline of things. I slipped down the stairs and into the master bedroom. I used the light from my cell phone and hurriedly checked the drawers in the dresser and the ones on the nightstand, sure that whatever Elise had left would be on top, but I came up empty. I looked in the closet. It was the size of a small room, and there was a small chest in the middle, but the drawers just held clothes. I was starting to feel a little panicky and forced myself to take a few breaths.

Then I had an idea. I went back into the hallway, stepped into the doorway, and waited to see where my eye went first, figuring that was what Elise must have done. It went to the tall dresser against the wall. I approached it even though I'd already checked all the drawers, but this time I looked up and saw a leather box on the top. I used my cell to look inside and let my breath out in relief when I saw it. There in plain sight was a ring that looked similar to the one I'd seen at Luxe. I picked it up using a sandwich-size plastic bag.

I dropped the ring on the stairs and was out of there in no time.

I rejoined Elise in the car and we crouched down, waiting for someone to show up. I had my phone set to silent, but my watch still vibrated every time Adele called wanting an update, which seemed like every five minutes.

Time passed and no one came. Finally, during one of Adele's update calls, I made sure she'd given them all the right time. She insisted she had.

"Well, that's it," Elise said, looking at her watch. "Adele told them we'd be calling the cops at eight, right?" I nodded, feeling upset that my plan hadn't worked. "I want to call the cops and give them the tip about the ring," Elise said. "They're not going to get me for tampering with evidence."

I asked her to hold off for a few minutes while I had a chance to think things through. I was still stunned that my sting hadn't worked.

Elise was getting impatient. "C'mon, let's go," she said. "I want to get out of here and then call the cops."

"I'm going to look inside first and make sure the ring is still there," I said. "Besides, we have to shut the lockbox."

Elise told me to hurry. As I was getting out of the car, my watch vibrated. I couldn't handle any more calls from Adele. I looked at the watch, prepared to hit the red button, that would reject the call. But I saw it was actually a text message. There were just two names. Then I saw that the text was from Mason and realized they were the real names of the girl from *Ethnic Smethnic* and the vegetable fairy that I'd asked him to research. I didn't think anything of them at first, and then I looked again. *What?* I was still trying to make sense of it as I walked down the dark street back to the house.

I was back inside in no time and went down the stairs to where I'd left the ring. It was gone. I listened for a moment and heard movement on the lower floor. I followed the sound to the scene of the crime and got there just as the sliding-glass door opened. I rushed forward and grabbed at the figure.

I thought I'd grabbed a shirt, but I heard a yelp as the person pulled free and I was left with a handful of hair. I didn't have to see the color; I knew it was Lara-Ann's wavy, glorious gray mane. She was on the patio before I could stop her, and I saw her raise her arm as she threw something off the side.

"You're wasting your time. The ring's gone. There's nothing to connect me with Tim's death," she said as she rushed to the gate on the patio that led to the stairway.

But I was on her like butter on toast and made a grab for her. It backfired as she whirled around, grabbed me, and pushed me face first against the metal gate. As my arms were pressed against the metal crossbars, my cell phone fell out of my hand and clattered down the stairway.

"That really worked," she said, half to herself. "It's from the Miss Miniver Mysteries."

As if I cared. I tried to move, but she had leverage on her side as she pressed all of her body weight against me.

There had to be a way out, I just needed some time to figure it out, and in the meantime I wanted to distract her.

"Your daughter is Paisley Wilson." I'd finally recognized the name on my watch. "Paisley is Cauli Flower. That explains why she looked familiar when I saw her standing outside the bookstore. I don't get it. She was one of Timothy's successes."

"Not if you ask her," Lara-Ann said. "She thinks he ruined her career and her life."

I felt Lara-Ann move her head around, and it occurred to me that she was trying to figure out her next move, no doubt thinking through all the books she'd read. It seemed to be to my benefit to keep her talking.

"But she's in a successful commercial," I said.

"You would think that would make her happy. Not my daughter. All I ever wanted to do was help her. That's why I went to hear Tim give that talk at the community college. She desperately wanted to be an actor, and I thought I could pick up some useful information. I talked to Tim afterwards and told him about her. I was thrilled when he agreed to meet her. He saw her star quality right away and offered to be her acting coach for almost no charge. The deal was that if she became successful, he could use her as a testament to his abilities. All she really needed was a little polish and some help getting through the entertainment business maze. In no time, he had her going to auditions."

I couldn't see Lara-Ann's face, but she grunted as if she was angry about something.

"If *The Girls' Club* hadn't come on the air and been an instant hit, none of this would have happened." Lara-Ann must have realized that what she said made no sense to me. I did know about the show, though. Deana had talked longingly about wishing she could have played the lead.

Lara-Ann explained that the very first audition Paisley had gone on was for the pilot for the show. "As soon as she saw that the storyline was about a woman her age trying to run a startup in Silicon Valley, she wanted the job in the worst way, even though there was no guarantee that the pilot would even get picked up. While she waited for a callback, Tim took her to audition for Cauli Flower. Paisley wasn't interested. She didn't think commercials were really acting. They made her an offer right away. She was exactly what the company's owner had pictured. She stalled about taking it, hoping she'd get a callback from the show. Tim kept pushing her to take the commercial, and he told me there was no reason she couldn't do both if the show offered her a part. When she still wouldn't agree, he got me to help talk her into taking it. A bird in the hand and all. It seemed great to me. She'd make money and get exposure."

I felt Lara-Ann's shoulders drop. Was this the chance for me to make my move? Before I could do anything, she'd shifted her weight again and I couldn't move. I needed to have a plan ready so when the moment arrived I could take advantage of it. It was hard to think with the metal bar pressing across my chest. The only positive was that she seemed anxious to tell her story, which kept her occupied.

"I thought I was doing a good thing. They filmed the commercial and it started to air. I'm sure you've seen it. And then we heard from *The Girls' Club*; they wanted Paisley to come back in. She read for them again, and they were all set to make her an offer until they realized she was Cauli Flower. They couldn't have her star in their drama if all anybody was going to think about was that she was the raspy-voiced girl in green dancing around broccoli, and that was the end of it." Her voice grew more forceful. "Tim had to know that could happen. If he'd told me, I never would have . . ." Her voice trailed off, and she blew out her breath.

"Paisley kept up her end of the bargain. He used her to advertise his coaching business and workshops. She even went and talked to some of his students. But she snapped when *The Girls' Club* started to air this month. It was an instant hit and became the show that everyone was talking about. All I heard from Paisley was that it could have been her and that it was Tim's fault. She started using drugs again. She fired the agent Tim got her together with. Then she told me she wasn't going to help him anymore and that I had to tell him she wouldn't be a special guest at the class he was giving at the community college. She blamed me for getting her involved with him in the first place."

"And Timothy didn't take it well?" I asked.

"I called him and told him what she said. He laughed and said no way was he letting her out of the agreement."

"Did you have some kind of contract?"

She laughed mirthlessly. "A contract could be gotten out of. He had something more. He said we should talk in person. When he said he had an offer I couldn't refuse, I knew exactly what he meant."

She went into the logistics, sounding proud of how clever she thought she'd been. She knew all about his drink habit and had come prepared for their meeting. She'd gotten the idea of the ring from a mystery she'd read, which came as no surprise. "I didn't wait for him to finish the drink. I turned the AC on high when I left. I didn't realize the ring was gone until I got home."

She spoke with particular pride when she got to how she'd

brought up the idea of the ring to the crochet group. She'd
overheard enough to know I was looking into Timothy's
death and thought it would eliminate her as a suspect. Yes,
she had left the drink for me and the note on my car in
hopes that I'd stop nosing around. It turned out she didn't
even know Deana and had just worn the hat to throw a
shadow on her face, like Countess Mara in *Death's Day Off*.
The ring being too big hadn't seemed like a problem; she had
put yarn around it to make it smaller, though it had turned
out to still not be small enough. "I overheard you talking to
Adele and that other woman, and I saw my chance to get the
ring back."

"You're the one who told the cops I took the scarf with
me," I said.

"I wasn't sure how it fit in, but I'd seen you put it in your
bag, and I heard that detective asking Adele about it. I figured it might be a way to get you in trouble so you would lay
off the amateur investigating. I pulled her aside on her way
out and told her what I'd seen," she said, sounding pleased
with herself.

I felt her shift her position, as if she'd made some kind
of decision.

"I suppose you want to know what the offer was. I might
as well tell you now that I know you'll be keeping it to yourself," she said, making me uneasy. I was going to tell her
that it was her business and I really didn't need to know,
but she had already started talking.

"It wasn't exactly an offer; that was just his weird way of
putting it. I told you that Tim wanted Paisley to take the

commercial and wanted me to talk her into it. That's when the truth came out. He had somehow gotten himself in the middle of the deal and stood to make some nice money if she did the commercial. He offered to split it with me if I got her to do it. The deal was that Paisley would never find out." She stopped to take a deep breath. "And Tim's so-called offer was that unless I got her to show up at the class and do whatever he wanted, he'd tell Paisley I'd sold her out. She would never forgive me and cut me out of her life. I couldn't let him hold that over me. Who knows what he would have tried to get me to talk her into next. Porn?" she said in an angry tone.

She was silent after that, and I felt her body tense as if she was about to make a move. When she said I'd be keeping what she told me to myself, her meaning had been pretty clear. I felt her arm searching for the gate release, and she mumbled something about *The Case of the Killer Garden*, and that's when I figured out her plan. She was going to let the gate swing open and I'd go hurtling down the steep concrete stairs right into the bougainvillea vines growing all over the bottom gate. From here the vines looked like a dark mass, but beneath the leaves and flowers lurked thorns that were like swords I'd become impaled on. It was not how I intended to end my days.

I heard the gate start to creak. It was now or never. My plan came together in a split second as I realized I had a weapon after all. Lara-Ann was momentarily distracted, and I was able to move my arm between the vertical bars on the gate. Now that my arm was free, I slipped my hand in my pocket and got ready to act. I swung my arm back and shoved the metal barrel, hoping to make contact with her body.

I knew I'd succeeded when I heard her make an *oof* sound of surprise, and I ordered her to get her hand off the gate and move back.

"I never thought of you as gun person," she said, swallowing a few times.

"Well, we're even, because I didn't think of you as a murderer. Now move."

I ordered her to go inside as I pushed the metal barrel against her back. I stayed on top of her as we went back through the lower floor. I was right behind her as I nudged her up the stairs. We were just at the top when the double front doors flew open and a bunch of cops charged in with their guns pointed at us. Then someone flipped on the lights. Detective Heather stepped around the uniforms.

"She's got a gun," Lara-Ann yelled.

Barry came in and saw me with my hand pressed against Lara-Ann's back. He shook his head in disbelief as he told me to drop it. "You're into guns now?"

The metal hit the floor with a clatter, and as he bent to retrieve it, he started to laugh as he held up the large hook holder.

Lara-Ann saw it and her face erupted in anger. "But you said it was a gun."

"No, you did," I said with a shrug.

Lara-Ann didn't miss a beat before she started to make up a story straight out of one of the mystery books she was always reading. How I was an overzealous amateur sleuth who had convinced her to come with me while I looked for evidence to get myself off the hook and then had turned on her.

"Part of that is right," I said. "I did come here about some evidence that ties Timothy Clark's death to the killer, which, it turns out, is her."

Lara-Ann rolled her eyes. "That's ridiculous. There's nothing to prove it."

"Really?" I said, and then I took out a plastic bag with a silver ring inside from my pocket.

"What?" she yelled. "But I threw it down the hill."

"Yes, you threw *a* ring. *The Average Joe's Guide to Criminal Investigation* says you shouldn't leave things to chance. I wasn't sure my sting plan would work, so I hedged my bet by using a decoy."

I held the plastic bag out to Barry. "You ought to find traces of cyanide in the compartment along with her fingerprints. There might be a few of Elise Belmont's as well, but that's another story."

"Are you going to tell me how you're involved with all of this now?" Barry asked.

"I plead the fifth," I said.

"I've heard enough of this 'she said, she said' business," Detective Heather said. She directed Barry to take Lara-Ann in one corner of the living room while Detective Heather took me to another. She pulled out a notebook and had just asked me to explain why I was there when the front door opened again and Logan Belmont charged in. He looked around at everyone and put his hands over his face in dismay.

Apparently, he'd gotten a call from the same neighbor who'd called him before to report that someone suspicious was fumbling with the front door and then had gone inside. He'd notified the police and then come over himself to see what was going on.

I was glad for the distraction, because I was still trying to figure out how to explain my presence without giving away everyone's secrets. But the distraction didn't last, and Detective Heather repeated her question and made it clear that she wasn't going to take any nonsense from me. Then the front door opened again and this time Elise came in.

"What are you doing here?" her husband said.

"You might as well know that I got my license," she said. "I showed the house to Molly and an undisclosed client— who still might make an offer on the house. I had hoped to prove my value by selling a couple of houses before I told you, and then I hoped you would see that we'd make a good team. Molly is completely blameless. It's not her fault. We didn't know that Timothy was dead when we were here the first time. And I moved the ring on the steps to keep clients from tripping over it. I didn't know it was the murder weapon."

Logan seemed uneasy as he looked at his wife. "There's something I need to tell you, too."

Detective Heather shook her head in annoyance and

sent the two of them to another corner of the living room, along with one of the uniforms carrying a clipboard.

Detective Heather turned back to me and started to repeat her question, but then she threw up her hands and called across the room to Barry. "She's too much trouble. Let's switch."

Lara-Ann took my place and I rejoined Barry, who was stationed at the granite counter which served as the separation between the main room and the kitchen.

"You heard what Elise said. Are we in trouble?"

"It will be up to the district attorney if they want to charge you and your friends with anything, but since you were here with Elise, who is a licensed real estate agent who claims she was showing you the house, you didn't break and enter." He stopped. "I get it now why you wouldn't talk. You were covering for your friends. I can only guess who the undisclosed one was. Right now the issue is how you happened to be here tonight and ended up with a ring that might be the murder weapon." He looked at me with a pointed stare. "And if we can do this in statements instead of your usual answering with a question, it will go a lot better."

"Okay, but I thought you were off this case," I said.

Barry made a face. "Even your statements come out like questions. I wasn't off the case, just off the part that involved you," he said.

"But even so, here we are." I smiled at him, and he gave me his serious cop face in return.

"Yes, here we are, and let's deal with this so we can all go home. If you could just answer the question."

"I don't think you really want to know," I said.

The serious cop face finally cracked and he looked frustrated. "It appears to me that you were here tonight to look at this house with your real estate agent and you just happened to have a big hollow crochet hook that you pretended was a gun because you found an intruder in the house."

"Sounds good to me," I said.

"And the ring in the plastic bag?" he asked.

"It was on the stairs and I didn't want anybody to trip on it, so I put it in the bag."

I looked at him to see if he was going to accept the answer. He was sort of shaking his head when he wrote it down, but then, after taking the ring, he let me leave. I noticed that Lara-Ann was still there.

I didn't find out until the next day that Lara-Ann had fallen for the "Why don't you tell me what happened so we can straighten it all out" nonsense and ended up confessing to putting the poison in Timothy's pink squirrel. She must have been surprised when she'd been sent straight to jail. The ring did have her fingerprints on it and there was also residue of cyanide. She was eventually charged with first-degree murder because it was premeditated. The jury didn't buy her story—straight out of one of her mysteries—that Timothy had been acting like a Svengali with Paisley and she was trying to save her daughter. She was sent to prison, where she acted like a mother hen to several younger inmates and had plenty of time to read mysteries.

Paisley was devastated when she realized her own mother had used her. At the same time, she found out that the vegetable company was replacing her with an animated fairy. She hit bottom and found a reserve in herself and pulled herself together. She got off drugs and used whatever connections she had to make a new start. Eventually she got her shot at a drama and realized her dream of being a serious actor.

Alexandra's idea for the human voodoo doll never went anywhere, and her beach movie bombed, but her *Babes Behind Bars: The Musical* became a campy hit, leading to numerous sequels.

Mikey got the Wonder Man gig at Universal and became a real superhero when he jumped on a runaway tram and saved everyone. A studio exec happened to be on the tram with his family. He was so impressed with Mikey that he arranged for him to star in the next Steel Man movie. Mikey was thrilled.

Sonia started taking acting classes at the community college. She was all about the journey, not the destination.

After posting Leo's before and after pictures on social media, Brett was besieged by customers wanting his services. The story made the news and he was offered a reality show.

Deana didn't get the drug commercial, but she was a standout in the equity waiver production. She got more chances to do small theater plays and collected lots of good reviews. She kept hoping it would lead to something bigger.

Detective Heather did her best to get me charged with

interfering with the investigation, but as soon as the prosecutor heard about crocheted scarves and rings with secret compartments that might have been moved around, he dismissed the whole thing and said all that really mattered was that the killer had been found, apparently with my help.

Chapter
Twenty-Six

"Such a shame about Lara-Ann," Mrs. Shedd said when she stopped by the happy-hour gathering the next evening. "It was so nice to have an extra pair of hands." She looked at me. "Mr. Royal and I will pick up the slack until we hire someone new."

CeeCee tried to get the conversation onto the baby blanket event and what we ought to work on next, but the conversation kept returning to Lara-Ann. I finally told them about my involvement, starting with my scarf. Since Elise and Logan had told each other their secrets, she felt free to talk about showing the house, though we both left out anything about Adele.

We were interrupted by Adele's arrival. The night before I'd called her as soon as Barry had let me go. She seemed shocked about Lara-Ann but mostly relieved that Elise and I had managed to keep her name out of it. Adele was all aflutter and seemed to have no concept that she was interrupting anything.

"Someone from the Craftee Channel called me," she

said, giving me a secret look. "It turns out a talent coordinator saw me on the news and wants me to be a guest on their *Everything About Yarn* program. And who knows where it will go from there. I can't wait to tell Cutchykins and Mother Humphries."

I had to hand it to Adele. One way or another, she'd gotten her shot at the brass ring.

I saw Elise brighten. She'd told me that she and Logan had straightened everything out. They'd made some kind of deal, forgiving each other's secrets, and agreed to work as a team. "We're making a plan to sell that house, together."

Dinah was watching it all. After I'd called Adele, I'd gone directly to Dinah's lady cave. She'd given me tea and cookies and we had talked until our voices were hoarse.

When the group wrapped up, I pulled Adele aside and asked about her workshop people.

"I called them all and told them what happened," she said. Then she let out a sigh. "They're begging me to stick with them. I suppose I could continue on as a sort of assistant. I was thinking it over, and I think Alexandra just made up all the mean things she claimed Timothy said. Hey, I got the guest spot. Which obviously means what he said *to* me *about* me is right. I am a born personality."

I was stunned by how she had managed to twist things around until they worked for her.

"You could thank me and Elise for not letting on that you were her unidentified client," I said.

"Thank you, of course. I appreciate your sense in not

wanting to stand in the way of my future. I'll be sure to thank both of you when I get my first award."

* * *

The phone was ringing when I got home from the bookstore.

"I think we need to celebrate," Mason said. We'd talked numerous times since my big moment with Lara-Ann and the cops. "You did agree to a second date," he teased.

"So I did," I said with smile.

He was still at work, so we agreed on the following night.

"We can go to the She La Las' show. They're debuting their new number," I said, and he agreed. "Don't work too hard," I said. "As for me, I have a date with a bubble bath, followed by a romantic comedy."

There was a momentary pause, as if he was considering what to say. When we'd been together before, he'd always ended our calls a certain way. "Love you," he said just before he hung up.

My house was quiet for a change. There were no cartons of takeout or Mystery Cakes on the counter since the ladies were resting their voices for the show.

There was a note from Samuel that the animals had all been fed and given outdoor time and that he'd taken in a floral delivery for me. A vase with a bouquet of roses sat next to it, a card addressed to me tucked among the blooms. I turned it over and read it.

It was from Leo and said, "Thank you for the lessons.

I'm ready to put them into practice. You said that I should go after who I wanted. And that's you. I will call you to make a date."

What had I done? I let my shoulders release as I walked across the house. I was thinking ahead to a hot bath and kicking off my shoes and stripping off my clothes as I went toward the bathroom.

I was down to a camisole and undies when I shut the bathroom door behind me, thinking of what kind of bubble bath to add. The thud didn't register at first until I looked back at the door and saw that the handle had fallen off. *Not again.* I picked it up and tried to screw it back on with no success. I looked through the hole in the door and saw why—the other half of the handle with the rod was lying on the floor. There was nothing for this half to fit onto. It took a moment for me to figure out that when I'd fixed it before, I'd had access to both sides of the door.

I tried sticking the end of a hair brush through the opening, but the door wouldn't budge. I tried other assorted tools, but nothing would push the metal mechanism back. I was locked in the bathroom.

Don't panic, I told myself. *There has to be a way out.* There was the window over the tub that looked out on the enclosed patio. It was really three windows—a big one that didn't open and two slim side ones that did. With great difficulty, I squeezed through one of the side ones and slid to the ground. The floodlights illuminated the small enclosure. What idiot had designed it? There was no gate to the outside, just the locked door that led to my bedroom. My only option was to go over the wall and hope the spare key was still in the garage. With bare feet, I gingerly climbed up the tiers of the fountain, finally grabbing onto the top of the wall and hoisting myself up. I sat on the top and looked down at the darkness below on the other side, considering the drop and how much it was going to hurt. I finally took a deep breath and turned around, prepared to face whatever. Just as I was about to let go, I heard a voice.

"Wait. Hold on and I'll catch you."

"Barry!" I said, surprised and relieved.

"I'm not even going to ask how you got there. It looks like I came to take care of Cosmo at just the right time." He positioned himself below me and told me to let go. I slid right into his arms.

"You brought me the scarf," I said, seeing it sticking out of his pocket. "And I hope the front door key."

He showed me the key in his hand. Since I was barefoot, he wanted to carry me, but I refused, though I did accept his jacket as he wrapped it around me and we headed to the front door.

"Thank you," I said.

He turned toward me, and his face was illuminated by the overhead light on the front porch. There was no cop face this time. Just Barry with a soft smile.

"You know I'll always be here to catch you when you fall."

CeeCee's Baby Blanket

The blanket starts out with three stitches and then increases on both ends, which forms a triangle. When the triangle reaches approximately 37 inches across, the decreasing on both ends begins and it will turn into a square. It makes a sturdy, stretchy blanket that washes and dries well.

Easy to make

Supplies:

2 cones Peaches & Creme yarn, 100% cotton, approx. 706 yds/645 m, 14 oz/400 g
Size K-10½ 6.50 mm hook
Tapestry needle for weaving in ends

Gauge: not important
Dimensions: approx. 27 × 27 inches
Stitches used: chain (ch), single crochet (sc), double crochet (dc), slip stitch (sl st), yarn over (YO)

Directions:

Ch 4
Row 1: Sc in second ch from hook and in next 2 chs—3 sc made.

Increase rows:

Row 2: Ch 1, turn; 2 sc in first sc, sc in next sc, 2 sc in last sc—5 sc made.

Row 3: Ch 1, turn; working in back loop only, 2 sc in first sc, sc in each sc across to last sc, 2 sc in last sc.

Row 4: Ch 1, turn; working in both loops, 2 sc in first sc, sc in each sc across to last sc, 2 sc in last sc.

Repeat Rows 3 and 4 until the piece measure approx. 37 inches across.

Decrease rows:

Row 1: Ch 1, turn; working in back loop only, pull up loop on first 2 sc, YO and draw through all 3 loops on hook, sc in each sc across to last 2 sts, pull up a loop in last 2 sts, YO and draw through all 3 loops on hook.

Row 2: Ch 1, turn; working in both loops, pull up loop on first 2 sc, YO and draw through all 3 loops on hook, sc in each sc across to last 2 sts, pull up a loop in last 2 sts, YO and draw through all 3 loops on hook.

Repeat Rows 1 and 2 until 3 sts left; ch 1, turn, pull up a loop in first 3 sts, YO and draw through all 4 loops on hook.

Edging:

Row 1: Ch 1, sc loosely around the blanket making 3 sc in each corner, join with sl st to first sc.

Row 2: Ch 2 (counts as first dc), dc around blanket
    making 3 dc in each corner, join with sl st to first dc.
Row 3: Ch 1, sc around blanket making 3 sc in each
    corner, join with sl st to first sc, fasten off and weave in
    ends.
Stretch to shape.

Molly's Incriminating Scarf

The scarf is worked the long way. The glow-in-the-dark yarn Molly used has been discontinued, and a substitute yarn has been given. Unfortunately, it doesn't glow in the dark. But it also won't implicate you in a murder.

Easy to make

Supplies:

For Scarf: 1 skein Red Heart Super Saver yarn, Carrot, 364 yds/333 m, 7 oz/198 g, 100% acrylic
Size J-10/6.00 mm crochet hook
Dimensions without fringe: approx. 68 × 3¾ inches

For Flowers: 1 skein Red Heart Super Saver yarn, Lemon, 364 yds/333 m, 70 oz/198 g, 100% acrylic
Size D-3/3.25 mm crochet hook
Dimensions: 2¾ inches across

Stitch marker (optional)
Tapestry needle to weave in ends

Gauge: not important
Stitches used: chain (ch), single crochet (sc), double crochet (dc), treble crochet (tr), slip stitch (sl st)

On the Hook

Scarf:

Ch 201
Row 1: Sc in second chain from hook and across.
Row 2: Ch 2 (counts as first dc), turn, dc across.
Row 3: Ch 1, turn, sc across.
Row 4: Repeat Row 2.
Row 5: Repeat Row 3.
Row 6: Repeat Row 2.
Row 7: Repeat Row 3.
Row 8: Repeat Row 2.
Row 9: Repeat Row 3, fasten off and weave in ends.
Add fringe to both ends.

Flowers (make 4):

Ch 10 and join with sl st.
Round 1: Ch 1, make 15 sc in the ring (recommended to mark first sc with stitch marker so easier to see), sl st to first sc.
Round 2: Ch 1, sc in first sc in previous row (the one with stitch marker) * ch 3, skip next 2 sc, sc in the next sc * repeat from * to * 3 times, ch 3 and sl st in first sc.
Round 3: *Sl st to move yarn into ch 3 space, sc, dc, dc, tr, dc, dc, sc * repeat from * to * 4 times, sl st to first sc, fasten off, leaving a tail of yarn to use to tack the flower onto the scarf.

Tack the flowers to the scarf.

Liza's Mystery Cake

1½ cup olive oil
2 cups shredded carrots
4 eggs
¾ cup organic sugar
¾ cup organic brown sugar
2 cups all-purpose unbleached flour
1 cup cake flour
2 teaspoons baking powder
1½ teaspoons salt
2 teaspoons cinnamon
1 cup chopped walnuts

Beat together the olive oil, carrots, eggs and sugars. Sift together the flours, baking powder, salt, and cinnamon. Add to the olive oil mixture, mixing just until blended. Stir in the walnuts.

Pour into a greased tube pan and bake at 350 degrees for approximately 50 min. Cool in pan before removing.